OTHER NOVELS BY SEAN DANKER

Admiral

Free Space

The Glory of the Empress

INNOCENCE

AN ADMIRAL NOVEL

SEAN DANKER

We wouldn't be here without Joshua Danker-Dake.

PROLOGUE

It was probably another beautiful morning in Cohengard, but I couldn't be sure.

The shield was down and muted, so nothing outside could be seen or heard. Rain was scheduled for this week, but I couldn't remember which day.

I pawed blindly in the dark, hoping for either the shutter control or my holo, but all I hit was the mute control. It shut off, letting in a little sound from the city. The hum of vehicles. Flyers mostly, since this was the seventieth floor.

The nice thing about this unit was that the window by the bed had a spectacular view of White Square. Not the real White Square; that was on Old Earth. This was just the fake one they put here after the revolt, trying to turn the site of a damaged building into what amounted to a big propaganda poster meant to be seen from space.

That was how Griffith would put it, at any rate.

Personally, I was glad to have a view of anything that wasn't just another sustenance block. Who wanted to look across the street at a giant white cube?

I still couldn't see, but there was a new sound, a sort of rattle, accompanied by a slight tremor. Whatever it was, it wasn't normal. I was groggy, but my nerves stirred at bit.

It was a harsh noise. This might be Cohengard, but it was still an imperial city. There weren't supposed to *be* harsh noises, especially so early. It wouldn't be polite to use verbal commands, but Inge was stirring. She shifted a little and sighed.

"What is it?" she asked.

"Do you hear that?" I whispered.

"What?" Her arms loosened around me a little, and I felt her head rise from my chest. The noise was getting louder.

"Windows," I said in a normal voice. If she was already awake, it didn't matter.

The wall vanished, revealing the pink and orange of the sky and the white of the city. We both shielded our eyes. It *was* getting louder.

"What is *that?*" Griffith asked, sitting up as well and pushing his hair out of his eyes.

There were lots of flyers out there, but they weren't making this noise. There was *definitely* a vibration. We could all feel it through the bed.

Griffith clambered over me and Inge to go to the window. I got up and joined him. Together, we looked out at the view, flinching as something rocketed past, racing up the side of the block. Griffith recovered and peered upward.

"That's a peacekeeper," he said, then sighed. "Someone's in trouble."

My heart was still thudding. It was just a drone, but it would only be moving that fast in the open if there was a raid or something going on.

"Empress," I said. Of course, we didn't have the right angle to see whatever was going on up there. The noise was fading. "Isn't it a little early?"

"Are they arresting somebody?" Inge asked from the bed. "Here?"

"Most likely," I told her, stretching.

She flopped down and groaned.

I picked up my holo to check the time, and a yawn died in my mouth. I caught Griffith's eye.

"It's not early," I told him.

"What?" He looked past me at the readout. "Oh."

"Oh no, come on," Inge opened her eyes and sat up, then crawled to the edge of the bed, putting on the face that she always seemed to think would change our minds. "Just stay."

"Hanging out in sustenance housing all day? Who *does* that? Not very fashionable," I said, stretching. Naturally, all three of us lived in sustenance, and that was what we did most days. Inge's unit wasn't any better or worse than mine or Griffith's, but we were usually here anyway. Her place tended to be tidiest, at least when it wasn't strewn with cast-off clothing.

But we needed to hurry.

"You should study," Griffith told her, following me into the bathroom. She leapt off the bed, but he hit the release and locked the door before she could get to it. "That just about killed me." He referred to the peacekeeper.

"The guilty flee where none pursue," I quoted through another yawn. He snorted.

"We aren't guilty. Yet."

"They say Imperial Security monitors debate clubs now, so you're probably already on some lists." That had been scary, though. I glanced at the ceiling, then at him. "I wonder who they're after."

Griffith stepped into the shower and activated it.

"Is it legal to lock her out of her own bathroom?" I wondered aloud, checking my chin in the feed and rubbing at my stubble. Well, it was sort of like stubble. It was sad and nearly invisible, but it was *there*, so I had that going for me. "Is she really that scared?"

"She's just doesn't want to study."

"She won't get anything done if she's worrying about us."

"You can stay and try to keep her on task if you want," Griffith suggested.

"I'm not backing out if you aren't." I faced him. "I'm just afraid we're doing more harm than good. Maybe we should go on a trip or something. Give her some time to herself."

Griffith paused in the act of lathering his hair and turned to look at me.

"I could go for that," he said.

"Hurry up," I said, pointing at my holo.

"I am," he said, frothing up the sanitizer. "If we're going to be bad subjects, at least we can smell good."

I felt the same way, but a sustenance shower was barely big enough for one, so I had to wait for him to finish. Thanks, Empress.

I went back to examining my chin.

"Have you got anything to wear?" Griffith asked.

"I thought we were doing blanks."

"We're pathetic."

"You said nobody would notice," I accused, chewing a sanitation capsule and drinking a cup of water.

"*We* notice," he shot back. He finished rinsing and stepped out of the shower. I immediately took his place as he moved underneath the dryer.

I made better time than Griffith did, and in just a few minutes we were emerging from the bathroom.

Inge had put on a robe and was at the counter, sipping coffee.

"This is your worst decision ever," she told us as we went to the closet.

"Citation needed," I told her, following Griffith.

I pulled out my blanks and held them up. This was the set of trousers and jacket that was given to everyone at graduation. It was just like the graduation uniform, but without school markings or embellishments. It was meant to be suitable attire for professional situations in the event that someone didn't have anything better.

And we didn't.

With a few alterations, a good set of original blanks could be quite a statement. In fact, there was some kind of high-fashion movement underway that was based on authentic Cohengardian blanks as some kind of symbol. It was one of those edgy things, but it was edgy to get people talking, not because anyone involved was genuinely rebellious. Which made for a pretty big contradiction, but nobody cared. Maybe the blanks would protect us; after all, real New Unity sympathizers wouldn't be caught dead in them. We weren't *real* New Unity; we were just going to go listen to New Unity people talking.

It'd be all right with me if we just looked like good subjects. Tourists. Something like that.

I'd only worn my blanks to have them fitted. They looked fine, but I still chafed at this. Did I really have nothing better to wear than clothes the Empress handed me as an absolute last resort? Was this really the best I could do?

Yes. The answer was yes. There was no way around it.

"Chin up," Griffith said, clapping me on the shoulder. "We won't always be poor."

"I'll believe it when I see it."

"They *say* they won't hold this against you," Inge said as we got dressed. "They say it's all right, that it's normal. But it's not true." She pointed at the window. "You saw that. This is Cohengard. What do you *think* that was about?"

"You know, you're starting to sound like you've got a little New Unity in you," I said, doing up my shirt. "Sure you don't want to come with us?"

"Oh, Empress. And kiss any chance I've got goodbye."

"Probably," Griffith said. I shot him a look.

Inge let out a disgusted groan. "Guys. Come *on*. I'm not going to be in sustenance forever. I could be somewhere better in six months."

That was true, but only if everything went perfectly.

"You will," I told her with confidence I didn't feel.

"Do my scarf," Griffith said.

"I'll do it," Inge said, putting down her drink and getting up.

"I've got it," I told her, waving her back. She scowled at me, and I tied Griffith's scarf and made sure it looked right.

"I've seen you looking worse," Griffith noted, brushing something off my lapel.

"Not worse than this," I said, checking myself in the closet's screen. "I look like I'm trying to get an apprenticeship."

"Is that *really* so terrible?" Inge asked coldly, folding her arms.

"Yes," Griffith said. "Do these for me." He held up his hands to show the little wrist fasteners. I'd barely been able to do my own.

"I'll get it," Inge volunteered, and I let her handle it.

"Right," Griffith said, and we sized each other up. "Are we presentable?"

"You are. I don't have the shoulders for this. Bad subjects should at least look good. I'm pretty sure that's in the Duchess' writings somewhere," I said.

"I'm pretty sure it's not," Inge snapped, giving us both a fierce look. "There's *nothing* I can say?"

"No." Griffith cut her off. "Don't bother. We're already late."

He hit the release and dragged me into the corridor. Inge stopped short of the threshold, holding her robe shut.

"I'll just tidy up," she said, glaring at us. "And study."

"Sounds good." We both kissed her, then closed the door. Shaking his head, Griffith started down the corridor. I smoothed my blanks and followed.

"We really do look like graduates," I noted.

"We *are* graduates," he reminded me, stretching his arms over his head as we walked. "It hasn't been that long. Empress have mercy. I'm so tired. Do we have time to get coffee?"

"We look like graduates that are trying too hard," I amended.

Griffith entered the lift, and I joined him. The ride down was always long and dull. "You don't *have* to come," he reminded me.

"I'm coming," I said. "It's fine. Don't make it weird."

"You're sure?"

"Starting to sound like you're the one that isn't sure."

Griffith sighed. "I'm sure when it's me. When it's you, I start having second thoughts."

I rolled my eyes.

The doors opened, and we left Sustenance Block Delta. It was warm outside, and the daylight hurt my eyes. Cohengard was having a loud day; the sounds of music, people, and vehicles filled my ears.

We turned and looked up at the block, but there was no sign of the peacekeeping crawler that had climbed our window.

"They should just take the elevator," I said.

"It'd be cheaper," Griffith agreed. We started to walk.

This was the problem with blanks: no one would confuse them with proper attire because from our school, they were all this same shade of gray, and no real tailor was turning out good formalwear in this shade for fear of it being mistaken for blanks.

Didn't that defeat the purpose?

And yet, just across the flatway was a guy about our age wearing *his* blanks and carrying a project case under his arm. That told the whole story. He was pursuing work, and doing a pretty good job of it if he was dressing up and giving presentations.

That was what Griffith and I were *supposed* to be doing.

I checked the time and hoped we wouldn't run into anyone we knew on the way.

"You said we could go on a trip," Griffith said.

"I meant something like that wouldn't hurt her chances."

"Where can we go?"

"Where can we afford to go?" I snorted.

"We could probably do something along the white line as long as we didn't go intercontinental," Griffith said. I looked over to see that he was actually thinking about it. "Where do you want to go?"

"Maybe Red Yonder," I said.

"That would be a lot of jumps," Griffith said. "I wish."
He was right. *Maybe* we could go off-world, but there was
no way we could save enough money to leave imperial
space.

"If she makes it, that's the first place we'll go. She's been
looking it up, then erasing her history," I told him quietly.

"How are you getting into her holo? But she wants to
go to Old Earth more than anything. She wants to set foot
in all those historically significant places. Says she won't feel
properly Evagardian until she does. Kind of worries me."

"Are any of us properly Evagardian? What does that
even mean?"

I put my hands behind my head and looked up. Flyer
traffic, high above, was just a sparkling grid against the
pinkish underside of the atmospheric protector. Beyond, the
suns shone through, the light skewed by the domes
protecting the city.

When I was small, I'd been convinced that those bright,
shifting patterns had really been dragons. Now I knew what
they really were: people who were prospering. People who
never had to wear blanks, who never had to set foot on
public transportation, who had homes with more than one
room.

"We could go to the coast," Griffith suggested. "That'd
be cheap."

"One of those physical trips? Doing stuff on foot and
sleeping outside?"

"Yeah. You can put it on your bio."

"I don't know if that stuff actually helps," I said. "I put
myself in the place of the person hiring, and I see that—I'd
be a jerk about it. So you had time to go soul-searching, but
you didn't have time to get an education?"

Griffith snorted. "Maybe it's good if you're going into the arts."

"I don't think that's me."

"You could be a singer."

"Not in this lifetime. How long's the coast thing take?"

"Like a hundred kilometers. That's a lot on foot. If we did something like that, we wouldn't get back until after she's done. Now that I'm thinking about it, it's sounding pretty good. We could do it. Better than wasting our time here."

I thought it over. It *would* be fun. "Can we leave today?"

"It's not like we got anything else going on."

We turned a corner, and ahead was the rally.

It was a big crowd. Usually we saw these from a safe distance, but today we were doing it for real.

The traffic was interesting to watch: there were others like us, moving toward the rally. And also a lot of people hurrying away from it, as though just being seen in the vicinity would do them measurable harm. As though New Unity's politics were communicable by proximity, like a biohazard. Like just getting close enough to one of these radicals was enough to jeopardize your whole future.

There were plenty of people who thought that was *exactly* what it would do.

"Who's speaking?" I asked Griffith.

"Suvari," he said.

"Isn't he pretty moderate?"

"Lately, yeah," he confirmed.

"Then we picked the right day for this."

"Did we?"

We were getting close. There was no one on the stage yet, but the noise level was impressive. It was quite a blend of people, not just young guys like me and Griffith; there were Cohengardians of all ages, thousands of them, and more rallies going on all over the prefecture. I wondered if they were all as well-attended as this one.

I'd have preferred to just leave for the coast. It might not help our prospects much, but it wouldn't hurt them. It might even help Inge. She needed to worry about her future, and having us around was a distraction.

A hand fell on my shoulder, and suddenly there was a woman between me and Griffith. Her outfit was casual but expensive. Not exactly flashy, but high-end that you'd notice. It was a trendy, classical Evagardian style, which wasn't something you saw much around here.

Her outfit wasn't very feminine, but the lady herself was pretty. She was about twice our age, and there was more confidence in her little finger than in both of us combined. Of course, that wasn't saying much.

"Boys," she said, and her smile stopped just short of smugness. "Can we talk?"

Griffith was just as startled as I was. She slipped her arms around our shoulders, and Griffith spoke up.

"Normally, yeah," he told her. "But we're attached."

She smiled. "This is business. And I insist." She called up her holo, which displayed a personal ID with a military seal. My stomach dropped.

This was awkward. Griffith was thinking the same thing I was.

"Can you insist? Legally, I mean?" he asked, playing it cool.

"Why would I *care?*" She firmly guided us away from the crowd and let go of us to walk normally, but stayed between us. "You're better off spending your morning with me than with that lot," she said. "Trust me. Those people aren't going anywhere, and there'll be another one tomorrow."

"Who are you?" Griffith was intrigued. So was I. Her ID hadn't specified which branch of the Service she was with. She didn't seem like a peacekeeper. There hadn't been a name—and if she could hide that on her ID, that meant she was probably pretty important. It couldn't be a fake ID; our holos had authenticated it. I was getting worried. And curious.

She steered us into the nearest cafe, which was mostly for professionals who wanted to carry their beverages out, but it still had a quiet lounge in the rear. The styling was typical for this kind of place: hard lines and a black-and-white color scheme. There were some real plants though, and that was nice.

She slid into a booth, gesturing for us to sit across from her as she absently keyed a thirty-Julian tab into the table's menu. Apparently she was treating us. I reached out before anyone else could and rapidly tapped the symbol for Titan milk tea five times, using up all the money instantly.

She stared at me, and Griffith snorted. He arched an eyebrow.

"Thirsty?" he asked mildly.

"For her," I said, as though that were obvious.

The woman gazed across the table at us, smiling patiently.

"Are you done?" she asked.

"What's your name?" I asked back.

"People like me don't need names," she replied, and Griffith leaned back, brows raised.

"Is this a salesman thing?" he asked. "Theater? Are you trying to impress us?"

"How does that impress us?" I asked.

"She's trying to act like she's Evagardian Intelligence. Or like Gagarin or something. They don't even try this hard in dramas." He rolled his eyes.

Gagarin was supposed to be a very elite sort of intelligence section, not actually a part of Evagardian Intelligence. There were lots of exciting dramas about it.

"Gagarin's not real," I pointed out.

"No, of course it is," Griffith said dryly. "They just do all that secret stuff. And they don't have names." He gestured at the woman, whose expression of saintly patience didn't flicker. "I know what she's here for."

"Really?" I was impressed.

"She's Imperial Security. IS wants to get to us first. Offer us some money to join New Unity and report on them. Where better?" He glanced at the window; the rally was visible outside.

Of course the government was well aware that we were poor. I looked at the woman with new eyes. Griffith was right. He was absolutely right.

"Wrong," the woman said. "Though I don't blame you for thinking that. I'd probably recruit you somewhere a little more discreet if that was what I was going for." She leaned forward and clasped her hands, and suddenly the eye contact was aggressive. "But I don't want you joining New Unity. That would be a waste. I want you to do something worthwhile. I'm not IS. I'm with the Service."

That was direct. Griffith and I both balked.

"You sure you have the right guys?" Griffith asked, glancing at me. I put my chin on my hands and nodded.

"We're not Service material," I told her flatly. It was all I could do not to laugh.

"Your aptitudes say otherwise." The woman shifted to let the arm from the ceiling put down the tea. She helped herself to one of the Titan milk teas. "Your aptitudes say you're wasted here. It's been almost a year since you graduated, and where are you? Dragging your feet looking at apprenticeships that you know you're not likely to get."

"We're still in the certification process," I pointed out, taking a sip from one of the teas.

"When was the last time you signed on a session?"

She'd been looking at our records.

"Who says we have to do anything?" Griffith asked. "Why can't we just get married?"

She smirked. "Inge Illamuerta. I know about her. I also know she is deeply beneath the both of you. Socially. Genetically. Intellectually, to be honest."

I wasn't exactly surprised, but I was unsettled. It was common knowledge that essentially all information about our lives was available to the Imperium, but it still felt weird to hear her saying these things so plainly. And if this woman wanted to get on our good side, saying things like that about Inge wasn't going to help her.

"She's got the best chance of getting an apprenticeship of any of us," I said.

"Maybe, but she'll squander it. She's too ambitious. She wants to leverage the internship into a scholarship to a Marragardian academy, but even if she's able to get that, which is unlikely, though not impossible, she won't be able to keep up when the time comes to deliver. She's in the wrong career, and she's going about it in the wrong way. She's greedy. Probably to impress the two of you. She thinks you'll drift away if she doesn't make it." The woman paused. "Will you?"

"I get that you're a big deal, but you're being kind of rude," I told her, and I must have said it in a particular way, because it seemed to take her off guard.

"Well said," Griffith murmured.

She cocked her head, then leaned back.

"Maybe I am," she said. "I apologize. But nothing I'm saying is untrue. The girl isn't being as prudent as she could. What she's doing won't work."

That was nothing that Griffith and I didn't already know. Inge's prospects weren't good.

"Then it's a good thing that advancing isn't really that important to us," Griffith said.

The woman put down her teacup and raised her hands in concession. "True love. And that's all well and good. I'm not here to talk you out of marrying her. Even if you're marrying down, she's marrying up. There's nothing wrong with that. She's very sweet, and from what I've read, the model subject. She's lucky to have you."

"You're not going to say she should serve too," Griffith said.

"Of course not. She'd never make the cut, not even for enlisted. But that doesn't mean she can't be an asset to the Empress. All the more reason for the two of you to stop dragging your feet. You had the academic aptitudes. If you'd been less distracted by other things in school, you could have done well in the private sector."

"Who's to say we won't?" I asked, trading a look with Griffith. "We're seventeen. Our lives aren't exactly over yet."

"I can't see the future, boys. Only the present. But your present doesn't look good. I wouldn't be here otherwise. You can't argue with that."

Griffith made a little gesture toward her. "This isn't normal. Does this really mean we're going to war?"

I was puzzled. "War?"

Griffith gave me a tired look. "Yes. Commonwealth encroachment in Free Trade space. it's been coming for ages. Imperials follow the rules poaching things, the Royals don't. There's been so much saber-rattling I can't believe we all aren't deaf. Read the news."

"Well, I knew we weren't on good terms," I said defensively. "But war? With the Commonwealth? That doesn't sound good."

"Are you sure you want him in the Service?" Griffith asked, pointing at me with his thumb.

The woman grinned, and something about it was kind of creepy. I wasn't sure why.

"I just don't want to see anyone squander their potential," she said.

"You must be desperate to come to us."

"Don't sell yourself short. So many kids in Cohengard don't even consider the Service. They don't think they'll make it, or they think that if they do, they won't be able to get anywhere because of where they came from."

"You do realize you came to us at a New Unity rally," I pointed out. "You have to know we aren't, you know, the *most* patriotic guys."

"This is Cohengard. Unless you're one of the people writing the articles or speaking at the podium, nobody cares," she said, waving a hand.

That was reassuring to hear, if it was true.

"This really is war prep," Griffith told me. "What better time to speed up recruiting than before the war actually starts? But even that doesn't explain you being here right now."

She shrugged. "I'm looking at you for officer candidacy," she said to Griffith. "If you applied yourself, you could be ready for the next selection cycle."

"Me? An officer?" Griffith smiled and folded his arms. He was trying hard not to laugh.

"What's to stop you?"

"There is nothing in my aptitudes to make anyone think that's realistic."

"I'm better at reading your aptitudes than you are. The Empress knows you better than you know yourself."

"What about me? You think I should enlist?" I asked. "Or am I an officer too?" This was outrageous. I wished I'd looked closer at her ID. Maybe this was some kind of prank.

"No. I have something else in mind for you," she told me. I wasn't sure what to make of that. "This is an opportunity. Whatever Inge is capable of, she's much more likely to achieve it without the two of you in easy reach. She can't apply herself when you're around, and you think you're being supportive, but you're just spoiling her. Your willingness to indulge her is working *against* her."

"Nothing we don't already know," I pointed out.

It still kind of stung to hear it.

"Of course. You aren't stupid. Which is why you also realize that the Service is perfect for you. It would get you out of her way. She'll sink or fly, but at least she'll have her best chance. And the two of you will come back with money, status, and a future. If Inge's doing well, good. If she isn't, you'll be in a position to pull her up. That is, if what you have really is true love," she added, still smiling.

"How long would we be apart?" Griffith asked, picking up a teacup.

"I want to send you to aptitude prep at the Walland. Six months there. If you do make selection, you'll do a year of basic, then a year of officer training. Then you'll be in specialization training. Depending on what your career field is, that could be one year, or it could be two or three. The longest school is three and a half. You'll be able to see her a few times during those first two years, and depending on where you go for your job training, you may be able to have her live with you while you're there. Some schools allow it, some don't. It's only for the first six months of basic that you're cut off from everybody. After that you get some dignity and freedom again. Within reason."

"But then I get ship duty," Griffith said. "If I end up out there," he said, pointing up, "then I'll be away most of the time. If we go to war, my commitment won't mean anything, and the Empress will keep me in it until I die or we win."

"Of course."

"I feel like you have a very poor grasp of how love works," Griffith said, gesturing with his hands. "It's this thing where you want to be *near* someone."

"Both my husbands say the same thing," the woman replied dryly, taking a sip. "We agree to disagree. Compromise, boys. It's all about compromise."

She reached into her jacket and took out two physical data cards. She put them on the table and pushed one toward each of us.

Griffith immediately picked his up and swiped it over his wrist to let his holo read it. He briefly considered the result, and his eyes widened.

"You're paying for passage and lodging. Pushing me to the front of the line. You want to give me a living stipend? This is special treatment. Why?"

"Because it's what's best for you, and what's best for us all," the woman said. "If you want it."

Griffith put the card down and sat back again, looking a little shaken this time. I could understand why; this *was* strange. I'd never heard of something like this happening. Sometimes teachers and recruiters would pressure people pretty heavily, maybe even with some kind of incentive, but not like this. They didn't *literally* pull you off the street. This was special.

"That's all," she said, finishing her tea. "You have to make up your own minds. I'm just here to give you the means and the push. It was nice to meet you both. Have a couple parfaits. On the Empress." She tapped the tabletop to key in another thirty Julians. "Of course, *everything* you have is on the Empress," she added, getting to her feet.

She smiled at us, and left without another word. Griffith watched her go.

"They're insane," he said after a moment.

"What?" I looked up; I had scanned the card she'd given me, and was reading the itinerary in it.

"She can't possibly expect us to consider this," he went on, shaking his head. "I mean, me? Maybe on paper I look good to these people for the Service. I *guess* you could read my aptitudes that way. But *you?* This has to be some kind of joke."

ONE

Now

I tried to dodge toward the stairs, but there were two other men with the same idea, and they were both pretty big. They bulled past, slamming me into the railing as they spilled into the stairwell.

I managed not to fall, but another shot rang out, and shrapnel bounced from the walls. There was a crackle of electricity, and I realized the handrail was metal. I let go as a distorted voice issued orders over the broadcast system. I wasn't interested in that, though. Heavy footsteps were approaching fast, and there were voices.

I scrambled away from the open doorway and fell to my knees, facing the wall with my hands behind my head.

Figures in armor crowded into the dim stairwell, and a bright light shone in my eyes. Less than a second passed, and the light vanished, but I was left with an eyeful of burning stars and an alarming tingle in my retinas.

The guards shoved me into the wall, and they were all clattering down the stairs. I counted to three, then got up and went back out onto the walkway, blinking my eyes and shaking my head.

There was a view from this floor: I was fifty meters from the yard below and still at least a hundred meters from the highest level. These walkways were open in the hopes that someone would dramatically fall to his death, but it also helped with the smoke by giving it somewhere to go. The guards had fired at least a dozen canisters onto the walkway, but I could still a see a little, and breathe. Now my eyes were watering *and* burning.

There was only the slightest shimmer to betray the atmosphere bubble, but the stars beyond didn't give much light; from here, space didn't look half as dark as the shadows bathing this transition block. Shadows didn't bother me.

Half a dozen inmates burst from the smoke and tore past at a sprint, a seventh trailing behind them. There was a shot, and he went down with a cry, tumbling to the ground.

I put my hands up and backed away as another guard materialized. He walked past me and stood over the dead man, confirming his identity with his holo.

There was nothing but smoke and stars. I didn't know the systems and nebulae of Free Trade space by sight, but I had to admit they were pretty. Lots of pink and blue and green out there.

A sliver of Oversight headquarters protruded against the view, and there were thin lines of distant, glowing viewports. I could just see a hint of the lights from Baykara City, high above it all.

The guard had his back to me now, his scattergun cradled while he took a box magazine from a pouch.

My shiv was in my hand, and I didn't hesitate for long, but it was still too much. He whirled on me, pulling his sidearm. I should have known better. This was New Brittia; there was always someone watching.

I rolled to my right as he fired, coming up and vaulting over the railing and into the open air. I caught the railing of the next level down and immediately let go, catching the next one. I clambered over to get out of the line of fire. These guards had rappelling gear, but I didn't think he'd follow me. If I was the focus of this raid, I'd have been dead ten minutes ago.

There'd been an opportunity to get noticed up there, but obviously it hadn't been a good one.

Two inmates who had been peering curiously into the stairwell turned to stare at me. There was no smoke down here.

"What's going on?" one asked with a thick Isakan accent.

"Couldn't tell you," I replied, brushing myself off and putting away my shiv. "Can I get down through here?" I pointed. I was going to be sore from that fall, but a bullet would've been worse. The raid didn't change anything; I wasn't going to use my time idling around this transition block. I'd have been moving on to the next section regardless, but the last stairway had been blocked. It had nearly gotten me killed.

The inmates nodded, and I staggered off. I'd been here twenty minutes and I was already annoyed, but I knew I'd miss the transition block after I'd left it. The people here were almost friendly. Once I got into general population, that wouldn't be the case anymore.

And the raid? Well, there was always something going on. If there wasn't, why would anyone watch? Why would anyone wager? How would New Brittia stay in business? If the moment ever came when nothing was happening in this place, the people that ran it would *make* something happen. They had an obligation to the subscribers.

Maybe that was what was happening now. Maybe they'd just chosen someone at random for a fox hunt.

Faded lettering on the grimy wall told me I was on deck 26G. I didn't have much time, and there was more than Oversight to worry about. This raid was slowing me down, and I couldn't afford it.

Inmates were hearing the shots and taking shelter in the bunk rooms. The walkways were all but deserted. I was two levels below the action but still close enough that people were keeping their heads down. These men were like me: new arrivals. They'd just come through processing, and they were probably intending to make the most of the time they had before they were required to move on.

Most of them weren't a threat to me, but it would only take one if I let my guard down.

I went to the railing and took a look at the yard. It was a crescent-shaped space teeming with people, and there were the housing blocks. New Brittia didn't make much sense when you looked at a map or schematics. It had begun as an asteroid, then become a mining operation and refinery, then a prison, and then a prison with a small city on top of it. Worst of all, it was a commercial attraction, so the people making the decisions were more interested in things being visually striking than practical. New Brittia would've been a chaotic sight even if it wasn't choked with inmates at each other's throats.

That guard had taken a shot at me, and he'd probably seen that I was holding a weapon. Now I was on Oversight's radar, and they were probably watching me at this very moment.

It wasn't much, but it was a start. I couldn't worry about that, though. I needed help, and if I didn't move fast,

I wouldn't get it. I had to think, and I had to move, so I'd do both at once.

I started to run. Now my feet could hurt like the rest of my body, although I was hoping that pain would go away any minute now. New Brittia's uniform shoes felt thinner than the fabric of my gray jumpsuit, and my ear still hurt where they'd stapled a tiny holo to it. I'd rolled up my sleeves, clearly revealing the new tattoos on my forearms: β-202. The same sequence was printed in white on the back of the jumpsuit.

I turned into a stairwell, hoping I'd put enough distance between myself and Oversight to have a moment of peace. And maybe I had, for all the good it did me.

There was a cluster of inmates on the landing above, and they didn't look as flimsy as most of the new arrivals I'd seen so far. A little reminder that for the most part, the people who were sent here presumably deserved it.

I didn't need trouble with these guys. One of them had arms bigger than my waist.

I kept my eyes off them and hurried down the stairs. Even if I didn't know the way exactly, I had to transition out. That was done via special gates at the bottom of this structure. As long as I could keep moving down, for now, that would be enough.

Down was forever, though.

The bottom was a lie; the Ganraen capital, Little Norwich. Nidaros, the *Julian*, Tessa Salmagard, a New Unity rally. The point of no return had come and gone so long ago that I didn't even remember what it had looked like when I tripped over it.

So I just thought about how poorly these shoes were cushioning my feet, which were pounding on flight after flight of metal stairs. If bad arch support was the worst thing that happened to me in this place, I could work with that.

I paused to get my breath on a landing. A paunchy Trigan was sitting in the corner, pressing a hypo to his wrist. He looked at me curiously.

"Where you going in such a hurry?" he asked.

I straightened up and went to the railing to look down. Still a lot of stairs.

"I'm moving on," I told him.

"Don't do it," he warned. "Don't do it before you have to."

I started down. The dark wasn't a problem, but I couldn't see around corners. I had to be careful, and the stench was starting to get to me in the enclosed space. At least the open outer walkways had some air circulation, but this stairwell was stagnant. There were breaks in the walls, and leaking pipes.

As I neared the bottom, I had to step over a dead body. Perhaps one in ten light fixtures still functioned, and where there was light, the walls were covered in scrawlings and crude artwork.

There were people in Cohengard who had learned that this sort of expression had once been used as a sort of political protest. When they'd tried to appropriate the technique for themselves, they'd found that the city's cleaning robots were more than a match for them. They'd taken to destroying the robots, then defacing buildings. All that, combined with avoiding the peacekeepers, amounted to a staggering amount of effort for what was at best a badly outdated form of protest.

Griffith and I had always had better things to do.

An imperial sustenance block was lavish compared to this. What an odd thought. There had been a time when no one ever would have been able to convince me that the day might come when I'd look back on sustenance with anything other than resignation. I'd always thought of sustenance as a prison, but if my life was a building, the very foundations were made of reinforced irony.

There was no map here. No directory but my memory, and that was one thing I couldn't fake.

I kept going, and listening. I passed a man making his way up, one hand clamped to the side of his bleeding head. Another man, hidden in the shadow of an archway, offered me stims in exchange for a fairly tame sexual favor. I didn't acknowledge him, but I wouldn't be able to close my ears forever. Sometimes looking like the beautiful Prince Dalton was handy, like when it had helped me get Salmagard on my side on Nidaros.

Here? Not an advantage.

The farther down I went, the worse it got. It was like descending into a lake of something black and sticky, feeling it soak into my clothes, inch by inch. Soon it would be over my head.

It was a long trip, clearly not meant for ordinary knees. My body tingled, and there was dizziness. It hadn't been as bad before, but the sudden exertion and repetitive climb down had made it worse. I didn't feel in control. It was like I was a guest in my own body, like my skin might grow wings and fly away.

It wasn't good, but it was still better than the withdrawal I'd dealt with on Nidaros, or the poison in my system while I'd been dragged around Free Trade space.

The bar had gotten pretty low.

I staggered off the bottom step and looked down at my hand. I stared at my new tattoo, then my palm. I opened and closed my fingers. It felt like my blood was angry. I'd never felt anything like this before, and when I was being Prince Dalton I'd gotten to feel a lot of different things. There weren't many chems a Ganraen prince couldn't get if he wanted them, though I'd mostly stuck to downers.

This wasn't a corridor, it was just an open space. There were thick columns, and debris, but I could see the archways. Each one was an exit. That was where I needed to go. The transition section was a mess, but it still had to function. There *had* to be a way out, and it couldn't be too difficult to reach; otherwise, it would defeat the purpose.

There were men in the gloom, but they weren't paying attention to me.

I wondered if my temper was really mine, or if my brain chemistry had gone to the same place my life had. I walked faster even though it wasn't prudent. I needed to be steadier, but a part of me was looking forward to this.

The processing blocks weren't just grimy and neglected; they were cramped. The outer walkways were nice because they offered a view, but they were still only about two meters wide. Down here, there was space among the columns, but what I really needed was to get into the open for real.

The arch led into a tunnel. There were cracks and stained outlines where machinery had once been. Automated vending, or maybe some kind of security checkpoint. New Brittia had grown and changed over time, always for the worse.

There was light ahead, but it was hazy because of some smoke or mist in the way. It wasn't an accident; this was here so there would be a recording of every transitioning inmate dramatically emerging from the tunnel. Hardly anyone would be paying attention to me right now, but that would change, and then that footage would be nice to have for the people running the show.

I stepped out of the cloud of theatrically billowing exhaust, into the open. This yard was maybe twenty meters wide and a hundred long. It was curved, tapering into a shape like a long teardrop.

The walls were at least forty meters high, and it was all ancient, rusted metal. The ground beneath my feet was metal too, and I was standing in a spot with particularly dodgy gravity that made me sick to my stomach. That hardly seemed fair; surely Baykara City had state of the art gravity, but down here in the prison, all we got was this?

Well, it wasn't as though it was the first time I'd been at the bottom of the socioeconomic ladder, although after being Dalton for so long, it was a bit of an adjustment. I'd spent almost three weeks in a sleeper after Shangri La; my mind knew that, but my brain felt like it had only been about twenty-four hours since I'd been sitting next to Tessa Salmagard on a shuttle to Imperial Pointe.

I wasn't even sure where the gravity was coming from. It could've been from a nearby ship, or it might've been a gravity drive inside the asteroid itself. That was probably it, going by how inconsistent it felt. The Baykara family had as much money as the collective populations of several star systems, but they wanted to leave people down here with a fifty-year-old gravity drive? That seemed kind of messed up.

There were a lot of inmates in the open. The atmosphere field gave the naked view of space a slightly yellowish tinge from this angle. From down here, I couldn't see much more than the processing block and the walls. There was a faint light up there, but it was so high up that I couldn't really see. That would be the city.

It was quiet. There had to be at least a hundred men in this yard with me, but they weren't making much noise. What was there to talk about?

I could even hear music, although it was a long way off. I wasn't sure if it was coming from the next section of the strut or floating down from the city.

I ignored the other inmates and started toward the far end. All the signs and markers were battered and faded, but

I no longer had to wonder where to go. This entire structure was built to funnel us toward this.

There were five gates. One inmate was seated cross-legged in front of one, gazing at it, resting his chin on his fists. He was around my age, with dark skin and long braided hair. He'd cut that soon if he was wise. The transition block had so far struck me as being pretty civilized, but things would be different on the other side of this wall. This guy knew it.

I passed him and kept on. Grates in the ground released hot steam, and I wasn't sure what that meant. Was there a legitimate mechanical reason for it? Or was it just ambience? I had my suspicions. There were obviously two aesthetics at work here, two sets of clothes for what amounted to the same person. Baykara City was glossy and beautiful, and New Brittia was grimy and disgusting. If you subscribed to the Baykara Network, you could take your pick.

Something for everyone.

A battered readout ten meters wide was above the five transition gates. It flickered, but I could still read the words.

WELCOME TO NEW BRITTIA

There was a nasty impact, and a cry of surprise went up behind me. I turned and looked back. There was a body lying on the metal near the wall.

I looked up at the walkways and openings stretching up into the haze. Thrown? Or jumped?

Probably jumped. That was probably common enough for people who got here and truly realized where they were. People who knew that no one was coming to buy them out and that they wouldn't make it inside. People who had been subscribers on the outside and consequently knew exactly what they were in for.

The high walkways certainly didn't make it difficult.

Or maybe, like me, he'd had to get acrobatic to escape something and he'd just slipped. I didn't have a monopoly on bad luck, even if it sometimes felt like it.

I turned back and headed for the gates.

A feed over the doors themselves resolved itself into the face of Abigail Baykara. Her features were washed out and indistinct but perfectly recognizable. Her glossy crimson lips curled into a smile, and the recording gave me a slightly challenging look.

"Are you ready to begin your sentence?"

Two

I rolled my eyes.

That was probably supposed to sound very meaningful and dramatic, but it was really just playing to the viewers. That was always the goal: finding ways to make real life look like a drama. Abigail's smugness was far uglier than her extensively modified face, and even if she *was* probably the single most influential woman alive, apart from the Empress, she was still trying too hard.

And did this thing actually want an answer?

"If it's not too much trouble," I said tiredly, and the doors opened. I didn't hesitate, and I didn't look back. There was a short corridor, and it was in much better repair than that oddly shaped courtyard. A second pair of doors lay ahead, and I couldn't help but notice how thick and serious they looked. I heard multiple locks sliding out of place.

There was a hatch to my left. Despite how awful it all looked, obviously some kind of maintenance had to be performed to keep this facility running. It would all be done by robots, and it would be just as secure as everything else. No one would escape New Brittia through something like this.

Not even me.

The second doors didn't open until the first had closed and sealed. Beyond lay a clean, bare room with a padded chair. Beside it was a small table. The chair and table were permanent fixtures that couldn't be moved. There was nothing else.

A sign directed me in both languages to sit.

The doors sealed behind me, and I looked around the room.

There was another hatch here, but it was harder to spot. This was a path for maintenance robots to get into this chamber, but it would probably be large enough for a very slight man to get through. There would be security measures and no way to open it locally. Technology was on my side, but only to a point.

I hadn't spotted any weaknesses so far. Then again, escape was the last thing on my mind.

I sat down, and the panel slid aside to reveal a plain, featureless robot. It was a cheap model in the shape of a human but too basic to be called an android. It had exposed joints and a hard, genderless body. Balanced on its hand was a tray with a glass. It stepped forward and put the glass on the table beside me. I'd heard about this little ritual, but I didn't have time for it. Tricks like this wouldn't even have worked on the old me.

"Can we speed this up?" I asked it, but it didn't reply.

A feed came alive, and Abigail Baykara's face appeared again. This wasn't a recording, but obviously Abigail

Baykara couldn't personally greet every new inmate. It was an AI using her face and voice to communicate, simulating her convincingly.

I didn't touch the glass offered by the robot. The liquid in it was amber, and it could be anything. Addictive stimulants, something to make me more aggressive, even an aphrodisiac—anything to make me more interesting to the audience. No, that was too cynical. It was just a stiff drink; an act of charity, a token of goodwill.

Or just a psychological cue to prime the inmate in the chair to believe what Abigail was about to say.

"Beta Two-Zero-Two," said the AI. "You have been incarcerated on multiple charges of murder and terrorism, calculated and converted by the Free Trade Charter. Your adjusted sentence is 42,991,900,074 days of confinement."

I wondered how often the AI got to read off a number that large. This was probably the first time. Another display lit up, showing the actual legal details of my predicament, but those weren't important to me at this point. For most people sent to New Brittia, the sentence was a little lighter—less than a lifetime, and therefore relevant to them in some way.

There was no point asking the AI to hurry up. It was going to say what it wanted to say. I'd have to take solace in the fact that it couldn't take *too* long because of the volume of inmates coming in at any given moment. Efficiency was needed for all this to work, and it *did* work.

There had been a similar orientation when I'd been taken off the transport and shuttled into the transition block, but for that one, I'd been chained up with thirty other guys to be inoculated, handed a gray jumpsuit and shoes, and told that if someone didn't buy me out of transition within sixty hours, I'd have to go to general population or be executed by Oversight.

It had now been nearly half an hour since then. It was probably uncommon for a man to make his way straight here this way. Someone would notice.

That was fine.

"But what if you could just make that sentence go away?" the AI Baykara asked. "You can. All you have to do is join the labor force. Your sentence, no matter how long it is, will be instantly erased. Then you can focus on getting out of New Brittia and back to your life—and you might even be able to go back a little richer. Think about it."

Abigail Baykara's face vanished, and a counter appeared. It looked like I had one hundred seconds before the doors opened. That was it. See? Efficient. They couldn't have us occupying these safe little closets for too long. That was what this was supposed to be, this chair and this room—one last moment to breathe before the real thing.

The AI made no mention of what the labor force entailed, or of the fact that every inmate of New Brittia was under constant surveillance and that all of the goings on—or all of the interesting ones—were being broadcast to billions of spectators at all hours.

We'd already been over all of that during my initial processing, but there hadn't been any need. It was common knowledge. Some of the people who ended up here were probably the types to actually indulge in New Brittia spectatorship out there in their normal lives.

Back in the Ganraen Royal Household, there had been a pair of executive maids that had been religious New Brittia viewers; they'd liked the romantic angle and were addicted to watching the love stories that would occasionally unfold among the inmates and laborers, and they would always be heartbroken when these men would inevitably die. Then a new one would strike their fancy, and their hearts would be aflutter again. There had even been people on my security detail that had talked about New Brittia openly.

Of course, Evagardians subscribed and watched as well, but they at least had enough shame not to talk about it in public.

And naturally, all of the Ganraen Royals, Prince Dalton being the only exception, were faithful patrons of the games up there in Baykara City. In fact, Prince Dalton had twice turned down opportunities to perform at the Baykara games. Once before I'd replaced him and once after.

The robot had retreated to its alcove and the cover had closed. Its real purpose was to force me out of the chamber if I refused to leave. Delivering that drink was its secondary function.

I left the glass where it was and pushed to my feet. Ethanol and I went way back, but it wouldn't do me any good now. Even if I drank it, I wouldn't feel a thing.

Ten seconds left on the clock.

It didn't matter who you were. Everybody knew about New Brittia even if they didn't subscribe to the Baykara Network. It was too ubiquitous, too culturally relevant. Evagard was only different because the Empress disapproved, hypocritically, of bloodsport, and so liking bloodsport was unfashionable. And being unfashionable was essentially un-Evagardian.

Lots of things were un-Evagardian, but even after all these years, it still wasn't clear to me what *was* properly Evagardian. Fortunately, that no longer bothered me.

Now that I was here, I wished I'd actually watched a few of these broadcasts. What little information I had was only data. It was all academic.

And so far, my meager knowledge hadn't proved particularly accurate or useful.

The exit opened, and in front of me were stairs leading down.

I descended into another yard, this one much larger than the one above. The walls were higher and the space was vast. It was packed with men and teeming with activity. Two guys immediately pushed past me into the corridor, ducking through the doors before they could close.

I ignored them and stepped into the crowd. Many of these men were wearing the gray of inmates, but there were also some in the amber of laborers.

I had to move. The space was hexagonal, and the middle was filled with structures and kiosks manned and operated by inmates. Men without the courage or stupidity to join the labor force could still earn something for themselves by supporting the laborers.

New Brittia's economy was an incomprehensible tangle of what was deliberately fed into the prison by the Baykara family, what was brought in by corrupt Oversight personnel, and the true black market, which was sponsored by organized crime, which was in turn sponsored by the extremely wealthy people who wanted very badly to influence the happenings within their favorite form of entertainment.

In the end, it amounted to no shortage of contraband, and plenty of money moving around. It was a Free Trade dream come true. Evagardians liked to think that they, the imperials, were the civilized ones. And they believed that everyone else, the galactics, anyone outside the Imperium, were the barbarians.

Places like New Brittia made that an easy to prejudice to cultivate.

Housing blocks surrounded the yard. This was Balkin Strut, so the proper name for this place was Balkin Square.

There were four housing blocks for sleeping, and at the opposite end of the square was the labor gate.

My view of Baykara City was better from here. It was still far away and dizzyingly high up, but at least I could see it up there, touching the stars. It was every bit as impressive as the Royal District on Little Norwich.

Former district. *Former* Ganraen capital station. And so on.

It was done up with an aesthetic that was borrowed from—or at least influenced by—the east of Old Earth, but without the evolution seen by proper modern Isakan artistry. Lots of tiers and curling architecture, all sitting on the gargantuan pile of metal and composite that made up the prison, which in turn sat on the rock of the asteroid. From a distance it was a peculiar sight, a lot of bright lights and delicate details perched atop a mountain of rust and ore.

Maybe it looked less tacky up close.

The gate to my right opened and another man in gray emerged. I wondered how many guys came through in an hour. And how many were dead by the time the next crop showed up. Obviously the numbers were sustainable; New Brittia had been doing this for a long time, and by all accounts, the business model was still expanding.

It looked like a lot to me, but this was only Balkin Strut. On the other side of the asteroid was Alpine Strut, which housed a facility just like this, with just as many men.

I moved away from the gates, but only enough to get out of the way. I took up a position beside a vendor that looked like it operated with some kind of physical data carrier, maybe a card. Quaint, but in keeping with New Brittia's culture. Digital money wasn't interesting to watch. A card was different, though. You had to protect it, or someone could take it from you.

I leaned against the metal wall and folded my arms, watching the people in the square. I turned in time to see a man deliver a powerful punch to another man's kidney from behind, staggering him. He grabbed him and dragged him through an archway into the sleep block. No one even spared the incident a glance. Not very romantic, but who was I to judge?

A moment later, a fight broke out in the direction of the stalls and kiosks. I couldn't see what was happening, but after a few moments of chaos, there was a noise that sounded uncannily like the unique note of a snapping spine, but it was hard to be sure over the music.

My eyes caught on a familiar face. I recognized him, even in profile, though I was having trouble recalling his name. My latest sleeper wakeup was to blame for that. Idris, that was it. Those two galactic freelancers had tried to sell me, Salmagard, and those other two imperials to this guy. He'd bought Salmagard and the other girl—but that other girl wasn't just anyone. She was Diana Kladinova.

There was no getting around it; I owed Salmagard and Kladinova a debt.

Kladinova especially. I was good at a lot of things, but forgetting wasn't one of them.

Idris' business model had been an interesting one. We'd never been meant to fall into his hands, of course. We'd been *meant* to be snatched away from those two freelancers long before they got anywhere with us.

And Salmagard and I had been meant to get to Red Yonder. And we hadn't meant to be stranded on Nidaros. And I hadn't ever meant to hurt anyone.

The joke was on me.

Idris was wearing gray; that made him an inmate, not a laborer. If he was here, he'd probably been picked up thanks to Salmagard and Kladinova. He was selling chems by some tables, and that made sense. He didn't look like the type to try his luck as a laborer, but he had to make his way somehow.

Time passed. I knew things were more subdued out here. These men were being broadcast wherever they were, but there would always be a powerful psychological block in place. People showed restraint in the open. In the comparative privacy of the blocks, things would be different.

If the men in amber knew what was good for them, they'd stay out of those sleeping blocks. And the men in gray couldn't get into the labor section. That meant this place, this square, was the common ground for everyone. It wasn't safe by any means, but it was as close to safe as anyone could get.

I was deliberately standing in shadow, mostly hidden by the vending box, but I still got a few curious looks. My resemblance to Prince Dalton wouldn't be *immediately* noticeable. My hair was short, and my features had been tweaked before my rendezvous with Salmagard so that I looked almost like myself. That didn't help much, though. Me, Prince Dalton—neither one of us had the right kind of look for prison.

I'd caught the attention of a laborer already. There was no solution to this, nowhere for me to go. Certainly no one was going to help me deal with him. I kept still and politely pretended not to notice him, but that wasn't an option once he got in close.

He was a head taller than I was, he had curly hair, and he wasn't bad looking. More importantly, he had a perfect shave, he looked very clean, and he even smelled good. So he wasn't just a laborer; he was a laborer that was doing well enough to finance some self-respect.

This kept getting worse. He wasn't completely made of muscles, but his frame was so much bigger than mine that those details wouldn't matter. At least, not under normal circumstances.

"Sorry, I'm waiting for someone." I waved a hand to shoo him away.

I had no reason not to be upfront. I knew the look on his face; I'd seen it before, just not on him. And there was nothing illogical about his interest. Hooking up with a laborer was a good idea for a guy who couldn't make it as a laborer himself. I still had Prince Dalton's height, but that alone didn't make me scary. Nobody was going to look at me and think I was laborer material. I was loitering in a new gray uniform in Balkin Square as though I had nothing to do. This had been inevitable.

I looked up at him, hoping my expression would convey to him that I meant what I said. I wasn't sure what I'd do if he didn't pick up on it and back off. I couldn't have trouble here; *this* spot was where I needed to be. I couldn't leave.

"Fair enough," he said, smiling. I let out my breath as he walked away.

I waited, but my luck couldn't hold forever. Someone else would accost me, and they might not be as reasonable. On the other hand, how long was I going to wait? There was a feed in the middle of the square, projected in the air. I could see what time it was.

I stepped out of the shadows, looking around. It was time to stop kidding myself.

I made for where the action was. In addition to the men in gray, there were a few of those androgynous androids out here as well. This was a marketplace, but there was just as much bargaining and gambling going on as buying and selling. Just as the viewers out there were betting on the laborers, so were the men here—men who could potentially have a hand in their fates.

It was simple enough to do. That laborer back there that had tried to pick me up, for example. I could bet against him, then let him take me somewhere private and hurt him somehow. If I walked away from that alive, leaving him injured would hurt his odds and potentially make me some money.

Which I wouldn't have for long; either he or someone else would take it from me, and I probably wouldn't enjoy or even survive the process.

I didn't want money. The currency here was just an arbitrary credit system, but it was a part of the Free Trade exchange, so it could be converted to real money if someone actually managed to get their freedom, which happened often. Not because winning freedom was so easy, but because the scale of New Brittia was so vast that while there were hundreds of men doing poorly at any given moment, at least one somewhere had to be succeeding.

There was no day or night cycle. No sun, no moon. Just the gradually shifting ceiling of stars. The lights were always dim, creating the illusion of evening or twilight, and the idea was to make the lights of the marketplace seem to pop, maybe even to create a festive atmosphere for the viewers.

There was nothing festive about the atmosphere in front of me, but the broadcasters were probably able to tweak the truth a little before it reached the spectators. Music, editing, lively commentary. They were good at their jobs; the Baykara Network was the most-watched entertainment programming in the galaxy.

I strolled along, absently rubbing my wrist and trying to avoid eye contact. Standing still for a while had helped. I felt stable, though I still wasn't myself, and things weren't looking up.

I'd put my faith in a plan.
I should've known better.

Three

Perspective could make the labor section seem to outshine the general quartering. It wasn't good by any means, but it would be noticeably less awful than the ruins that the inmates wearing gray had to sleep in.

Without an amber uniform of my own, I couldn't get in.

There were at least a dozen other inmates doing precisely what I was: gazing at the labor corps. A couple of them were probably about to walk into those recruitment cells. They were gathering their courage, and I respected that.

But I wasn't one of them. I wasn't there to make up my mind; I'd already done that. I was watching the scoreboard, scanning the names of the laborers. I didn't see what I'd hoped for, but I hadn't expected this to be easy.

"Looking for me?"

I turned. It was the big guy from just a minute ago. He wasn't following me; I'd have noticed that. This was coincidence.

"I'm looking for a guy called Atlas," I told him. "Do you know him?"

"Tattoos?"

I tried to remember, and there was a spark of hope. "I think so. Here." I touched my neck on the right side. "His suit might have a spider on the back." That was all I had to go on.

The blond man nodded. "I queued with him. It was a day or two ago. Haven't seen him since."

I pointed at the scoreboard. "He's not active right now, but is there a way to find out if he's in there or out here?"

He appeared to consider the question. "You could join labor," he said.

"I'm not the type."

"You don't look *that* weak."

"I'm not a fighter," I told him honestly.

He snorted. "I guess you could ask one of us to go in and look for him."

What a subtle guy.

"Fine." This was the fastest way, and I didn't want to risk signing on as a laborer myself. The blond man looked pleased, but I cut him off with a look before he could speak. One of us had to take a risk here, and it wouldn't be me.

"If I bring him out here, then there's two of you," he pointed out. "What if you decide to change the deal?"

"Bring a friend."

He considered it.

"I'll be here," I told him. He didn't bother to threaten me or warn me not to try to weasel out of my end. That all went without saying. He just gave me a genuinely good-natured look and jogged off toward the nearest labor entrance.

This wasn't a great move, but I didn't see a better option.

I immediately broke my promise to wait in that spot and found a shadowed corner. Standing in plain view would get me an endless stream of propositions until someone turned up that wouldn't take no for an answer.

It wasn't easy to keep a lookout; there was too much going on. Even though the men in amber stood out easily among all the inmates in gray, I wasn't confident in my ability to spot Atlas in the crowd.

And I wasn't making it easy for him to find me, but I'd waited by the gates already. What more could I do? He hadn't shown up.

More minutes passed, and while the peculiarities in my body faded gradually, my nerves didn't. I was clenching my hands so hard that I nearly broke the skin. I needed to loosen up, but that wasn't going to happen. I'd been in some awkward situations before, but nothing like this. There was no loosening up here, not really. How many people died here each hour? Each minute?

The noise level didn't change as the minutes went by. These men did not get tired of shouting and fighting, and at least two romantic liaisons took place behind the next stall over while I waited. They could get a measure of privacy from the other inmates, but there was no privacy from the broadcast.

At least a few people were enjoying themselves. I waited twenty minutes before the blond man emerged from the labor block.

He was alone. My heart sank, and he looked a bit disappointed too.

"I don't think he's in," he said. From the amount of time he'd taken, it seemed like he'd made a real effort to find Atlas for me.

"Thanks anyway," I told him absently. I was already thinking about what I was going to do next.

"Going to look for him? I can help," he offered.

That was flattering. "There are easier ways to get laid." I had no more use for this man, and his offer to accompany me would probably last until we were somewhere reasonably isolated. Then I might learn that his good manners were dependent on witnesses. It wouldn't end well. I had to shake him off now, and for a second time, he fell back without protest.

That was encouraging. There were reasonable guys in here. I had no place to judge; after all, there was no one in all of New Brittia with a sentence like mine.

It was a shame I couldn't show the details of my conviction to my suitors. I didn't look like someone with twenty million murders to my credit. Though, to be fair, what *does* someone like that look like?

I slipped into the fray among the stalls.

I needed somewhere high-traffic where I could find someone who knew a lot of people. Idris. I'd spotted him once, but he wasn't at that spot anymore. That was a pity, but I couldn't stop. What was the most critical necessity? Water?

Water would be attainable inside the blocks. So I needed something else, something basic, something that everyone needed. How about calories? There were a lot of people and androids peddling foodstuffs.

Somewhere, there had to be food that didn't need to be bought. New Brittia was a business, but this section of it was also a prison, so by Free Trade law, a man in lawful confinement had to be provided with certain things, which included a certain ration of calories. As a private prison, New Brittia was exempt from some rules, but there would still be food and water.

Using hunger to ratchet up the drama and tension in the broadcast certainly wasn't beyond them, but there would be a protein dispenser somewhere. That would be the best place to start looking.

Each block had its own canteen. None of them were covered; there was no rain, no weather of any sort here. The sky was a ceiling of energy, a nearly invisible bubble that enclosed the entirety of New Brittia, along with Oversight and Baykara City. Actually three bubbles: the main protector, the backup, and the purely visual holo-filter that made it look pretty.

There were a few obelisks with taps and water filters, and old protein dispensers. Even now, a pack of maintenance robots were at work repairing one. Inmates were less apt to abuse the prison's facilities here because they were in the open, vulnerable to sniper fire from Oversight. They could smash up the inside of the blocks all they wanted, but out here, the guards would probably shoot people that broke things meant for common use. A protein dispenser was expensive to replace, but an inmate wasn't.

There was a lot of old equipment that clearly did not work, and since Oversight rarely set boots on the floor of Balkin Square, there was no one but these robots to clear away refuse. Things that were too big to move that way, like a broken vending pylon, would just sit here as part of the scenery indefinitely.

There were tables and benches, all synthetic with simple, heavy construction. Nearby was strength-training equipment, and that stuff was getting a lot of use. Survival was the first concern in New Brittia, but the adoration of the spectators was the next most important consideration.

Inmates and laborers alike wanted to be strong, and to sculpt their bodies. Exercise was one of the best uses of one's time.

I had yet to be surprised by anything that had happened here, but that didn't mean my visit was going well. It was time to follow my intuition—by the look of things, it was all I had. This wasn't like the surface of Nidaros. There was no one route to victory, and there were no convenient imperial trainees to watch my back and pick up the slack. I needed help, but I had to keep my eye on the bigger picture.

I picked out a young man that looked safe to approach. He was alone, visibly melancholy, and no bigger than I was. A bowl of some kind of protein and an improvised spoon sat in front of him, but he wasn't eating.

I sat down and caught his eye.

"Hi," he said. There was a touch of Earth East or Isakan in him, but not much; it was really only visible in his eyes. His accent was Commonwealth Colonial, and he didn't seem unfriendly. My luck was holding, if that was what it was called.

"I just got here," I told him. "I'm looking for a laborer named Atlas."

"Never heard of him." He absently stirred his protein.

"I'm not surprised. But how do I find somebody like that?"

"Do you know for sure that he's on this strut?" the boy asked.

"Yes."

"Ask one of these guys wearing yellow."

"I did. It didn't help. How do you find people?"

The boy seemed genuinely intrigued. "I don't know," he said. "Ask around?" He shrugged. "I don't really know what you're asking me."

"Neither do I, I guess. I was hoping for a miracle."
There was no directory. No system in place for one inmate
to locate another. A part of me had known.

He snorted.

I ran a hand through my hair. "Where can I go for
communications?"

"To the outside? Spirluck." He pointed his spoon at a
block on the other side of the square. He saw my look of
relief. "It's not free," he added, looking sympathetic.

"Naturally. Thanks." I pushed to my feet.

"No worries."

What had this kid done to end up here? I couldn't think
about that; we all had a story.

It wasn't much to go on, but if Atlas and I had missed
each other, and it seemed that we had, he'd be going for
comms. Even if I was wrong about that, *I* needed comms.

Maybe the way I felt could be blamed on something
other than being a lightweight. It had been so long since I'd
been at my best that I was starting to wonder if that had
ever been real. The way my heart was beating made me
think of waves, of being in an ocean, just a small object
absolutely at the mercy of something vast and
unfathomable. It was supposed to be the other way around,
and it *was*.

It just didn't feel like it.

Even in my former life in Cohengard, I hadn't been
completely aimless. I'd had Griffith to follow around back
then. Our goals hadn't been anything much longer-term
than having fun, but things had started to take shape after
we met Inge. Even before Griffith, there had always been
Evagard. Society. The path, the funnel, the corridor made
up by culture and expectations. You always knew what to
do. You just had to do what other people did. Get an
education, make yourself useful.

You could even just sit around in sustenance housing until you grew old and died. People did it. It wasn't a desirable option, but it was theoretically available to everyone.

Then I'd become Prince Dalton, and ever since, I'd been asking how it could have come to this.

Gamma Block looked the same as the other blocks, but there was someone in there with influence. Spirluck, the boy had said. It was a weird name, and whoever he was, someone was propping him up—maybe the Baykara family, maybe some Free Trade gangsters. Cartels, whatever. Who could keep it all straight?

New Brittia's interior lifestyle wasn't sustainable; to keep things moving, to keep the mix of men in here at its most volatile, the showrunners had to take a hand in things personally. Someone like this Spirluck would help regulate the flow of goods and services.

There was no official means of communication with the outside for inmates, but there would be some unofficial ones. It was ironic: Oversight was actually more isolated from the galaxy than the prisoners. Oversight guards and staff were absolutely cut off, not only from the broadcasts, but from anyone who had access to them. They had too much power over the inmates; obviously they couldn't be allowed to bet—nor could they communicate with people who could bet. They didn't work shifts; they worked tours, like soldiers, except with contracts that amounted to indentured servitude.

The pay was good, but they were prisoners too.

At least inmates could pay exorbitant prices to send and receive messages on the black market. Some avid Trigan mining baron would reach out and place a bounty on the head of his most-hated laborer or inmate, and men like Spirluck would try to collect it. It seemed like ugly business, but my understanding of New Brittia was far from complete. Not a minute went by where I didn't wish I'd paid closer attention to it when I'd had the chance.

But it went against my upbringing. One of the Empress's core teachings was that bloodshed for entertainment lowered everyone involved. The only place in the empire where an Evagardian could lawfully and honorably take another Evagardian's life in front of an audience was Valadilene. And that was, at least officially, not for entertainment.

On the outside, everything about New Brittia was the opposite of the Evagardian aesthetic. But was it? It was just survival of the fittest. Sure, in Evagard, pretty much everyone survived – but it was the same principle. *Success* of the fittest.

So this was just like home.

That didn't cheer me up; it was starting to look like there was nothing here but me and my best guess. It was a punchline for the ages, but no one would ever hear it.

Coming here had been my idea, after all.

There were no guards at the archways. No one cared if I just strolled into Gamma Block; I was entitled to be there, in theory. I was an inmate, so I could look for a bunk in any of these blocks.

It was dark. There were portable light sources inside some of the cells, and the feeble glow would spill into the halls.

Outside, everything was dirty. In here, the filth was more severe. The smell was almost enough to stop me, but the relative quiet almost made up for it.

There were no lifts and no windows. Without a view, there was no advantage to being high up in the block. That meant that rooms here at the bottom would be the most valuable, which explained why there were so few people around. These cells and these bunks were spoken for by people who weren't to be trifled with.

There was a hint of amber, and I stopped, backpedaling to look into a cell. There was a laborer's suit hanging on the wall, shredded and covered in dark stains. A trophy.

It was too big to belong to Atlas.

And there was a boy sleeping on the bunk. His ankles were tied.

I still had my shiv. There was no one to stop me from cutting him free. But where was there for him to go? Whoever had tied him up might catch up to him if I freed him, and in that scenario, had I really done him a favor? Maybe my meddling would just get him killed. But this was New Brittia, and he'd be dead soon anyway. I could only do for him what I'd hope someone else might do for me. I was already on record as being responsible for so many deaths that one more wouldn't make any difference.

I cut him loose and gave him a shake to rouse him. He came to, but I was already gone.

I didn't have time for this. It would take more than a few random acts of misguided kindness to get my karma out of the red. That would take miracles on top of miracles, and I hadn't even seen one yet.

Spirluck's enclave wouldn't be so far from the exit, but I didn't know the way. I should've asked someone how to get to him. As for what I was going to do when I got there—well, that was where things would get interesting. These people wouldn't let anything go without payment. There was no easy workaround; I'd have to do what I had to. The stakes were too high for me to take any unnecessary chances.

The synthetic walls gave the place the acoustics of an Old-Earth cathedral. I heard a snort of laughter and the impact of a punch or a kick. The snap of a bone. A groan of pleasure. There were ghostly sounds in front and behind.

There was a stairwell leading down. I hadn't realized there were lower levels as well.

There were cries of pain.

I kept walking. A man came out of the cell ahead very suddenly, startling me. He'd been pushed, but he just shook it off and brushed past me. There were four men playing cards in another cell by the light of a readout.

The dark worked in my favor. People would notice that I wasn't as big or built as they were, but they wouldn't notice much else.

My luck wouldn't hold forever, though.

There was a bark of laughter, and two men emerged from a side passage, naked and glistening with water. They were both carrying gray jumpsuits, but one of them also had an amber one over his arm, and it was wet and dripping.

It wasn't easy to see, but my eyes caught it: crude, black stitching in the shape of a spider.

That suit belonged to Atlas.

Four

I watched them go, then went into the narrow passage they'd emerged from. Running water was loud in the air, which wasn't quite as foul here.

The shower was another wide, low room. The walls were tiled, and it wasn't in any better repair than the rest of the block. The taps were permanently on, but the drainage was obviously lacking, because there was half a meter of standing water.

Water tinged with pink.

There was a man on the other side, face-down, sprawled across the steps that ringed the outside of the room, motionless. His mouth was only partially above the water.

The tattoos covering his dusky skin were all on display.

I stood in the doorway for just a moment, then stepped in, my jumpsuit immediately soaking through. I splashed across the shower and dropped to my knees.

The size of the jumpsuit in the man's arms back there had looked right. I still hadn't expected it to *be* right.

Atlas was bleeding from a brutal head wound, a dent in his skull that he'd never seen coming. His eyes were open, but the left one was bloodshot. His breaths were shallow and ragged, and he was choking. I turned him over and elevated his head, cradling it. He couldn't see me. Tearing gasps bubbled from his chest, and there was pink foam at the corners of his mouth.

I sat back against the wall, and water fell on either side of us.

I was grateful for the noise; it almost drowned out his pitiful breathing.

He gave occasional, violent shudders, but he wouldn't move again, not in any meaningful way. The water was lukewarm, but it felt like ice. Atlas' blood spread in tendrils, highlighting the lazy currents leading to the drains that still functioned.

The man in my arms was a total stranger. I'd never met him, but the future had been in his hands.

I locked my arm around his throat, shut my eyes, and squeezed. He'd already breathed some water. I could feel the rattle, the wrongness in his chest as he labored for breath.

It felt like it took a long time for him to go still.

A long time ago, a Cohengardian woman had been leaning precariously on her apartment balcony in Inge's sustenance block. A peacekeeping shuttle had sped past quite low, where normally there would be no flyer traffic. It startled her, and she fell.

It was a nightmare scenario that got an enormous amount of exposure. It wasn't a blunder on the part of the peacekeepers, and it certainly wasn't the woman's fault. It wasn't anyone's fault; she fell more than a hundred meters and died instantly.

Evagardian medicine had *still* been able to put her back together. She lost a certain amount of brain function, and an enormous percentage of her body had to be replaced with prosthetics and regrown. It was said that she wasn't quite the same person that she had been before in addition to having lost a step intellectually—but that didn't change the fact that a splattered mess had been restored to a walking, talking human being who had gone on to have a life.

The same story was common during wars, for soldiers who suffered enormous wounds but were put into stasis in time and repaired later. I'd seen it myself with Nils back on Nidaros. And Salmagard, who like that Cohengardian woman had been medically deceased.

For Atlas, all it had taken was a bump on the head.

It should have been a killing blow, but some quirk, some twist of fate had kept it just short of that. There was no medical care for him here, much less care at an imperial level. Say what you want about the Empress; if you're going to get hurt, Evagardian space is the place to do it.

Even a normal prison in any but the least enlightened corners of space would at least have an infirmary.

But who would want to watch people convalescing?

There was no help for the wounded in New Brittia. Maybe I could find some basic first aid supplies out in the square, but those wouldn't have done Atlas any good. Maybe nothing could have saved him. After all, what were the odds that this was coincidence? It hadn't been coincidence that I'd found myself on Nidaros of all planets.

And it hadn't been coincidence when those two freelancers ruined my plans with Salmagard.

I sat there for a minute. It would've been longer if someone hadn't showed up to shower.

The man glanced at me holding Atlas' body and promptly ignored me. He folded his gray jumpsuit and put it on a dry spot in the doorway before stepping under the nearest stream.

And he hadn't recognized me. If coincidence had taken Atlas, then it was handing me this—that would've been very tidy, if I hadn't stopped believing in coincidence such a long time ago.

Atlas was dead. Sitting in a shower holding a corpse wasn't the way forward. I let him go and got to my feet.

"Idris," I said. My voice didn't carry; the water was noisy. But Idris turned around, brushing his bangs out of his eyes.

He'd bought Salmagard, and she'd promptly escaped. It was no surprise that this man had ended up in New Brittia. Whether he'd been busted on his own time or taken down because Salmagard reported him, he was a criminal. Even in Free Trade space, criminals still occasionally went to prison when they got caught.

It took Idris a moment to recognize me, and by the time he did, I had closed the distance between us. He could no longer easily escape, even if he obviously wanted to. He backed up until he hit the wall. Prince Dalton was still tall enough to loom over someone like him, and that was what I did. There was nowhere for him to shrink back to, although he tried.

"How long have you been here?" I asked him over the roaring water. I made an effort to keep my voice even, but I wasn't going to be able to just slip into a facade of calm.

Whatever my face looked like, it made Idris want to be somewhere else.

He just put on a defiant look. He wasn't young or pretty, but he wasn't hideous, and worst of all, he had a small frame. In a place like New Brittia, that above all else identified someone as a victim. I could tell from his face that he'd already seen his share of hardship. He hadn't been anyone outside, so in here, he was less than nothing.

But he was still alive, and whole. That said something about him.

"You've been here before, haven't you?" I pressed.

He nodded.

"How long?"

Hesitation. "Forty days," he replied, holding my gaze.

Despite everything, I was impressed. Idris didn't look like much, but to survive that kind of time in New Brittia, he had to be tough, or at least resourceful. And whoever he was now, it wasn't the same person he'd been before his first stretch here.

That was good news.

"I need your help," I told him.

His tough act was good, but I'd seen better. I grabbed his throat with my right hand and pushed him into the wall, then lifted him off his feet.

"I don't have time to negotiate," I said.

He choked and nodded vigorously, face red, clutching at my wrist. I dropped him with a splash and stepped back, then crouched in front of him as he got to his hands and knees. His eyes were wide, but they weren't on my face. He was looking at my arm, wondering how such puny muscles could have picked him up so easily.

"How much time do you have on the clock?" I asked.

"Two thousand days," he gasped, rubbing at his throat.

"Were you planning to do the time? Or join labor?"

He shook his head, grimacing. "I don't know."

"Helping me could get you noticed."

That got his attention. He sagged against the wall, squinting at me. "Who *are* you?" he asked.

"A terrorist."

"An imperial. I remember."

"Don't worry, I don't hold grudges. I have things to do."

"Like what?"

I got to my feet and glanced at Atlas' body. "Like getting out of here before what happened to him happens to me." There was a shred of truth in what I said; I wasn't a very popular guy, and events in here could be influenced by people on the outside. Enough people wanted me dead that if I didn't keep moving, my sentence would be even shorter than I wanted it to be.

He picked himself up.

I'd suspected that Atlas might have come into this block to try to broker a deal to use Spirluck's communications equipment. From the look of things, I'd been at least partially right.

None of that mattered now.

Idris was by no means onboard with my proposition, but with no play to make, he had no choice but to play hostage.

He pulled on his jumpsuit, and I pushed him into the shadowy corridor. Nowhere was safe. There was no place in all of New Brittia that we could let down our guard, but it was less perilous out in the open. We needed to get out of this block and back to Balkin Square.

Idris was looking for an opening, but I wouldn't give him one. I kept my hand on him with enough grip to make my point. He was intrigued by what I'd said, but that alone wouldn't earn his trust.

This was my life. I just couldn't close my eyes without waking up to a new reality. No one wanted to show me the way; everyone else had it easy, with orders to follow.

A plan.

I'd had a plan once, but it hadn't included a stint in New Brittia. I thought of the Vanguard.

It was a prestigious Evagardian position that could only be held by one person at a time in the entire empire, always an Acolyte. The Vanguard was the very best that the Empress's Garden had to offer. Although Acolytes served alongside the Service, they were actually a separate entity with their own little hierarchy inside the Garden, much closer to the Empress herself.

The Vanguard was a symbol. Acolytes were already those with the highest aptitudes and the most training. They used a weapon that even soldiers in the Service didn't have access to: nanotechnology. Tiny machines inside the body, undetectable to scans. In the dramas, the nanomachines always materialized as swords for exciting duels, but in real life, they had more important duties, like regulating body chemistry and countering threats like targeting computers and smart weapons. An Acolyte full of Evagardian nanomachines would be hard to hit with a bullet, and even then that might not be enough to stop them—the nanomachines would influence the nervous system to minimize pain, all the while repairing the damage far faster than the body ever could on its own.

Someone like that would be hard to deal with.

The Vanguard was supposed to be the best of all of them, a single figure. Not a leader in terms of policy, but a more literal physical leader. A single human being at the very front of a formal, uniformed Evagardian assault. Those didn't happen often, but when they did, they only ended one way.

Even the Vanguard, whoever it was at the moment, had things easier than I did. They were just a weapon. A blunt instrument; they had all of the Imperium to point them in the right direction.

The Vanguard never had to question anything.

From the outside, it might look like the Vanguard was the one forging the path ahead, but that wasn't true. The Empress was the one making the decisions.

She was always the one making the decisions. She was only one woman, and she could only have her own hands on so much, if she was even real. But it was her thinking, even if it was only imagined, upon which it had all been built.

All roads led to her in the end. Yet at the same time, it was all but impossible to meet her. The big Evagardian joke: everyone knew it, but it just wasn't funny.

We emerged from Gamma Block, and it was sad that the colorful but dim lights of Balkin Square were bright enough to make me squint. The smell wasn't as bad, and my standards had gotten low enough for that alone to lift my mood.

Even New Brittia could seem welcoming at the right moment, with the right perspective.

Idris and I were still soaked, but there were nude inmates and those who had altered their jumpsuits, or colored them to form elaborate costumes. Many of the laborers wore pieces of improvised armor, some of which were pretty outlandish. No one was going to spare a glance for us just because we were wet. I let go of the back of Idris' neck, and he reached back to rub it.

"What do you need me for?" he asked. "You want to know who killed that guy back there? You'll never find them. It could've been anyone. It happens all the time."

"He doesn't matter. There's someone else here," I said, still gazing at the lights. "That guy in there was going to help me find him. Maybe you can help me instead."

FIVE

Stay in plain view and risk being accosted by anyone passing by? Or go somewhere private, and invite more aggressive, predatory behavior?

I didn't know which was worse. I sat down at an empty table and leaned back. It was cooler out here, and wet clothes weren't exactly comfortable.

Discomfort I could live with; I was still better off than Atlas.

"Griffith Karlsson," Idris said, sitting down beside me. "I feel like I've heard that name before." His voice was wary, but he was expecting something from me that wasn't coming. I didn't have time for the past. It didn't really matter that Idris and I had met before; if I hadn't run into him, I'd have just found someone else and bullied them instead.

My distaste for him was the last thing on my mind, and he was starting to pick up on that.

"You probably have," I told him. Griffith wasn't as famous as Prince Dalton, but he'd made his share of headlines.

"You know he's here?"

"He should be," I said, gazing up at the gargantuan housing blocks. "As of a few hours ago." But people died here every minute.

"Is he a friend?"

"My only friend."

"But you don't know where he is."

I gestured vaguely at the chaos. "I was going to have help finding him."

Idris sighed, giving me a vaguely disdainful look. "I don't know what you think I can do. How is this going to get people watching?"

"I told you. I'm a terrorist. I matter. Just being with me will get you noticed. You've been here before. Think. How would you do it?"

"I'd talk to people," Idris said.

I shook my head. "I don't have that kind of time. Every time you walk up to someone in here you throw the dice. The law of averages isn't on my side." I opened and closed my fingers.

"Why do you keep doing that?" Idris asked, and I stopped.

"Don't worry about me. There are records. A roster. Everything's tracked."

"Yeah."

"How do we get at that information?"

He stared at me. "Oversight has it."

"But how would you *get* it?"

He considered it. "There are workarounds for Oversight's blackout."

"Inmates who get information from the outside, then feed it to Oversight so they can make moves?"

Idris nodded, scowling. "It can't be very efficient, but I've never gotten near that stuff. We all know it goes on."

"But that communication channel exists? From us to Oversight?"

He chewed his lip, then shrugged. "It has to. But it won't come cheap."

"How secure can their systems be?"

Idris cocked his head. "You're a breaker?"

"No, but someone here is."

"And they're not running a charity," Idris reminded me.

Everyone kept saying that, like I didn't know.

"Let me worry about that," I told him.

"As long as you don't think you're going to trade me for anything."

"I wasn't planning on it. How do we do this? Who is this guy they call Spirluck?"

"I don't know. He's big. He's over in Gamma." Idris pointed.

"Was he here the last time you were?"

"No."

"Then he's not one of these lifers like you see in the dramas?"

"Those don't exist." That was a pity, but it made sense. You got out, or you died.

"He'll have someone who can do what I need done. All we have to do is find him."

"Then what?"

"Diplomacy," I replied.

"The same kind you're using on me?" Idris asked dryly.

"Confrontation isn't my strong suit."

"If you try to scam them, they'll find you," Idris promised. "No one will tell *you* anything for free, but it's different when it's Spirluck's guys asking. You can't get away from them if you do something stupid."

"I don't plan to be here long enough for it to matter."

"You don't look crazy," Idris said. "But then you open your mouth."

I glanced over at him. "Plenty of people have gotten out before their sentences were up."

"Laborers. And corpses."

"And guys like me."

That gave Idris pause.

"Think about it," I told him. "This is a business. Every day the viewers get to watch the usual." I indicated with my eyes where a guy was taking a savage beating between two stalls. "Viewers like to see something different. And what the viewers like, the network likes. Maybe even enough to help out."

"You have something up your sleeve."

"I did," I said. "But now he's floating in that shower. If Spirluck has what I need, let's go see him." I got to my feet and Idris got to his, looking pained. "You were living in there, weren't you? Why are you afraid to go back in?"

"I was hiding," he said.

"In plain sight? You thought if you walked around the first level like you owned it, people would just assume that you belonged?"

"Something like that."

We gazed up at the block. If I'd known a little less about Idris, I might've been starting to like him.

"What do they do with bodies?" I asked.

"Your friend? They'll take him outside, and the robots get them."

"Do you know where we have to go once we're in there?"

Idris nodded slowly. "I can *find* it. Not sure I want to."

I wasn't expecting it to be easy. Frankly, easy only would've made me suspicious.

There were three archways leading into Gamma Block and there were people outside all of them, but they weren't guards, though most of them probably worked for Spirluck in some capacity. I'd gotten past them once by looking confident, and I could do it again.

Idris knew what he was doing. He was no Atlas, but his relative competence might be enough to tip things my way.

"What happened to them?" Idris asked as we passed through the archway. We got looks, but no one bothered us as we traded the light of the square for the shadows of the halls.

"Who?"

Talking would help us sell the illusion that we felt at home.

"The girls."

"I don't know."

Idris sighed. "That's the problem with you imperials."

"What?"

"You're just trouble. All of you."

I smiled in the dark.

He gave me a funny look. "Were you *all* terrorists? You and the girls?"

"Just me, but the others will be in trouble for being seen with me. That's why we have to hurry."

"Why?"

"Because Evagard wants me, and by now they know I'm here."

"You think they'll come for you?"

"They already are."

That took Idris aback. "If you're such a scary terrorist, why haven't I heard of you?"

"You have."

He didn't' reply to that. We turned a corner, passing by a guy about my size. He didn't seem interested in us. He moved on without a word.

"I can stay ahead of them. This might be the one place in the galaxy that there aren't any imperial spies," I said. "It's the one place I'm safe."

"All they have to do is go to the Baykaras."

"And they go to Oversight, and Oversight comes in here and kills me. I know," I said. "It's just a matter of time. Or it would be, but there's something you're forgetting."

"What?"

"This is Free Trade space. Abigail Baykara doesn't have to cave to the Imperium. Maybe I'm more valuable to her alive."

"People do like an underdog," Idris said, glancing into a cell. It was hard to tell if the man in there was dead or passed out. We kept walking.

The deeper we went, the worse the smell got. We had already taken two turns. I wasn't lost yet, but I was developing an appreciation for the possibility. If the time came to move fast, I'd have to be careful. It was a simple grid, but the figures in the dark, the smell, and the sameness of it all conspired to make navigation difficult. Idris could also be walking me into a trap, but I didn't think he was. He'd had no opportunity to set anything up, and I hadn't gotten the impression he had a lot of friends.

There weren't many exits. It would be easy to get boxed in, and Idris wasn't lying when he said that Spirluck and his men would hit back hard if I did something they didn't like.

Threats could work in the short term, but if you were going to make it in here for any period of time, you had to make good on them. My strategy of faking everything would only work as long as I kept moving.

Spirluck wasn't going to like me much. I'd just have to stay one step ahead, but there were no windows, no convenient escape routes.

The things I was saying for the whole galaxy to hear, the fact that Evagard was no doubt talking to the Baykara family about me at this very moment, and what had happened back on that walkway with the guard all meant one thing: there were eyes on me right now. Not very many, but some.

Soon there would be more.

I was happy to entertain the viewers. It meant I was playing along, doing what the system wanted me to do. If I did it well enough, they might return the favor.

"What are you going to do if you find this guy?" Idris asked as we walked.

"We'll leave," I said.

"Oversight heard you say that. But I guess everyone loves a jailbreak."

I hadn't said anything about a jailbreak.

There were stairs ahead. I followed Idris up, the accumulated filth making my flimsy shoes stick to the synthetic surface. Someone was coming down, and Idris moved aside. So did I, and as the figure passed in the dark, there was a powerful odor of ethanol.

Spirluck was based on the second level. He was still conveniently close to the bottom, but with an added layer of security in case some contraband rival came at him in force. Just like there were only a few ways out of the block, there were only so many stairwells within.

"Is there any kind of plan? Or are you just making this up as you go?" Idris asked.

"Find me who I need," I told him. "I'll take it from there."

He wiped his face with his sleeve and climbed the last few steps to the corridor. There were a few cheap portable lights stuck to the walls, but it was far from bright.

It was still a bit hushed on the second level, but not to the same degree as the first. The acoustics were even stranger, but I could hear laughter coming from one of the cells nearby, and some loud swearing in the opposite direction. Someone was playing music, and someone in the very next cell up snored loudly.

Again, there was no real security. I'd expected more, but I was expecting the worst, and I was thinking about the real world. This was prison; things were different.

These men were all criminals, and while there would always be exceptions, it was probably true that brighter criminals mostly made a point not to end up in New Brittia.

But these men were used to dealing with other men like them. There wasn't much trust, and they understood the need for vigilance. There had to be something in place, something to keep someone from just walking into Spirluck's block and taking something valuable.

And yet, maybe not. After all, if you took something from him, where could you go? Another block? The farthest you could get from here was less than a kilometer away.

But there had to be shortsighted people who would try things anyway.

I paused, listening. The sounds coming from around the corner were unmistakably and genuinely feminine.

"Android," Idris said distractedly, pointing. "Come on."

It made sense. Out in the civilized part of the galaxy, when people didn't feel like having sex with other people in the flesh, they turned to VR, but VR collars were on the short list of genuine contraband inside New Brittia. Management didn't want that level of escapism; inmates could never be allowed to forget where they were.

So while there were no actual women in New Brittia except under special circumstances, there could be androids in female form. And it made sense that comfort androids would be controlled by men like Spirluck. They would be in demand, and would command a lot of bargaining power. Chems would be the other really powerful commodity.

I'd been right to gamble on Idris. He seemed to understand how things worked, even if he didn't seem quite certain where he was going.

"You've never been up here before, have you?" I asked him. Someone was coming, and we both moved to the side of the corridor, leaning on the wall in the shadows.

"Once," he whispered.

The man that passed was huge, and wearing the amber of a laborer. He didn't pay any attention to us as he disappeared down the corridor. Sudden laughter made us both jump, but it was just someone in the next hall over.

I wondered what Idris' words were worth. He was making a good show of playing along, but I doubted I'd actually sold him on my company being to his advantage. He knew if he was going to have a chance to get away, it was going to be soon.

We couldn't ask for directions if we were pretending that we belonged. The sparse, pitifully inadequate lights worked in our favor by not letting anyone get too good a look at us, but our luck was going to run out.

Idris faltered, and I saw why: there was a cell up ahead, and there were two men outside it. They weren't loitering; they were guarding it.

I was glad to see that, even if Idris wasn't. It meant he was right, and we were getting close. And we couldn't turn away; that would be suspicious. I put my hand on his back to keep him moving forward. We had to cruise past these guys, and we did. They looked, but they didn't say anything. Idris was caught between me and Spirluck, and he was starting to show some nerves.

"Follow the music," he murmured as we approached the next junction. I took him at his word, and we made the turn, running into a man coming the other way.

He was an inmate in gray, but he was big. He'd cut the upper portion of his jumpsuit so he could pull it off his torso and tie the arms around his waist to go shirtless. He had a lot of recent-looking scars, and there was a dull sheen of sweat on his chest.

"Who the hell are you?" he demanded, looking more curious than alarmed.

It was a fair question under the circumstances.

"Who the hell is *that?*" I replied, staring past him. He turned to look, and I slammed the blade of my shiv into the base of his skull. There was virtually no sound except for Idris' strangled gasp of shock. I caught the big man as he started to fall and used his weight and momentum to drag him out of the corridor and into the nearest cell, where there was another man fast asleep on a bunk.

Quietly, I laid the big man out. Idris ducked into the cell, spotted the sleeper, and froze. I held my finger to my lips and made a calming gesture toward him. Then I lifted the body's arm and opened his axillary artery.

Careful to stay out of the quickly spreading pool, I took the dead man's hand, extended his index finger, and dipped it in the blood. Then I used it to write. I'd seen this in a drama.

I wrote the letters S-P-E-R, then made it dramatically trail off. I'd done it without getting any blood on myself.

Idris, appalled, let me pull him out of the cell. I wiped off my shiv on his shoulder and put it away, keeping a firm hold on his collar.

All communication was verbal in New Brittia, and these were criminals. It wasn't a very sophisticated ploy, but it would confuse the hell out of them, and that suited me. It wouldn't matter that I didn't know how to spell Spirluck.

People would get the idea.

Six

The cell was filled with body parts.

They weren't real, of course. It made sense that comfort androids in a prison would see a lot of use, and it was clear that the residents of New Brittia did not treat their mechanical companionship gently. Arms. Heads. Torsos. A set of hindquarters lay on the bunk, artificial skin and panels lifted, exposing the musculature and electronics.

Most of the bodies were female, but not all. There were different skin tones on display, and some contrast that suggested a lot of patchwork repair had taken place. It was clear from the tools and components scattered around that someone was working very hard to keep these androids in working order. There were cleaning supplies, and tools. The cell had been turned into a workshop, and it wasn't exactly neat, but it was conspicuously clean.

There was no one there.

But we could hear the chaos that had arisen from the body of the man I'd killed, and the message I'd used him to send had let us get this deep into the block. People were much more interested in the murder and its implications than a pair of figures in the dark, but it wouldn't take long for the two to be connected. Once word got around, figures in the dark were exactly what these men would be on the lookout for.

I was counting on that.

Raised voices echoed up and down the corridor. Idris pressed his back to the wall and closed his eyes. He wasn't deaf. Confusion would turn to aggression, and aggression would turn to bloodshed.

We were deep behind enemy lines. Idris didn't have a military background, but he could read the room, and it was obvious from his face that he fully appreciated the situation he was in. Up until this moment, he'd been looking for a chance to get away from me, but now I was his lifeline. Idris believed he wasn't getting out of this block alive without me.

Now we had a proper working relationship.

This was a gamble, and our survival depended on our presence going largely unappreciated in this deeply disorganized setting. Spirluck had men that worked for him, but there were no comms, no formal hierarchy, no chain of command. It was a dark block with a corpse in it and a lot of scary, dangerous men who hadn't managed to stay out of prison.

Of course, none of that bothered me. I was Evagardian, after all. This? This was all supposed to be beneath me.

I was the adult on this playground, and these inmates were the children running around my ankles. They could misbehave and make a mess if they liked, but whatever happened, at the end of the day, we would all know who was in charge.

We had the Empress to thank for that, and that was exactly that kind of thinking that a New Unity terrorist would hate more than anything.

Idris needed to stay calm and keep up the act. I gave him a warning look, then went over to the improvised shelf. There was the head of a pretty, relatively recent android. It had green eyes and dark hair, but the skin had taken some damage around the chin and some of the hair was missing.

I looked over the mechanic's improvised power supply and connected the head. The eyes came to life. The speech driver was in the skull; without the rest of the body, it couldn't move its mouth, but an android didn't need to move its mouth to speak.

"Hi," I said to it. "What's your name?"

"Shelly," the android replied. There was a very slight distortion in her voice, but probably nothing you'd notice during use.

"Do you know where your body is?"

"No," the android replied.

I looked at Idris. "Can they put her on another body? Spare parts?"

"They probably just use the head," Idris said. He was clearly distracted—he wasn't even looking at me. He was watching the corridor instead.

I cringed. "Look, someone's working on you. Do you know the name of the man trying to repair you?" I asked the head.

"Gingham," the android replied.

"Thanks," I said. I put the head back on the shelf and scrubbed my hands on my jumpsuit. "Gingham. Who names their son Gingham?"

"Frontier people," Idris said.

"Really?"

"They're going to find us in here."

"They might," I said. "But what will they think when they do?"

"That we don't belong."

I didn't reply to that. I was looking around the cell for anything worth taking, but at the moment, I didn't have a use for any tools more complex than my shiv.

"Are you judging?" Idris asked, watching me from the doorway as I took one last look around. "You just killed a guy."

"I'm Evagardian," I said, straightening up. "We disapprove of this kind of reliance on machines."

"I thought your Empress was just afraid of AI."

"She's not afraid of anything. I think the Imperium would phrase it that she has a healthy respect for the dangers associated with AI," I corrected him. "Not that I'm an apologist."

"Where were the guys like you on my security staff?" Idris grumbled, peering into the corridor again.

"You're lucky your security was no good," I said.

"Why?"

"Because if those two imperial girls hadn't gotten away from you safely, you'd be dead right now. They would've been rescued, and I hope you're not naïve enough to think you'd have survived it."

"Bullshit. Which one was yours? Or was it both? You said you were a terrorist. Did Willis and Freeber *interrupt* something?" The notion seemed to amuse him, but then something caught his attention, and he moved away from the doorway. "Someone's coming."

I went to the other side of the door to wait. Maybe this next one would pass, like the last two.

Eventually, whoever worked on these androids was going to show up. That was the one I needed alive. Anyone else—well, it just wasn't their lucky day.

The man who came through the door was thin. He had a limp, and lots of wild, tangled hair. He wasn't what I'd pictured, but he was probably my guy. Things were getting noisy outside the cell, and with chaos building in the block, I'd been hoping Gingham would return to his nest.

He spotted Idris, but I spoke before he could say or do anything.

"Is your name Gingham?" I asked, arms folded. He turned on me, eyes wide.

There was some shouting going on not far from us. The inmates were taking my bait and running with it. In a block full of people with good judgment, or any judgment, this never would have worked. Being in a prison did have its perks; I wasn't up against the galaxy's elite.

The man looked back at Idris, then at me again. He didn't have to answer; the look alone was enough.

I straightened up. "I need your help."

He wasn't listening. Arguments outside, strangers in here—he was doing the math, and he was a little brighter than the other ones. I snapped my fingers loudly in front of his face. "Focus," I said, and he did. "You're going to help us out."

"With what?" He had options to deal with us, but he was scared, and he didn't have the courage to try anything. No nerve. He fit the profile: someone whose particular skills were enough to make them a pet, to secure for them the protection of stronger men.

This would be easy.

"We need to get at some Oversight data. Or Management data, whichever's easier. I need to know if a certain inmate is still alive and where he is. Can you get that for me?"

"No."

I stepped close very suddenly, pushing him against the wall and leaning close. I put one hand on the top of his head and squeezed.

"Time's an issue."

"Maybe," he amended, losing some color.

I pointed at the android parts. "These have connectivity."

Gingham shook his head. "They're all disabled. They don't make it that easy for us."

Well, that made sense. These androids had to be brought in by someone, and whoever that was had removed or disabled parts of their systems that could be used to communicate with the outside.

That wouldn't stop a man like Gingham; he had that look, and it reminded me of Nils. He'd been my most valuable asset on Nidaros, and Gingham was going to pull his weight for me in New Brittia. Techs and breakers. These were the people that kept the galaxy running.

Guys like me were the ones that came along and messed it all up.

"What do you need?" I asked him.

"A connection point and something I can use to interface."

"Do you not have those?"

"Not both," he said.

So his owners were careful with him. Giving a guy like this too many tools would be dangerous. I hoped that meant he was good. As good as Nils? Probably not. Less backbone, too.

"Where do we get them?" I asked, then went on before he could say something he could regret. "We *are* going to get them."

But it wouldn't be easy. If connectivity was controlled, then anything that had it would have value and thus be guarded. But an input device should be easy to get; any old holo would do. Outside of prison, everyone had one on their wrist, their ear, or implanted somewhere. It was what you used for everything: talking to people, searching the nets, transferring money. There would be a few floating around in here.

"Without too much of a mess," I added. "Your time's up. You're going to help us. If you do a good job, you can get a head start out of it."

He'd already picked up on that much. The gears were turning, but I decided to help them along.

"When this is over, do you want to look like an accomplice or a victim?"

"There's a way," Gingham said, swallowing.

"Tell me," I said. I couldn't just have him lead us off blindly. I would listen to his plan and decide if he was telling the truth or trying something stupid.

"There's one model that has a connection," he said, glancing at the android parts. "It's new. With that and a holo, I can get the roster."

"How do we get those things discreetly?"

Gingham glanced at the doorway. "We can go get a holo. And I can ask someone to get the android. I can have them bring it here."

"What would people think?" I asked, putting my arm around his shoulders. "If they saw us as friends?"

"I don't know. Did you kill Patrick?"

I snorted. "Who? Do I *look* like a killer to you?" I asked, guiding him into the corridor, keeping our backs to the men down in the next junction.

Idris followed, staying close. I stayed friendly with Gingham as two guys jogged past. I was impressed by the way they moved around in the dark so confidently. The dim twilight outside never changed, and inside the blocks it was always night.

Yet I couldn't find it in myself to be surprised. New Brittia wasn't here to cheer people up. Eternal night was appropriate. I kept an eye on Idris; I couldn't have him bailing on me just yet. I still needed him.

"How many androids do you have?" I asked conversationally, steering Gingham out of the path of another big man, who looked at us as he passed, but kept moving. Then he stopped.

I spoke before he could, tightening my grip on Gingham, who winced. "What's going on? Gingham said somebody's dead."

The big guy looked at Idris for a moment, and that was a stroke of luck. Idris had been hiding in plain sight in this block for a few days, so people had seen him. They didn't know him well, but he wasn't a complete outsider like me.

"Someone stuck Patrick," he said, and pointed at Gingham. "Get upstairs."

Gingham nodded nervously.

The big man went on his way, and we moved forward. We turned a corner, and there was a man emerging from a cell ahead. From the way I felt Gingham stiffen at the sight of him, I knew that either this was our destination, or this man was a problem.

"Hey," I said before anyone could do anything, and the man, who had been about to call out to us, hesitated.

"Inside," I said, jerking my chin at the cell. "We need to talk."

This guy was wearing a laborer's jumpsuit, but it wasn't his. There was a knife at his hip, and he had some gaudy necklaces and jewelry. Leathery skin. Lots of muscles.

Someone's idea of security.

He looked taken aback, and a little angry. I shoved Gingham into him, putting on enough force to send them both staggering through the doorway and out of the corridor. The man in amber couldn't keep his balance, and he and Gingham went down in a tangle; neither one of them could present any kind of defense. I bent down and slipped my shiv between the guard's floating ribs as he tried to get free. I pushed Gingham off of him.

The guard took a moment to expire, and I kept his mouth covered. Gingham and Idris would have both loved to run at that moment, but I was between them and the door. The guard went still, and I got to my feet.

"Jesus," Idris said, and I wiped my shiv on his other shoulder this time. He gave me a dirty look but didn't protest.

Gingham was not, as I'd expected, frozen. He was pale and sweaty, but focused. I shouldn't have been surprised; he was a New Brittia survivor. He'd seen worse than this, and though I didn't have much to base it on, I didn't think he cared very much for the men running Gamma Block. They owned him and protected him, but I wasn't getting the impression that his owners used him gently.

I saw the girl on the bed, and the sight of her shocked even me. I stepped back into Idris, who also saw her and flinched. That got Gingham to look up from the body, and I pulled myself together.

"Is that what we're here for?" I demanded, pointing. Idris went to the door to keep watch.

It wasn't a real girl, obviously. Just an android styled to look like one. And she had no arms.

Comfort androids were rare in Evagard, but in the Commonwealth, they were everywhere. The whole point was that they were idealized, and that often manifested as youth, but not quite this *much* youth. This one was obviously meant to look like a child.

Gingham nodded.

I'd just killed somebody, and this was what made me queasy.

"Judging again?" Idris asked, raising an eyebrow. I ignored him.

"Grab it," I said. Idris tried to pick it up, but he quickly put it back down.

"It's heavy," he complained, giving Gingham an accusatory look.

"I said it was new," the sweaty man said weakly. "Not top of the line."

"I can't carry that," Idris said. "My shoulder was dislocated. My hands are still messed up. Those imperial girls," he added, giving me an accusing look.

"So turn it on," I said, irked. "It can walk." I kept my hand firmly on the base of Gingham's neck. We needed to move.

The android's eyes opened, and Idris pulled it to its feet. Though it was annoyingly heavy, the thing was disturbingly lifelike even without arms. What had happened to the arms? And it had to be new, because the transparent negligee it was wearing was all but pristine.

"Don't make a sound," Idris said to it, and the android nodded.

I led Gingham out into the corridor. Don't mind us, anyone. An imperial terrorist, a guy very obviously under duress, and an inmate leading a little girl with no arms dressed for grownup things.

My plan to keep a low profile wasn't going to work.

SEVEN

Even with the dark and confusion on our side, we wouldn't last long in the open. I pushed Gingham hard to lead us to whatever he needed to get my information.

Moving fast would limit our exposure, but if we went to a bad place, we'd be going in on the wrong foot. There was no strategy here, only tactics, and this place was determined not to let me make a good showing. I was just digging myself deeper.

When things like elegance and logic are just broken pieces on the floor, there's still nerve. Aggression could never fill in all the gaps, but a little audacity could go a long way. This was typical of the path I'd taken since shedding Prince Dalton after Little Norwich.

Forward. Always forward. I still had a long road ahead, and my odds of seeing the end of it weren't getting any better.

Gingham's holo was in his own cell, hidden carefully beneath his bunk. I'd seen inmates and laborers wearing holos in the square, but those had been different, something unique to New Brittia, like the tiny earpieces we all wore. I'd had one stapled to my ear along with everyone else when we processed in.

Gingham's device wasn't really a holo. It had no holographic capabilities, only a screen. He called it a holo, but it was really just a portable terminal.

It seemed these devices were more carefully controlled than I'd thought. Gingham was owned and operated by Spirluck, so he was positioned to have access to the best that could be found inside the prison, and more or less anything could be gotten in here. This tiny android we had trotting along behind us was evidence enough of that.

But this was just sad. The terminal was a palmtop model, styled to look like the primitive devices from the twenty-first century, before holographic displays took over. It was compact and battered.

But it would display data, and combined with the android, it could potentially get me what I needed.

There was nothing to definitively tie Gingham to what was going on, but people would catch on and come looking for him. Even if they only expected to find his body, this wasn't the best moment for us to get that attention. My seeds of disorder could give us a boost, but they wouldn't carry us. There were now two bodies in Gamma Block, and no one had seen anything. It wasn't safe to be a stranger here.

The men rushing around out there didn't know that I was the one they wanted, but I *was* the one they wanted. They wanted me dead, and they weren't the only ones. Evagard and the Commonwealth were on the long list of people who wanted me gone, and every moment I spent stationary brought me closer to that.

Gingham had shifted into exactly the right mindset. He was determined to appease me. I was worried about Idris, though. He was scared, and that wasn't helping. But he led the little android along behind me.

This was a labyrinthine network of cells and corridors on the second level of a block with an indeterminate number of ways down and a finite number of ways out, which would shortly be blocked, if they weren't already.

Idris' world had rapidly become pitch black, and from where he was standing, I was the only beacon of light. He couldn't run. With bodies already cooling off, there was no turning on me now. He was part of this.

And we could hear the echoes of Spirluck's men, who were doing everything but howling for our blood. It wasn't very relaxing.

We'd put some corners between ourselves and Gingham's cell; I planned to take advantage of the next quiet spot to put Gingham to work, but we ran into two guys emerging from a staircase. They were coming down from an upper level, perhaps to investigate all the noise.

Even if I liked fighting, fighting wasn't something that winners bothered with. Murder was better in every way. In the dark, and with the element of surprise on my side, it seemed almost unfair.

In bumping into me, the first man had served himself up. My shiv had opened his axillary artery before he even knew what was happening. Blood flowed, and he looked surprised. I just pushed him to the ground. He might take a minute to bleed out, but he wouldn't get up. His companion bolted back into the stairwell, and we heard his footsteps fleeing upward. He thought he was outnumbered. He had no way to know that I was the only threat in our party; he just saw three and a half people, and he didn't like those odds.

He was fleeing up, not down. That was fine. I hoped the viewers were enjoying themselves. If they hadn't been watching me before, there would be some now.

I dragged Gingham a few steps down the corridor and pushed him into a cell.

"Get to work," I told him.

He was already on it. He dropped to his knees in front of the android. "Turn around," he told it. Smiling, the android obeyed. Gingham was using his thumbs to input data into the little terminal. It wasn't that I had no technical skills; I did, but mine were narrow in scope. I *was* qualified to do this, but not with these time constraints. I could handle primitive technology, but I didn't know my way around a comfort android.

Gingham did. Already, he was using his terminal to take advantage of the android's connectivity, normally used for remote handling and downloading updates—but a connection was a connection.

The only light was the screen of Gingham's handheld terminal, and Idris looked pale in it. He was staring at the interface panel in the back of the android's neck. It was a little unnerving to see skin peeled back and synthetic materials beneath.

Odd thing to be squeamish about, but I didn't care for the sight of it either. The machine was perfectly lifelike. Androids were frowned on in Evagard. Androids modeled on children, particularly for this purpose, were *extremely* frowned on, and probably illegal. What was the point of an android like this? Obviously it made sense in New Brittia— there was no VR here.

But who manufactured this? Why? VR was a cheaper and more practical outlet for this stuff.

I caught myself there. That was Evagardian thinking, and this was Free Trade space; the imperial perspective just wasn't relevant here. Galactics were barbarians, and they could do what they wanted.

That was also Evagardian thinking.

My fingers tingled, and I could see every bead of sweat on Idris' face. He was thinking about the guy that had gotten away. He was going to tell people what he'd seen.

Data scrolled on Gingham's screen.

"Copy as much as you can," I told him.

"I don't have much memory."

"Get me names and whatever you can that might help me navigate. Use the trackers or the grid, something to give me a location."

"Those are timecoded into these logs," he said distractedly. "This is a capture. It's not current. It's almost an hour old, but it's safer to get at the archive servers."

"Safer?" I raised an eyebrow. "What are they going to do? Put you in prison?"

"They could raid the block and shoot me," Gingham replied, his voice surprisingly conversational. I wondered what he'd done to end up here. Breaking, obviously. But whose systems had he been messing with?

There were footsteps in the corridor, and voices. A light flashed. People were coming, looking for the intruders who were wreaking havoc on their block. I was out of time.

Idris wanted to say something, but he just moved away from the doorway. Other footsteps were fading, but a figure appeared in the corridor, shining a light in at us. I couldn't see him; his light was blinding us—but he was alone.

"Gingham?" he sounded uncertain; Gingham's back was to him.

I stepped into view. I was holding my shiv down by my side. I turned the blade so that it caught the light, and that froze the guy in the corridor.

"Don't stand out there," I told him. "Come in."

He ran.

"Are you insane?" Idris demanded.

I ignored him. "Almost finished?" I asked Gingham. "You're going to have to part with that reader."

"I know," he said.

I'd gotten my hands dirty. I'd made myself interesting.

There were people watching. There would be a pool running on how long I had to live at this very moment. Thirty seconds? A whole minute?

The noise in the corridor spiked; that would be that guy who'd seen us getting back to his friends and telling them what he'd seen.

Management could decide they didn't want me to have this list. They could authorize Oversight to come in and take me down, or use a pulse to kill the device—they had plenty of options. But they wouldn't use any of them.

Interfering with me was the last thing they wanted to do. I was still probably only a small attraction at this point, but I was an attraction nonetheless.

They would want to let me grow.

They wouldn't bother me because they wanted to see what I was going to do next, and they weren't the only ones. If they hadn't been before, Evagardian Intelligence, Imperial Security, and the Commonwealth would be watching now as well. I didn't have to protect myself from the network, just the inmates. And that would be difficult enough.

"If your friend's here, he'll be on that list," Gingham told me, getting to his feet and holding out the terminal. His eyes flicked toward the doorway. Indeed, we could hear his rescuers getting close. He was probably wondering what he was going to tell them. Idris was against the far wall, as if he thought if he pressed his back to it hard enough, he could somehow get out of this cell.

"You have no faith," I told him, taking the reader from Gingham.

"You are crazy," he said. "I knew it."

"Close her up," I ordered Gingham, pointing at the android. He turned to obey, and I reached around to cut his throat. Idris swore loudly, pressing himself even harder against the wall. I caught Gingham's hair and pushed him to his knees, pulling back to tip his head and let the blood flow. I leaned him forward a bit, and it splashed onto the floor of the cell.

Idris made a move for the door, but it was much too late for that now; they were out there and coming this way. He couldn't escape without being seen and chased, but he would gladly risk that over being in a room with me.

It sounded like there were half a dozen people on the way, at least.

I tripped Idris as he tried to get by me, sending him spilling into the blood. He retched and tried desperately to get to his feet.

"What are you *doing?*" he wheezed, his hands slipping on the slick floor. He was covered in Gingham's blood. "They're coming!"

I wasn't deaf.

I pressed my shiv into his hand and closed his fingers over the handle. "You talk to them." I pulled him upright and gave him a hard shove out of the cell, where he literally stumbled into the arms of the approaching inmates in the dark.

I stepped back and leaned against the wall in the shadows. Idris didn't have time to say a single word. I waited, ready in case someone came in for a closer look at Gingham's body, but no one did. They had their killer, at least for this moment, and a moment was all I needed.

I slipped my hands into the pockets of my gray inmate's uniform and left the cell.

As I left Idris behind, he wasn't the one I was thinking about. I was thinking about the android, and the way it just stood there, facing the bunk as instructed with its neck panel open, its back covered in blood.

Blind obedience. There really wasn't anything more dangerous.

As for Idris—well, if he had suffered, it had been only briefly. These inmates weren't interested in retribution; they just wanted to eliminate the threat. Poor blood-soaked Idris had probably been simply tackled to the ground and stabbed in a businesslike fashion. That was what it had sounded like to me, at any rate.

I didn't have much sympathy for him.

Only a man who could look at that little android and feel no disgust could make the mistake of trusting me. Idris was a businessman, and a reptile.

When Willis and Freeber brought me and Salmagard to him, along with Sei and Diana, he hadn't known who we were apart from being imperials.

Was he so far gone that he really believed I'd just let that go? That anyone would? He had bought two people as though they were objects.

Did he think I would just forget who he was, what his line of work had been, and what I'd seen? Maybe that had been hope on his part, but I didn't think so. Idris had been dead from the moment I laid eyes on him, and he should have realized that.

Even in Evagard, ironically one of the more liberal and tolerant cultures at large, mistreating another person's romantic partner was not considered good business. It was as close to a universal law as anything. I wasn't aware of any culture where that sort of behavior went unpunished, at least at a personal level.

A man who wasn't bothered by a comfort android shaped like a child, a man who thought I could overlook our first meeting—he was so far out of touch that there was no helping him.

And he didn't have my excuse.

I was judging people even as I was killing them; the Empress would have been proud. *She* probably wasn't watching, though.

Not yet.

EIGHT

It didn't hurt my eyes to leave the block this time; they were adjusting faster now.

It was all starting to catch up and even out, finally. I'd even stopped sweating.

The lights of Balkin Square were welcome, and the air was cleaner. I could breathe. I kept my hand on the terminal in my pocket. Everything I'd done had been to get my hands on this device and the information it contained. This was my lifeline, and I wasn't about to let it go.

Inmates streamed around me. They all had lives to live and no reason to notice me. Even if they knew something was going on inside Spirluck's block, they probably didn't care. I hadn't been able to avoid getting a little blood on my jumpsuit, but compared to the amount that I'd spilled, it wasn't much at all.

At least I hadn't done any bleeding yet, but it was only a matter of time in this place. So far I'd been the one with the element of surprise each time. Sooner or later, I'd be on the receiving end. All I could do was keep my guard up and try not to stay in prison any longer than I had to.

These guys didn't know that I was anything out of the ordinary, and who was to say I was? I could hardly be the only man in New Brittia who wasn't what he looked like.

I'd gotten out of the block without any difficulty, but I wasn't naïve enough to think that I'd walked away clean. People had seen me. Those guys would eventually put it all together, my description would go around, and Spirluck would be coming for me.

Maybe he wouldn't care about those people who had been collateral damage, but I'd killed Gingham, and he had value.

I didn't know Spirluck, but I knew his type.

If I actually sped up as much as I should have for every person who wanted me dead, I'd have been approaching relativistic speeds at that point. I wasn't.

I wasn't going anywhere.

The dubious safety of isolation? Or the even more dubious safety of the open?

Maybe something that had happened in Gamma Block had made me a little less alluring. Inmates looked at me as I passed, but no one stopped me.

I left Gamma Block behind and moved into the stalls. There was a certain charm in there, where I could smell food and drink. There were lights, and it was here, in the midst of it all, that it was as close to bright as New Brittia ever got.

There were inmates of all shapes and sizes, some of whom were doing relatively convincing impressions of being female. There probably wasn't much you couldn't get here, interestingly. This was probably the only detention facility in existence with such a developed economy.

It was necessary. Commerce was motivation, and people needed motivation to act. People had to act to entertain, and viewers had to be entertained to renew their subscriptions to the Baykara Network.

I found a stall that looked nice and lifted the curtain to lean in. There were a few seats, but only one man seated at the counter. He was a laborer. The guy behind the counter was ancient, but the heavy curtain muffled some of the noise and gave a little privacy.

I wasn't feeling cautious.

"You serve grays?" I asked. Some people wouldn't sell to inmates, only to laborers. The old man shook his head.

"Sit down," the laborer said without looking up. He was my size, but with more muscle, and a few years older. He had the makings of a beard, heavily bandaged hands, and he wasn't paying any attention to me. He was drinking something that was mocked up to look—and possibly taste—like Evagardian Ale. He was visibly drunk.

The old man didn't want to argue. I took a stool.

"You got ethanol? What do you have?" I asked, fumbling for the money card I'd taken from Gingham along with the terminal. It was all he'd had in his pockets. I'd gotten him out of New Brittia, even if it probably wasn't the way he'd have chosen for himself. The least he could do was buy me a drink.

The old man gestured at his little cooler. A pathetic inventory by the standards of literally anywhere else, but in a prison, it was a kingly selection.

"Give me that Asahi," I said, and swiped my card.

The bottle was cold. He didn't give me a glass. I had to open it by leaning it against the edge of the counter and striking the top. Quaint.

Griffith and I used to do this for fun.

I took a long drink and got out the reader, setting it on the counter to swipe through the list. There was probably a more efficient way to search, but I wanted to browse.

Encountering Idris had gotten me thinking. What if Griffith wasn't the only person in New Brittia that I knew? Idris hadn't done anything for me that some other victim couldn't have, but still. There might be some advantage in running into an acquaintance.

I had energy. I hadn't done much; my exertion had been minimal. I hadn't even done much running, not since making that escape back in the transition section.

I still should have been exhausted. I wasn't. Everything was razor sharp, even my brain. My eyes weren't sandy. They didn't burn. My fingers didn't shake.

I read every name.

The man behind the counter was politely making a point of not looking at what I was doing. The drunk laborer wasn't. He watched with interest. His amber suit was thoroughly faded. He'd had it for a while, but obviously it was still functioning. Surely Management would give him a new one if he really needed it. There were some belts and bandoliers on him.

From the number of empty bottles in front of him, he had to have some money. He was probably a popular and respected laborer. Presentable. If he could handle himself, it was easy to imagine him catching the fancy of the viewers.

But he was making himself vulnerable by getting this drunk, and he knew exactly what he was doing. He knew how easily his life could end in New Brittia.

He didn't care if he lived or died. And I didn't care if he watched me. I wouldn't hurt him as long as he didn't bother me.

These guys didn't seem so bad. I looked up from my list for a moment, then went back to scanning.

"Either of you know anything about Spirluck?" I asked. "I'm new."

"I can see that," said the laborer. No he couldn't. My jumpsuit was indeed new, but it was damp and bloody, and getting grubbier by the minute.

"Gamma Block," said the man behind the counter. I nodded.

"What kind of reach does he have?"

The older guy snorted and didn't reply. I didn't blame him; it was a stupid question. Even if these guys knew, how did you articulate something like that?

I kept looking through the names. It was amazing how quickly I'd gotten used to the New Brittia ambience. The sounds of the interactions of hundreds of inmates in every direction was less troubling than the harsh acoustics inside the housing blocks.

I still didn't like having my back to a lot of people. Knowing that the curtain was there didn't help. I shifted my body a little to get a better peripheral view. The presence of people was an uneven comfort. I was vulnerable here, but I was vulnerable anywhere.

The laborer kept drinking. It was like he was playing a game to see if he could empty out the vendor's little cooler all in one sitting. That could be fun; there were some interesting-looking drinks in there. Bottles I'd never seen before. Exotic labels from all over.

"Where's your inventory come from?" I asked.

"Spirluck," the old man said. Of course.

I found Griffith on the list. So he'd still been alive an hour ago, at least. I was relieved to have located him at all, but a lot could happen in an hour.

He was booked under his real name. The line in the log belonging to him contained only a few details: active laborer status and his various transition dates and timestamps—and that was where I saw something strange.

There was a prefix on his ID that was different from the name above his. And the name below it. It was different from mine.

I realized that the inmates and laborers were divided by more than the just the colors we wore.

They were segregated by which strut of the New Brittia facility they were housed on.

I put down my bottle. After a moment, I put my chin in my hands and closed my eyes. I was calm. Everything was still clear. After several moments, I opened my eyes, picked up my bottle, and drained it. Not that ethanol could help me now.

"I'm on the wrong strut. I don't suppose," I said, flicking a glance from the old man to the drunk laborer, "that there's a convenient way to get to the other one?"

The old man just stared at me. The laborer snorted.

I hadn't thought so.

New Brittia was not a space station; it wasn't arranged with those three-dimensional sensibilities. It was more like something on the surface of a planet, just a very small planet.

This was Balkin strut. It housed a processing station, temporary quartering, a general population component—that was where I was now—and a labor section.

There was a tear in the canvas that made up the rear wall of the stall, and I could just barely see the lights of Baykara City. High above, past the labor section, was the asteroid itself—and Baykara City was on top of it. On the far side of all that was Alpine Strut, which was more or less identical to Balkin Strut.

The maximum security holding section was over there too.

From where I was sitting, to the left of the city and far beneath lay the ore mines. And on the right, the Oversight section was wrapped around the side of the asteroid like a belt.

Whichever way I wanted to go, there was something big standing between me and Alpine Strut. The fastest way would be to get a shuttle and fly over there, but that wasn't really on the table.

Pity there wasn't a way to get Griffith to come to me.

I couldn't get from here to the city without an invitation.

Oversight was the obvious weak link for inmates who might not be inclined to serve their sentences, and that was why Oversight was always wary. The guards had an important role, but they were isolated in more than just their communications.

Baykara Management owned Oversight but did not support them. If inmates hurt or killed Oversight personnel, no one complained. It was good entertainment. Indeed, it was my understanding that New Brittia broadcasts spun Oversight—in their ominous black armor and helmets—as the oppressive antagonist. The people who paid the guards *wanted* to see the inmates get the best of them. To compensate, Oversight offered excellent pay and benefits.

Oversight had its supporters, of course. With as many viewers as the Baykara Network had, everyone had someone out there cheering for them.

Even me.

Right now there were probably plenty of people interested in the nameless Evagardian who was going about as if he owned the place and leaving a trail of bodies behind. They could hear every word I said; they knew exactly what

I was doing: trying to reach Griffith. There were no secrets in New Brittia. Everything could be seen. It was just a question of who was watching what at any given moment, how much they knew, and how they interpreted what they saw.

And even if no one was watching, everything was recorded.

By now there would be people following a broadcast focused on me. A lot of them. The Network's attention was drawn to action, and as I made myself increasingly interesting, they would promote coverage of me more aggressively. At this point, I didn't know where I stood in the great scheme of all that was going on at New Brittia, but I had a feeling I was rising fast.

I'd been in the spotlight before. As Prince Dalton, I'd been singing or dancing or telling jokes, not stabbing people—but an audience was an audience.

Oversight wouldn't expect someone to try to infiltrate their territory in the interests of reaching the other strut; it would be like breaking out of New Brittia just to break back in again. But that element of surprise wouldn't do me any good. I'd just look like someone breaking out, and that much they were ready for. Besides, if it was that easy, why *not* take a shuttle and joyride over to wherever Griffith was?

No, there was only one way to get over there. I rubbed at my eyes out of habit, not because they needed it. And even the route I had in mind didn't carry any guarantees.

There were no limits. No rules. There was no logic. Every time I thought my life couldn't go any farther out of control, there was something like this. It was normal, and there'd been a time when I'd believed I knew what that word meant.

I got up and left the stall.

The narrow spaces between the stalls couldn't really be called alleys, but they were tight and dark, providing the same sort of privacy you could hope for in an actual housing block, but without as much risk. It wasn't privacy from the broadcast, but it seemed like the inmates didn't care much about that. At least, I didn't see a lot of people acknowledging that they were on display.

Even if they weren't alleys, that didn't stop anyone from using them like they were. I was barely able to slip past one happy couple. I squeezed through a gap that probably wasn't meant to be squeezed through and moved forward without a sound.

The temptation to stop and think was strong, but that was the worst possible thing I could do. Momentum was about the only thing I had left. I couldn't let it go; if I did, I might not get it back.

There was someone up ahead, hidden in shadow near the opening. I could see men passing in the square beyond. This man was alone. And he wasn't hiding. He was watching.

Was he watching for me?

If Spirluck's people had rallied quickly, it wasn't out of the question for them to be looking for me already, and it wasn't hard to guess where I'd go next. I was stuck in a bottle with Spirluck; there was only one possible place for me to try to run: labor recruitment.

They knew what I looked like, and they had a guy watching the approach to those doors. Probably more than one. That wasn't a good sign; it meant Spirluck was serious about getting even. I could hardly blame him for that, and if he let people walk all over him, his position of power would weaken.

Getting past this obstacle wouldn't save me from Spirluck; it would just make his job a little more difficult.

Maybe this guy was watching for me, maybe not. I'd never know.

I stole up behind him and broke his neck, dragging him back and dumping him behind a pile of dissolving cargo boxes. The viewers would probably prefer splashier confrontations to my underhanded tactics, but that wasn't really an option.

I went to the opening and looked out. Lots of open space, lots of people. I didn't hesitate. What would be the point? If there were more lookouts, I wasn't going to spot them; there were just too many people. And even if I did spot one, what then? What did it change?

I emerged, keeping my pace leisurely. It wasn't like Spirluck's guys were only ones I had to worry about.

People looked. They bumped my shoulder as they passed. There were too many men for me to seriously watch them all. I didn't let myself react; I just kept my eyes forward.

Ahead of me, the structure stretched up and away, one more wall between me and Baykara City, which stood between me and Griffith.

There was a shout behind me.

Of course, there was a lot of noise and indeed a lot of shouting going on at any given moment in Balkin Square. But my instincts hadn't kept me alive this long because they didn't work.

I just kept walking, hoping to get lost in the crowd, but I wasn't that lucky. There was running, and commotion. I looked back to see no fewer than three men charging across the square, knocking inmates aside to get to me.

I ran, closing the distance to the nearest hatch and hitting the release. I stepped back as the safety lines on the ground lit up.

"Would you like to have your sentence commuted?"

The voice that asked belonged to an AI, but it was doing another good impression of Abigail Baykara.

"Might as well," I replied, watching the three men sprint toward me.

NINE

EIGHT YEARS AGO

"You don't feel patronized?" I asked as we struggled out of our graduation uniforms.

"I did," Griffith replied, loosening his scarf. "But that was before he'd been talking for two hours and I realized he was just getting started."

I knew how he felt.

"Was he not supposed to go that long?" I hung up my jacket and looked around in annoyance. The light in Griffith's closet was broken, and his place was set to a dim lighting scheme already. Worse, the lights would only listen to his commands, not mine.

"I guess it's not classy to call him out on it. He was up for Grand Admiral at some point. I guess he can talk if he wants to."

"There hasn't been a Grand Admiral in fifty years," I said.

"And that guy hasn't been lucid in longer than that," Griffith replied. "Who talks for that long? To a bunch of graduates at the beginning of their lives? How far gone do you have to be to think that saying that much without saying anything that matters is a good idea? Anyway, I didn't want to go, but now I do. At this point it's not even about wanting. I *need* a drink. What are you going to wear?"

"I'm not sure."

"They're calling it a semi-formal event, so we can't just wear whatever."

Anxiety hit me. "I didn't know that."

Griffith waved a hand. "It's on the walk, so you want to at least dress like it is. You know? Everyone else will be wearing their graduation uniforms."

"Can we do that? Or is it beneath us?" I asked.

"I don't want to make an issue of it," Griffith said. "We've got these." He pointed at our blanks, hanging side by side in the closet. They'd only been awarded to us yesterday and were still in their protective bags.

"I'll never wear that," I promised.

"Me neither," Griffith agreed, shoving them aside. "Let's just be at least tolerably fashionable."

"I'm *always* fashionable."

We got changed and left. As Griffith coded his door, he looked thoughtful. "You think this is some kind of test?" he asked me.

"Hmm?" I looked up from my holo.

"I mean, where did this tradition come from? Why send us out to something like this after graduation? It's not mandatory, it's not supervised. There's no meaning in it."

"It's a celebration," I replied, shrugging. "It doesn't need to have meaning. Or that is the meaning, I guess."

"Is this lift under maintenance again? Empress," Griffith complained. Something was always broken in his sustenance block. We headed down toward the next lift. "I think it's a test. I think they're watching to see who goes and gets wasted and who actually spends the time networking."

"Want to stay in?"

"I'd like that," Griffith said. "But we're committed."

We stood in front of the lift, waiting. Waiting for those doors to open.

It seemed like we did this a lot, but that wasn't true; it was just that this wait was such a noticeable, conspicuous pause. It was the part of our day where everything stopped, if only for a moment. A lull. It stood out to me, but at least I wasn't waiting for lifts alone.

The venue for the post-graduation reception and social was a commercial hospitality strip on the walk, one of Cohengard's more attractive artificial canals. The nice thing about it was that there were no particularly ugly incidents from the revolt associated with it. The night cycle had begun, and Cohengard's sky field was tinted with a nice blue and teal. The light of the stars was magnified, and there weren't any decorative clouds in the way.

The walk was lit up in its best form, and everyone was out. The social had interesting, rustic lanterns ringing it instead of the normal light globes that usually lined the canal. Of the five thousand graduates in our section, it looked like about three quarters of them were attending. More than I'd expected, but no one would've expected me and Griffith to show. I'd actually been hoping Griffith would call it off.

But it wasn't so bad. There was live music and lots of white serving tables rolling around. There was human hospitality as well, and if it was subsidized by the city, it was doing a good job looking like it wasn't.

There were, of course, peacekeepers, but they were being discreet.

Nemerov wasn't a rich or even a particularly well-regarded school. With that in mind, this was a good showing, but I was still wrapping my head around the idea that my mandatory education was over.

Griffith pulled me through the crowd, through the tables and the milling people. We shook hands with everyone we knew and exchanged some congratulations. We avoided our enemies and did our best to track down most of our friends.

No one was going out of reach; where was out of reach? But after tonight, it might be a long time before we saw some of them again face to face, if ever. Nemerov kids or not, a few of them had actual futures to look forward to.

"Griffith," said a voice, and we both groaned and turned around to see Tim Woodhouse pushing through the crowd. He was still wearing his ceremonial uniform and grinning widely. "Where are you dragging my boy?"

"Did you make it?" Griffith asked him bluntly. Obviously he had; Woodhouse wouldn't be looking so smug if he hadn't. He'd passed officer aptitude for the Service. I didn't try to hide how impressed I was, because I couldn't. That annoyed Griffith, but there was no helping it. It was a huge achievement.

"I start selection in a week," Woodhouse said.

I shook his hand. "How long's that take?" I asked.

"About six months."

"Then what?"

"Training. Three years at least before I have a commission."

I whistled.

He sighed. "Yeah. But it opens up a little once I get past a certain point. I get a little freedom."

"What are they going to make you do?"

"Hard to say from just my test scores, but I'm hoping for something in Bio. Medical."

That took me aback. I'd been surprised to learn that Woodhouse thought he had a chance of making it into the Service at all, much less as an officer. But he'd made it as far as selection, and with his sights set on such a prestigious and technical field.

Apparently I'd never given him enough credit.

He looked confident. Woodhouse thought he was going to make it, and at this point, who was I to say he wouldn't? And the thought of three years in the imperial oven didn't seem to bother him at all.

Three years. In three years, Woodhouse could have his commission in the Service. Decent income, enormous prestige, and a genuinely good chance of elevating his bloodline even if he didn't particularly distinguish himself.

Where was I going to be in three years? I'd be nineteen, just like Woodhouse. But where?

"Where's the selection?" Griffith was asking.

"I don't even know yet. At some point, my holo's going to have a shuttle ticket, and I'd just better be on it," Woodhouse said, grimacing. "I've been grinding it out for this for so long, but now it's so sudden and so opaque. I don't have a good feel for what's coming."

"Don't complain. It's a good deal," Griffith said. He felt the same way I did.

"I'm not. I'm just scared."

"You'll have to have all the fun you can before that shuttle leaves. How much of a gap is there between the selection and you going into training?"

"Probably not much."

"Live while you can."

"I'm not sure I know how anymore." Woodhouse shrugged. "I can't do anything without thinking that I should be studying. Once I get out there, I won't have any time or any choice at all. At this point, it'll be a relief."

I knew what he meant.

"Take care, guys. And send me a message once I'm in there, remind me how much fun you're having out here. You'll either make me miserable or help me get through the day. So one of us wins no matter what."

"Nobody wins in the military," Griffith said.

I rolled my eyes. "Come to our place later."

Woodhouse looked grateful. He really was dealing with some nerves. He was *supposed* to be happy.

"Thanks," he said.

"Am I even here?" Griffith asked when he was gone.

"We're not going to leave him in the cold just because he makes us feel bad about ourselves," I told him sternly.

"Why are you so nice to him?" He gave me a suspicious look.

"Why shouldn't I be? I never thought he'd make it," I said.

He rolled his eyes. "Where's our table?"

I checked my holo. "It's by the stage."

"Let's go. I'm done talking to people."

Great. This was supposed to be a celebration, but Woodhouse had just butchered the mood. We sat down, and I wasn't surprised to see that our table was nearly empty, but Larsen appeared and took his chair.

"Where's Velma?" I asked, settling in beside Griffith.

"Doing an interview," Larsen replied, turning to wave at a passing drinks cart. It spotted him and rolled toward us.

On graduation day? That was a really good sign.

"What's wrong?" I asked. Larsen didn't look good, and that didn't make sense. "An interview for what?"

"She got first percentile in aptitudes. Enlisted combat roles. She's been prepping for selection behind my back." He looked calm, but he wasn't calm. He was shell-shocked. His eyes were vacant and he didn't seem to know what to do with his hands.

The cart rolled up, and he just took a glass at random.

"Empress," Griffith breathed. "She's joining up? Is she *leaving* you?"

"I don't know." He shook his head and drained the glass. He'd obviously already had a few. "She says she was keeping it from me because she'd be embarrassed if she didn't make it, but if she's scoring that high—I mean, how could she even think she wouldn't make it? So I think she is."

"Larsen, she didn't keep it from you because she's leaving you," Griffith said, eyes wide. "She kept it from you because of your debates. She was protecting herself."

Good point. Larsen had been the vice chair of the political conversation committee, and he was serious about it. He'd attended New Unity rallies and even contributed to some of their little publications.

Of course Velma hadn't told him she was pursuing the Service. It stood to reason.

But what was she thinking? What was *he* thinking? How did something like this happen? They'd been together as long as Griffith and I had known them. And running in opposite directions the whole time? This couldn't be the whole picture. The cold feeling in my stomach that had come from running into Woodhouse was getting worse.

I wished there was something I could do for Larsen, but it looked like he'd spent a long time digging blindly and only just now noticed how deep his grave was. I hadn't had any idea, and neither had Griffith.

Larsen was the one person in Nemerov that Griffith actually admired. Larsen knew what he believed. He knew it and he wasn't afraid to speak up.

Griffith worshipped him. Seeing Griffith seeing Larsen like this—I was starting to get a little emotional.

But Griffith was acting tough.

"This isn't what you need to hear right now, but she's going to cut you loose," he told Larsen frankly. "When she goes up for secret clearance, having you on the radar will not help her. It'll limit her opportunities."

Griffith was right. He was thinking clearly, even if he wasn't being sensitive.

Not that Griffith was *known* for being sensitive.

"I know." Larsen wasn't stupid. They'd been such a great couple. And Velma—I'd always liked her. The Service. Was *everyone* joining? Had we just missed this? Had they all been hiding it? Only one percent of Evagardians had good enough aptitudes and scores to join, but it seemed like more than one percent of our friends were deserting us for the uniform.

Larsen didn't stay to mope. I watched him go, and Griffith just stared at his drink.

"They probably made her do it."

"What?"

"Priority picks," Griffith said. "When they're recruiting people they really want. They've got people that come out and talk to them. Guide them. Help them have the best chance. That person's the one who told Velma to shut him out."

"That's a conspiracy theory," I said, taking a drink. Then I sat up a little straighter. "Have you been reading that New Unity stuff again?"

"Larsen's our friend. I keep up with his stuff."

I stared at him. "You— you're going to get into trouble."

"I'm not running for office."

"But," I began, but I stopped. There was no point. "At least this much is legal now," I said, touching the lip of my glass.

"Right. We're technically of age." Griffith snorted. He put down his glass and pushed it away. "Takes all the fun out of it."

"What about us?"

"What *about* us?"

"What if we did an assessment?" I asked.

"What?"

"It's not like we have bad aptitudes. We're a little behind everyone else, but that doesn't matter. We can catch up."

"Are you serious?" Griffith stared at me, stricken. "Are you trying to make me start flipping tables?"

"There's a *reason* they're all going," I said, gesturing at the party.

"Not all of them."

"Everyone who *can*. This is Cohengard. We'll always have to work harder, always have more to prove. The Service makes sense."

"Look," Griffith said. "Relax. It's where we are. They're all going—I know how you feel, believe me. But those aren't the kind of feelings we act on. Be rational. And besides, just thinking about you going off to die for the Empress makes me want to..." he trailed off, shaking his head.

I'd known he was going to say that. He was right about one thing: being legally allowed to drink ethanol after graduation *did* make it less interesting. I drank anyway.

"You're not mad because I invited Tim over, are you?"

He snorted. "Just for tonight."

Then he smiled.

"What?" I asked. That was a quick reversal; I'd worried that I was going to have to spend the rest of the evening trying to get his spirits back up.

"Nothing," he said. "I was just thinking about you in the Service. Just the idea of it."

And he started to laugh.

TEN

Now

The doors shut. I'd had longer waits in my life.

There was nothing as melodramatic as pounding on the other side; Spirluck's guys had still been ten meters away when I got through.

I wasn't kidding myself; I wasn't safe from them. If Spirluck wasn't a laborer himself, he'd at the very least have laborers in his pocket. The environment inside the labor corps would be slightly less treacherous than general population, but I didn't imagine it was any kind of haven. It was my understanding that outright murder was frowned upon inside labor quartering, but a lot of things were frowned upon in New Brittia. That didn't stop anyone, me least of all.

I was in a room identical to the one that had transitioned me from processing into general. There was a chair and a feed, and a robot would be appearing any second.

The panel slid aside, and it emerged with another drink.

Abigail Baykara's face appeared on the wall. She was a work of art. Although the Baykara clan no longer held Evagardian citizenship, the Empire was where their roots were. Though the Baykara family was a Free Trade icon now, they still probably favored Evagardian medical care. Everyone did. Everyone who could afford it, at any rate.

Sensibilities varied enormously across the Evagardian systems. Depending on where you were, people would have different views of what it meant to be an Evagardian. Some believed beauty was a product of the universe and best appreciated as it developed naturally. Others liked to take a more active role in satisfying vanity, approaching it more like art.

In some places, that meant the removal of blemishes or minor tweaks. In others, it meant treating the human body as a blank canvas.

Abigail Baykara was at least sixty. Not even middle aged by Evagardian standards. This digital representation of her wore sensible galactic business clothes, and underneath the outfit, her body would youthful to the point of looking like the idealized caricatures on display in VR pleasure apps.

Keeping the body young and strong was common enough for people who had the means to do it, both in the Imperium and elsewhere.

What the Baykara clan did with their faces was a bit less common, but you'd still see it from Evagardian aristocrats if you knew where to look, and in plenty of eccentric galactics as well.

Abigail Baykara's face had been carefully sculpted into what I considered an optical illusion. There were images that two people could look at and see very different things, and even just a shift in angle, thought, or concentration could tip the balance. In Abigail's case, the balance hung between exotic beauty and something completely alien.

The corners of her eyes were drawn up and back, and her eyes themselves were somewhat enlarged. Her irises had been recolored to shine brightly. Her nose and cheekbones had been altered, and so had her chin. Her ears were slightly pointed, and every strand of her glossy black hair was meticulously arranged.

Her lips were painted extravagantly, and a lovely green cosmetic at the edges of her eyes created quite a picture when that massive, glowing gaze was turned on you.

Her skin was smooth to the point of looking artificial, and there were a few small, restrained decorations: a primrose on her jaw and a Trigan emblem on her cheek.

She was interesting to look at. I could understand how some people found this sort of thing attractive. It wasn't my preference, though.

I glanced at the closed doors on either side of the chamber and sat down. It felt good to breathe freshly recycled air and to be somewhere clean. The little androids couldn't keep it pristine, but compared to where I'd spent the last hour, it might as well have been the Empress's Garden.

"Beta Two-Zero-Two," Abigail said, smiling warmly. "Welcome to labor orientation. If you choose to join the labor corps, your sentence will be forgiven and erased, as will any records of criminal activity in Oversight's databases. These records will continue to exist in the files of the law enforcement agency that committed you to New Brittia. However, upon joining the labor force, you will receive provisional immunity that will be honored by the following agencies."

She began to list them. A part of me was curious, but I didn't have the mental energy to pay attention. It was a long list, but it didn't include any imperial peacekeeping organizations.

"Unfortunately, just becoming a laborer only cancels your sentence. It does not give you free passage out of New Brittia, but it does give you a chance to earn it," Abigail was saying.

I leaned back and closed my eyes.

"As a laborer, you'll enjoy better quality of life than you did as an inmate, but chances are, your ultimate goal is going to be to leave here and go where you please. There are several ways to make that happen. As you know, activity within New Brittia is open to spectators, and among those spectators are recruiters on both sides of the law. Private security, private military, and privateers—they all look to New Brittia for their staffing needs. By distinguishing yourself as a laborer, you can catch the eye of these recruiters, who may purchase your passage, traditionally in exchange for a contract of indentured servitude similar to the one you'll commit to in a moment if you choose to proceed."

The comfort I was getting from the chair was psychosomatic. I wasn't really tired. I wasn't even sore; there were twinges from my arms and shoulders because of that daring leap much earlier, but that was all. I was fine. I just sagged in the chair because I felt like I *ought* to need it.

"Martial prowess isn't the only way to get attention. For detailed information on notable personalities who have succeeded in escaping New Brittia by taking advantage of the spectator system, consult any public information terminal inside your laborer housing facility."

True, out in Free Trade space there were plenty of people getting by on celebrity status garnered in here—

celebrity status that had nothing to do with their ability to acquit themselves in labor challenges. It was all about getting people interested, being recognizable. Building a brand.

There were plenty of corporations out there who wanted to hijack a brand built on someone else's work in the hopes of elevating their own. And New Brittia, with its uncountable legions of spectators, was a good place to find faces that people could be trained to recognize.

"On top of the billions of spectators outside New Brittia, there's one more recruiter to think about. Me. If you don't know about the Baykara Games, consult a public information terminal. Before you accept entry into the labor corps, understand that there is a price—the price of your freedom is your life. In joining the labor corps, you enter an agreement of indentured servitude under me personally, an agreement that is not subject to the protection of the Free Trade Servant Protection Act."

Nothing I didn't already know, but I was curious to hear Abigail Baykara's phrasing. She couldn't lie about this.

"As a laborer, you will be required to maintain your laborer status. Failure to do so will result in your summary execution."

Well, that was direct enough. This clause was to prevent inmates from joining labor just to get out of general population. This guaranteed that all laborers would at least try to do something interesting with their time. Those that didn't would die. There was no transitioning back; once you joined labor, you were in until you got out or died. There was no third option.

Abigail had done a nice job on this speech.

"Maintaining your status isn't difficult, but it is dangerous," she said, then launched into a description of all the ways a laborer could keep his status. Most of it was focused around the core notion of scavenging in the mines, but hostile encounters and headhunting were also accepted forms of payment. That was thoughtful of the Baykaras; there was something for everyone. You don't like killing people? Don't. Just kill or destroy whatever obstacles they put in the mines. Don't like killing things at all? Just scavenge.

I was surprised there was no reward for having sex. It was well-known that a large segment of the New Brittia fellowship was more interested in that stuff than in the adventures in the mines or the action up at the residence.

Things like what had happened to Atlas were exactly what those people wanted to see. But no—on the labor side, it was no longer about degradation. What they wanted here was something a little different. Charming.

I wished she'd hurry up and finish. A part of me wouldn't have minded sitting around for a while, but I couldn't. The whole galaxy was after me, but time was the only enemy that mattered.

I gazed at Abigail. I'd heard that all the Baykaras favored these little cosmetic touches. No one thing that Abigail Baykara had done to her face or body was too jarring, but cumulatively it was like looking at a new species. I'd seen pictures of Evagardians and other galactics that took it even further, but not many of them. And I'd certainly met some odd characters when I'd been Prince Dalton.

Abigail Baykara owned the single largest entertainment franchise in the galaxy, and she had deep ties to Free Trade regulators. She was the richest woman alive after the Empress, and based on my understanding of the Baykara Network's still-growing popularity, she would only get richer. Indeed, she was about to get a *lot* richer.

Because if it wasn't widely known yet, it would be soon. I didn't know if the galaxy would present this as

Prince Dalton himself being in New Brittia, or just the man who had pretended to be Prince Dalton. However that played out, I would bring more eyes to New Brittia than the Baykara Network had ever seen before.

If I lived long enough.

Celebrities were made in New Brittia, but they did not end up *in* New Brittia. And I wasn't just any celebrity—I was the celebrity who had destroyed Little Norwich, the Ganraen capital station, and brought about the ceasefire in the largest war the galaxy had seen in a century.

"Beta Two-Zero-Two, do you understand the parameters of this agreement? If not, we can go over it again, or I can elaborate on any point that you request."

I got up from the chair.

"What's the meaning of life?" I asked.

"I'm sorry, but I only have answers for questions relating to the transition from inmate to laborer status. If you'd like to me to start again or go over any of the—"

"I understand. Show me the contract and let me commit."

Abigail Baykara's image smiled at me.

"I applaud you, inmate Beta Two-Zero-Two. It takes a certain kind of man to put his life on the line to improve his lot. The possibilities for men like you are endless." Her smile grew, and the contract began to materialize. It seemed unlikely that anyone really took the time to read it.

I certainly wasn't going to.

ELEVEN

I emerged from the transition room feeling exactly the same as I had going in. I wasn't a new man, and I wasn't rested or refreshed by the brief break from New Brittia. My fingers still tingled, my skin was hot, and I saw and heard everything with perfect clarity.

This was probably what it felt like to be an android.

I wore the amber of a laborer, and that was nice. The suit was sturdier than the gray jumpsuits of the inmates, and it had a lot of features with utility: adjustable sleeves, a double-breasted front, a high collar, and most importantly, actual boots. It wasn't exactly armor, but it felt appropriately substantial.

I rolled up the sleeves to my elbows and fastened them, loosened my collar, and took in the labor block.

It was wide open, no different from Balkin Square, but smaller and less crowded. There wasn't as much junk, and things were generally cleaner and less abused, but clearly this place had seen years of hard use.

Instead of crude artwork, the walls were adorned with advertisements for food and drink available through the automated vendors at outrageously low prices; every company wanted people being broadcast eating and drinking their products with the whole galaxy watching.

Terminals, protein combiners—the necessities of life ringed the square. There was very little cover, probably so Oversight snipers could theoretically kill an underperforming laborer, or force them to hide in specific places that could be easily cleared—or, ideally, to flee into the mines.

More efficient execution methods existed, but highly visible violence was more interesting. Oversight didn't get fancy toys to play with; they only had guns.

There wasn't much to do in the labor square; that was probably why so many laborers chose to go back out into Balkin Square to amuse themselves, dangerous as it might be. It wasn't more dangerous than the mines, and if they blew quota, they could try to hide in the blocks out there, but Oversight would just do a raid, track them down, and shoot them. We didn't have kill chips, but we were all under surveillance, so hiding wasn't really viable.

It was brighter here, and the air seemed cleaner. Everything felt better in the labor corps, but what good was it, in the end? It could've been all luxury, but it would still have the mines looming over it.

The mines of New Brittia were a part of my future now. To think I'd once been nervous about going onstage as Prince Dalton and singing. Being a galactic music sensation had been easy, though. Everyone had already loved Prince Dalton. He'd done all the work, and I'd just stepped in and done more or less what he'd done.

Everybody loved Dalton. Not everybody loved me.

I turned to return Spirluck's gaze.

He was only a few steps away, standing just inside the nearest gate. I'd never met him before and I didn't know his face, but it was him. Right on schedule.

He was taller than I was, and older. He had a narrow frame and a pointed chin.

He wasn't a real inmate. He was a plant. It wasn't possible for someone to rise to the top like this; anyone who showed that kind of excellence would be recruited out of New Brittia in short order. He could only be here because he wanted to be.

He belonged to the management. He was a specialized piece of the complex machine that made New Brittia work. A professional conduit.

But that didn't mean he didn't have to play the part of the kingpin. I'd made him bleed, and he was obliged to deal with me. Or to recruit me; that was his other option, but I didn't think that was what he had in mind, and I couldn't take him up on it in any case.

I returned his vaguely hostile look with one of profound disinterest.

There probably wasn't any point in trying to warn him off. He wouldn't listen.

Maybe he would respect the rules and wait for a better chance at me in the mines. It was very impolite for laborers to engage in hostilities here in their little grotto.

It was best if I didn't bait him into anything. With a little luck, he'd pull back to think, and I'd be gone before he made up his mind. I broke off the aggressive eye contact and headed for the nearest wall.

Combiners, taps, and data feeds. This was another perk of being a laborer.

Much of the data were directly related to laborers and New Brittia: rankings and standings, active rosters, and information about the mines.

But there was also data from the outside: feeds from galactic news outlets and even entertainment broadcasts.

This wasn't an amenity added out of kindness or a reward for the bravery of laborers, although it could be seen that way.

It was a calculated move to galvanize us. These broadcasts were a window to freedom: they would only strengthen a laborer's resolve to get out of New Brittia, and it was working. I didn't know the exact number of men who went into the mines each day, but it was a lot.

I found the broadcast commands and started to swipe. It was a good selection of feeds, and I wanted news.

I found a Free Trade broadcast talking about the past and future of Evagardian and Commonwealth relations and encroachment in contested space. It sounded like the ceasefire between the Imperium and the Ganraen Commonwealth was still in effect.

That would be the main thing on everyone's minds until after the peace talks. People were wrong when they said that the destruction of Little Norwich ended the war.

The loss of so many royals and so much of the Commonwealth's military leadership had effectively stunned the Ganraen Navy, the way a punch to the gut can double a man over and leave him vulnerable.

Vulnerable but alive. And more or less whole.

Rather than letting the Empress take advantage of that vulnerability and deliver a killing blow, the Ganraen State Department issued a peculiar mixture of ceasefire and surrender that the Empress surprised everyone by accepting.

It was an obvious desperation play, but it didn't truly signal the end of anything. From the outside, the destruction of the capital looked like a decisive blow. Unfortunately, there was more at work. More than anyone realized, and most Evagardians didn't appreciate just how large the Commonwealth really was.

Yes, a large piece of the top tier of Ganrae's leaders had been obliterated, but the rest of the Commonwealth had been left largely untouched. And there was no shortage of people ready to fill that leadership vacuum. After Ganrae recovered, it would become clear that the loss of the capital had not seriously affected the Commonwealth's ability to wage war. The Ganraen Navy was still largely intact.

The war would only truly end if the peace talks succeeded. The Empress had to come to an agreement with the surviving Royals and Commonwealth leaders about how to move forward with their respective expansions, and *then* she would have to convince the Free Trade shot callers to play along.

If she succeeded—and if history was anything to go by, she probably would—then the war would be over, at least for now. At the moment, it was only on hold. There had been force reductions on both sides after the ceasefire, but that was just for show. Everyone was ready to go back to work if they needed to.

I continued to swipe through the feeds until I saw my own face.

My face was beside Prince Dalton's. As expected, no one seemed sure what to make of me. They were pretty sure I was an Evagardian spy, which was true, but of course, Evagard was denying any responsibility for my actions and telling everyone that I was a dangerous terrorist. By the look of things, people weren't really buying the denials from the Imperium, but they would keep denying because the only person who could disprove it was me.

Evagard needed distance between me and the Empress. If I was a terrorist who did it all because I wanted to, that was all right. If I was a spy who had gone rogue, that was bad but still workable for them.

But if I'd destroyed Little Norwich—if I had killed all those people on the Imperium's orders—everything would change, and it would change in ways that could never be undone. The truth wasn't that simple, but the truth wasn't important.

The only thing that mattered was the narrative.

A spy replacing a foreign dignitary was one thing. It wasn't pretty, but it wouldn't derail the peace talks. The Imperium ordering the destruction of a station full of innocent people—if that became the accepted truth, there wouldn't even *be* any peace talks.

Awkward stuff for a lot of Evagardians. Doubly awkward now that I was on the loose with the whole galaxy watching. Evagard certainly found it scary and embarrassing to have me at large in hiding. But at large in public? I'd hate to be the one in charge of the unlucky task force that was supposed to be tying up loose ends.

I looked at my present face and Dalton's beside it. Sometimes, when I thought about this, I could see the resemblance—it could seem almost uncanny. And sometimes I'd wonder how anyone had looked at me and thought I'd make a good Dalton.

I'd undergone a lot of changes to become him. Nothing as radical as Abigail Baykara, but still. Tweaks to my face. My body reprogrammed in many ways to mirror his physiology—even down to where I grew hair, and what color. Not that it mattered, because Dalton had always been completely hairless except for his flowing locks, the care of which had occupied almost as much of my time as my actual mission. Totally worth it, of course.

I'd reverted some of those changes after Nidaros, mostly the ones to my face. But the deeper changes, particularly those made to my actual frame, were still intact. The most difficult part of becoming Dalton had been the change in height. I didn't mind it so much now that I was used to it.

It looked as though there was still some doubt. There were a lot of people out there, and different theories had taken hold with different groups. Those who believed I was an imperial agent acting on the Empress's orders. Those who believed I was an imperial agent gone rogue. Those who believed I'd been a New Unity radical from the beginning. Those who believed I was being set up. Those who believed I was the real Prince Dalton. Those who believed the destruction of Little Norwich had been staged by the Frontier System Congress or Kakugo to put an end to the war before it spread to their systems.

The fact that Prince Dalton had been replaced by a double was gaining traction, as was the notion that double was an Evagardian spy. The connection to Little Norwich was following, right on schedule.

As long as I was alive, I was going to be a problem for someone.

It was an ugly picture out there. Murky. A nightmare for the imperials trying to spin it all the right way to support the Empress, because just as there were Evagardians who wanted my head, there were also plenty trying to defend me.

They said that if I *was* a spy, I was a proper hero of the Imperium, and that Evagard's denials were disgraceful. That was sweet of them, but naïve.

The feed abruptly cut; the woman talking about me had just shifted to the subject of my appearance at New Brittia. These feeds couldn't include any coverage that might give one laborer an unfair advantage over another. No coverage of New Brittia could be seen from the inside.

The word was out, though.

They had my face and they knew I was here. Grains of sand were falling from my hourglass, each of them an infinity charge large enough to destroy a world.

Or an empire.

Or maybe just a capital space station with a trifling twenty million people on it.

Because of what I had become, my name, records from Cohengard, even my most fundamental identification numbers had been purged. There was no longer much tangible evidence of who I was—or who I had been. I had my own memories, and there were the memories of people who had known me back then, but those wouldn't have much impact, not in the face of an Evagardian counterintelligence campaign.

The records did exist, somewhere. Whether they came out or not—and when—well, that would be interesting, but it wouldn't be my problem. My real identity would be powerful support for the picture they were working to paint of a Cohengardian boy with a grudge against the Empress. A boy who would do something horrible and try to leave the Imperium with the credit for it.

In the end, there was a good chance it would be my past, not my present, that would convince everyone that I was exactly the terrorist that Evagard was describing.

And speaking of terrorists, there was another feed. A major attack was in progress at Sterling Station. That was a galactic station, but a civilized one. The newscasters were speculating that it was the work of New Unity. They were probably right; there'd been a couple big New Unity attacks brewing for a while, and this could easily be one of them. Imperials loved to look down on galactics and call them savages, yet right now there were Evagardian terrorists out there using physical violence, the most primitive tool of all.

It hadn't escaped me that Spirluck was behind me, probably with a couple of his guys. I was just lost in thought, watching the feeds. Savoring the moment.

It was a pity there wasn't time for me to learn more about that business at Sterling Station. Catching up with the news felt good. It was almost something a normal person would do.

To the right of the feed was another broadcast, but this was an internal one showing which laborers were inside the grotto and which were active in the mines. One of them had just emerged, and I recognized his name. I'd seen it earlier on the roster, and that he was nearby now—I took that as a sign that it was time for us to meet again.

Break time was over. It had been nice while it lasted.

I turned around and struck Spirluck in the throat. He dropped to the ground, choking. I'd destroyed his windpipe; nothing could save him but stasis and good medical care. His chances of getting those here probably weren't good.

The two men who were presumably his bodyguards stared at me in shock. Then they stared at Spirluck as he writhed at my feet.

I didn't have time to let him chase or harass me. I'd have liked to make a deal with him, use him to my advantage, but there was no guarantee he'd play along, and I didn't have time to give the matter the thought and effort it deserved.

The bodyguards didn't make a single move toward me. One of them actually backed away.

That's the thing about authoritarian-types: ruling by fear will get you results, but only as long as you've got a pulse. Fear and loyalty are powerful motivators, but that's the only thing they have in common. They aren't the same thing. Spirluck had influence, but he didn't have popularity.

And no one's ever sorry to see an unpopular ruler take a fall.

TWELVE

I left the bodyguards there to debate how they could best spin Spirluck's abrupt demise to their advantage. One of them might be the one to step into his shoes, or maybe Management would find someone new on the outside and send them in. It would take a brave man to accept that job, but Spirluck had, and so would others like him.

It was impressive what people were willing to put themselves through for material gain. I'd been there once, a long time ago.

Would murdering a laborer outside the mines endear me to Management? I didn't care. Normally it wouldn't, but it was uncommon, and anything uncommon was good broadcast.

It was just a little proactive self-defense, in any case. Proactive self-defense didn't get you a lot of traction in most courtrooms, but I was already in prison. What had the law done for me lately?

People stared as I crossed the grotto, but no one approached. All these guys could handle themselves, but they were already laborers. They were already exposed to plenty of risk. Why take on more?

Ahead, wide arches opened on stairs leading down. It reminded me of something I'd seen on a tour on New Earth, a tribute to public transportation from the twentieth century: underground transport that ran on a schedule and moved people around a city. This was like one of those stations where people would go to wait for the next trolley.

I descended. Below lay the transition point, a long chamber with all the entrances to the mines.

Freeber walked past me without even a twitch. He hadn't noticed me at all.

"Really?" I said, and he turned and looked back.

I watched recognition spread over his face, and he tensed. But his look quickly hardened. He faced me and squared himself, and I was impressed. He didn't rattle.

Probably because he was twice my size.

I didn't know Freeber particularly well. I'd recognized his name on the list that Gingham had gotten me, and I knew his face, but we'd only been in each other's company for a few hours. He had been a freelancer partnered with his wife. They were the ones that had kidnapped me and Salmagard from Red Yonder. They had tried to sell us to Idris. As for why they'd chosen us as targets—well, some convenient information must have fallen into their laps. They hadn't been freelancers—not really. And they hadn't been agents. They'd been a pair of gloves, gloves for hands already so dirty that I didn't know why they'd bothered.

And they shouldn't have. Something had gone wrong, and Willis and Freeber had succeeded in selling Salmagard and Diana. Unfortunately for Idris, Salmagard and Diana had not been content to stay sold.

Sei and I had parted ways with Freeber when he'd handed us off to shady buyers that actually just wanted sacrifices for their weird cult, which was unaware that it itself was the real sacrifice and that they were in fact intended to be tossed into a black hole.

Charming people in Free Trade space, really.

In a sense, Freeber had been the one to put me in New Brittia, but it wasn't that simple.

No one thing had brought me here. Mistakes that I had made, bad luck—these were only half of the walls that boxed me in. And luck had nothing to do with it. Luck, good or bad, was something I'd left behind a long time ago. If coincidence was real, it only existed for other people.

Freeber hadn't done me any favors, although he had inadvertently gotten me away from Salmagard. That had probably saved her. She deserved better than what had been waiting for her if I'd had my way. It was a good thing.

I could try to look at it that way, anyway.

So with that in mind, maybe Freeber was a friend after all. Not that it mattered.

"We should talk," I told him, continuing down the stairs. I motioned for him to follow and didn't look back. He wasn't afraid of me; the difference in size between us would make it hard for him to see me as a threat. And me, a threat? I really did just want to talk. He also didn't know that I'd been killing a lot of people lately, so he had no reason not to hear me out.

There were benches at the bottom. Ahead lay the entrances to the mines. There were a dozen of them, spaced wide apart. It was a cavernous space. There were a few laborers in view, but not many, and it was pleasantly quiet. It would've been peaceful, a profound improvement over general population, if not for the clock ticking down every laborer's life. Of course, everyone's lives were ticking down, but the men wearing amber had less time than everyone else.

I sat down on the bench in front of the nearest set of doors. After a moment, I sensed Freeber behind me. So his curiosity had gotten the best of him.

"Sit down," I said. He didn't.

"What do you want?"

I wondered what he was thinking. This had to be an odd situation for him. After all, I was his victim. Of course he wouldn't be completely comfortable talking to me, but I wasn't sure exactly which kind of discomfort he might be feeling.

"Your wife," I said.

There was a pause. "What about her?"

I turned and looked up at him. "Where is she?"

"I don't know," Freeber said.

"I remember someone saying you'd been here before." Was that true?" No reason not to be upfront.

He hesitated, then sat down on the far end of the bench. "Yeah," he said.

"Where'd you meet her?"

"Who?"

"Willis."

"Why are you asking?" He was less suspicious than curious.

"Because I'm thinking about asking for your help. This is going to sound weird, but I was really impressed with your relationship. You and her."

He just stared at me. I shrugged and went back to looking at the doors ahead.

"You don't have to get it. I just think it must be really nice to find someone you can be yourself with," I said. "No secrets. You guys seemed to have it right. How long were you together?"

He looked at me for a long time, face unreadable. He was wondering if I was being serious.

"A while," he finally rumbled.

"You remember the girl I was with?"

He was too intrigued to walk away. This wasn't going where he expected it to go.

"Which one?"

"The normal one," I said.

He nodded. Of course he remembered: Salmagard had the face of the Grand Duchess. Even galactics would recognize that.

"I barely knew her. I'd just met her, really." It was true. There had been Nidaros, then just a few hours together before we were kidnapped. The amount of time I'd spent with Tessa Salmagard didn't even add up to a full Old Earth day cycle. "But that was still long enough to know this is for the best," I said. "I guess you helped us both out that way. Do you want to see her again?"

"Your girl?" he asked mildly.

"Willis."

"Why are you asking?" he repeated.

"I have a friend," I said. "He's on the other strut. I want to get him out of here."

Freeber snorted.

"The only way to get to Alpine Strut is through the mines. Isn't it?"

He smiled. "I don't even know if that's possible."

"Of course it is. You run into laborers from Alpine down there, don't you? It all has to be connected."

"I guess."

"I have to get through. Then I'm leaving. What's the sentence for kidnapping?" I asked him. "How long are you in?"

His eyes narrowed, and I realized I'd made a faulty assumption. There was probably more than just abduction on his list of offenses. Still, I was right. His sentence had to be long. He didn't answer, but he didn't have to.

"Did you get out last time through labor or time?"

He hesitated. "Labor."

"Think you will again?" I asked. "How long did it take the first time?"

"Three weeks."

That must have been hell. Three weeks didn't sound like a long prison sentence, but with the clock ticking, the constant threat of execution—Freeber could handle himself. He'd seen and done things, and that made him the perfect man to have along. He really could help me reach the other strut.

"Helping me get through the mines can't be any more dangerous than whatever you'd be doing otherwise. And crossing to Alpine might get you some attention. It could help you out," I said. "I've been busy. If you come with me, you'll get some eyes. How much do you know about what's waiting down there?"

"Doesn't matter. They change it all the time."

"You still know more than I do. Have you ever heard of anyone crossing to Alpine?"

"No," Freeber said. "What's the point? We don't even know what it's like over there."

"Just like this," I said, shrugging. "The point is to get attention. Especially if no one's ever done it."

I was making a good point, not that it mattered. It had been easy to bully Idris into helping me, but it wouldn't be easy with Freeber. It was better if I could recruit him with temptation.

Proposing a jailbreak from New Brittia wasn't a dangerous thing to do. Or rather, it wasn't any more dangerous than business as usual. The only thing the spectators liked more than escape attempts were escape successes. And what the spectators liked, Management liked.

If Freeber didn't buy into a jailbreak, he might still be interested in making a splash. The problem was trust, and the question of what I brought to the table for him.

"So? Are you in or out?"

"You're serious."

"You know the mines."

"I don't *know* the mines," Freeber said. "Nobody does."

That was fair; if anyone truly knew the mines, that would defeat the purpose.

"But you've been down there. If you want to get out of here, you're going to have to take some risks. Why not take them with me? Or do you have a lot of friends?"

He snorted again. "Why are you even talking to me?"

"I only have one friend left," I said. "If he was here, I wouldn't be."

"You want me to protect you."

"I don't need protection, but I just got here. I can't learn how to survive the mines overnight. My chances of getting across are better with help. Why are you having such a hard time with this?"

"I'm not going to partner with you," he said bluntly.

He meant it. Freeber wasn't an idiot, and I'd known this would be his reply.

"Why not?"

"You know why not."

"You are a big part of the reason I'm here," I told him.

"You were coming here anyway," he added, glancing over at me. "You don't get sent here for getting sold. Unless someone sold you into this place. Is that what happened? If it was, I think you'd be a little more pissed."

"That's not what happened," I said. "I'm a terrorist. And I'm not staying," I repeated. "How about you come with me? What if she's watching you right now?"

"Nice try."

"How do you know she's not? I'm really asking."

Freeber looked bemused, but he turned and joined me in gazing at the doors to the mines.

"I don't know," he said after a moment. "I hope she is. It means she's free."

"Why don't you know? I feel like you would know. Were you two into New Brittia?"

He shook his head. "We only did spectator stuff when we couldn't do VR instead."

"You had the whole galaxy to fly around," I said. "You had your own ship, you had the woman you loved. Why wasn't that reality good enough for you?" I didn't actually mean to say that, it just came out. "Sorry," said, rolling my eyes. "None of my business."

Freeber stared at me.

I turned my eyes back on the doors. "Why wouldn't she be watching? If there was someone in here that I cared about, I'd be watching. I would've been watching if I'd known my friend was here."

"You didn't know?"

"We were out of touch for a long time. I was working."

"What did you do?"

"You know. Terrorist things."

"What did you really do?"

"You don't have to believe me. Do you keep up with the news much? The war?"

"The Commonwealth and the imperials? It's over. Nothing to keep up with now."

That was not true, but it was believed by a lot of ignorant people. They all *wanted* the war to be over. They were confusing their hopes with reality.

I had hopes too.

I grinned. "Then who I am wouldn't mean much to you."

"Fine."

"Why wouldn't she watch?" I pressed.

He didn't answer that, but I didn't have to be an empath to see through him. He was doubting. That was good, but it wasn't enough, and I didn't have any more time to waste trying to woo him. It had been one stroke of good luck to get my money's worth out of Idris.

Demanding that lightning strike twice was greedy. I wasn't going to convince him to be my new friend, but I'd known that from the beginning. I didn't need to.

"You won't come with me," I said at last.

"No."

And he wouldn't be talked into it.

"Can you at least help me before I go in? Tell me what you know?"

He rubbed face with his hands. One of the gates opened and three men emerged. They went straight to the stairs.

"Can you do that much for me?" I pressed. "Square us up?"

The footsteps faded. No one wanted to be anywhere near these gates. No one but us. That was no surprise; it was a little gloomy, and who would want to stand around and look at the entrances to the mines? It was where most of these men would die. No, they'd rather spend their time in the grotto.

It was as quiet as a tomb.

"All right," Freeber said.

THIRTEEN

There was no Evagardian equivalent of New Brittia. There were contests of strength and prowess, but Evagardian law was very clear about what could be commercialized as entertainment.

Things were looser in the Commonwealth. There was combat sport, but people weren't killed. They occasionally died, like in any contact sport, but competitive events in the Commonwealth weren't focused on bloodshed. There was plenty of competitive savagery done in VR for broadcast purposes, but nobody cared about that. Not when there was *real* stuff they could watch instead.

Imperials liked to look down on Ganraens, and it was easy for people at the other end of the galaxy to forget that Ganrae was only one of the three systems that made up the Commonwealth. Yes, it was the most influential, and for all intents and purposes the face of the alliance, but it wasn't a good idea to sleep on the others. It was true that the Frontier system wasn't the most enlightened, but the Kakugo system was culturally almost on par with Evagard, and with a much less controversial government.

If Kakugo could ever get free of the Commonwealth, they'd likely have the same kind of immigration draw that the Imperium did. And if the Ganraens could get free of their royals and reform their government, that system had a lot of potential as well.

None of them lived and breathed Evagardian perfection, but compared to the chaos and depravity of the Free Trade systems, even the Commonwealth seemed jarringly civilized.

There was a whole category of Evagardian comedies about galactics uprooted and put in imperial settings and having to adjust. And of the opposite: imperials trying to deal with galactic sensibilities. Even after years of being a Ganraen prince, I was still that guy. That entitled Evagardian used to the Empress's way of doing things, shocked and disgusted by how real people went about their lives outside the Imperium.

I was grateful for that feeling. It was a taste of home.

Freeber and I made our way back up the stairs and into the grotto. He'd agreed to at least share some wisdom with me, but I wasn't sure why. A sense of fair play? Nothing else better to do?

Or, like me, did he have something else in mind? I really would have liked to learn from him, to patch up some of the holes in my understanding of this place. I wasn't sure that would happen, but I could hope.

"Most of what you know must be out of date," I said, following him toward the outer wall.

"The details change, but it's all the same." He paused in front of an advertisement for flavored air filters for private shuttles. That seemed like a peculiar ad to run inside a prison, but who was I to question the wisdom of people who did marketing for a living?

"Just pretend I'm Willis," I told Freeber.

He stared at me. "Are you coming onto me?"

At least he had a sense of humor. "I *do* remember you have a thing for Prince Dalton. But seriously, you'd want Willis to survive. Give me the advice you'd give her."

Freeber snorted, reaching out to key to the broadcast. He cycled until he hit a placeholder image. It was a view of New Brittia from the outside. It showed the asteroid, both struts, the Oversight wing, and the city. It was a publicity image, probably the closest to a map that anyone in here was likely to get.

"Which is which?"

Freeber gave me a disdainful look and pointed at the strut on the left. "This is Balkin. If you really want to get to Alpine, I guess this is what you want to pay attention to." He indicated the bottom of the Oversight structure.

"What's down there?"

"The dock. That's how outsiders get into the mine."

"Like when they bring in people to hunt you guys in there."

"Right."

"How do you know that?"

"Because it's also how they get people in here without processing them."

I realized he meant against their will. I didn't let my surprise show. It wasn't that I hadn't known about that, but it was a jarringly horrible concept. Even to me. Obviously everyone in New Brittia except for the people who were planted were here against their will. But they were prisoners with access to the labor system and the potential exit that it offered.

There were also people brought here for other reasons. That was the thing about Free Trade law. There weren't many regulations to hold you down, but there was also very little to protect you from being victimized. If you ended up on the wrong side of it, there wasn't much you could do about it. Who would you turn to? Free Trade peacekeepers were all privately owned. What if the person abusing you was one of them? Or the person who owned them?

Being born in Cohengard was bad. People from Cohengard had to work harder to get anywhere, but at least they were already imperial subjects. Free Trade people would face suspicion and prejudice wherever they went, and they'd have a much more difficult time getting there. A Free Trade ID was the last thing an immigration office wanted to see. Kakugo forced anyone with a Free Trade background to *buy* their citizenship.

"How does that help me?"

"There's only one dock. I don't know—" Freeber looked thoughtful. "I don't know if *anyone* knows if there's a way through at any other point, but the system has to have access to both struts there." He tapped the display. "There might be some doors or locks. I don't know."

I smiled. He was really giving this some thought. I *had* gotten through to him. He still didn't want to come with me, of course.

I understood what he was getting at, and it was throwing me off. He was right, and that was alarming, because he was right about something that *I* hadn't fully thought through.

It was good news, though. It meant it was at least theoretically possible to get through to the other strut.

"So in relation to us, that's over there somewhere." I turned and looked, but of course there was nothing to see but the wall of the grotto. "What's the layout like in there?"

"At first it's easy, and there are options. The deeper you go, the weirder it gets. It's not just the mine anymore. They've changed it. Added to it."

"I've heard things, but I don't know how any of it fits together," I said. "How far have you gotten?"

"Pretty far," Freeber grunted. There might've been a note of pride there.

"If I wanted to get through, I'd make my way down and that way. I'd just take every right I saw, guess."

Freeber looked curious. Was he just now realizing I planned to go through with it? I couldn't blame him for being skeptical, but he thought he was free to be amused by the challenge that lay ahead of me because he mistakenly believed that he wasn't coming along.

I'd hoped that I'd be able to convince him to come along, but he'd gotten out of New Brittia before, and he seemed to think he could do it again. He was better at dealing with this place than I was. Why would he follow my lead? Especially when he couldn't possibly trust me.

"I'm with you," I said. "But is it really that simple?"

He just shrugged.

"Well, what do you do when you're in there? What do you know? Do you have a route?"

"I used to," Freeber replied, looking grim. "But even if it hasn't changed, I was on Alpine. I was going in from the other side."

"But what do you do in there? Do you do collections? Or paint veins?"

"Either," he said.

"How does that work?" I asked, looking at my wrists. "Do I need gear?"

"No, your holo will tell you when you're close."

I reached up and touched my ear. The tiny earpiece had come with the laborer jumpsuit, but it hadn't actually done anything yet. It wouldn't activate until I was inside the mines. Another perk of being a laborer, presumably.

New Brittia hadn't always been about entertainment. It had begun as a neo taaffeite mine and refinery, which had failed as a result of hostile indigenous life in the asteroid itself. The neo taaffeite would have been valuable if simply mined and sold, but it was worth exponentially more as a component of New Brittia's entertainment model.

Laborers could locate and even help mine new veins; that was one of the ways to push back the death sentence. But mining wasn't very interesting to watch even though the concept of doing it by hand had to be a bit novel. It was trying to work in such an intensely perilous place that made it so entertaining to the spectators, not the mining itself.

I wasn't planning to do any mining, but nothing was guaranteed here. If something went wrong and my sentence crept up on me, I had to be prepared to do something about it. My transition had bought me an hour to live as a laborer, but just a minute ago I'd killed Spirluck. That would buy me some time. I checked my holo to be sure and blanched.

I only had thirty minutes. They hadn't given me credit for Spirluck, probably because I hadn't done it in the mines. That was dirty. No, it was the network's way of giving me a nudge.

"And what's in there?" I asked, turning to look back at the stairs leading down.

Freeber shrugged. "Everything."

Because laborers could kill other laborers for credit toward their death sentences *inside* the mines, it was already dangerous down there, but not colorful enough for the spectators. Management fed new threats into the mines to make sure they never got too safe, or too predictable.

"While that might be true," I said, "I don't think it helps me. I've heard things, I've seen advertisements. What have you actually seen in there?"

"With my own eyes?" Freeber considered it, watching the other laborers in the grotto. "Trigan headhunters," he said.

That took me aback. I was aware that Management liked to hire people to come into the mines and hunt the laborers, but Free Trade space was already so full of unscrupulous ruffians for hire that it seemed inefficient to import them.

"Why Trigans?" I asked.

"I don't know. I didn't stop to ask them," Freeber snapped.

"Seems odd," I said. "Are these guys armed?"

"Not well. That would be too unbalanced. They give them antique weapons."

"How antique?"

"Old Earth."

"Too much Old Earth in my life," I grumbled. "You sold me to people living in a replica of a twentieth century village. It was kind of nice, actually."

"Really?" Freeber looked impressed. "I just assumed they were going to—"

"To what?"

"I don't know. But going off the books like we did doesn't bring much."

"And usually those people want to eat you or kill you. Or kill you and eat you." I waved a hand. "I know. They were crazy, and yes, they were going to kill us."

"If they'd pay that little, they couldn't plan to keep you long."

"Thanks for being sensitive about this. Was it worth it?"

Freeber snorted. "Did you get loose or what?"

"Let's stay on topic. What about the things, the xenos that drove the miners out of here before the Baykaras got it?"

"I don't know about those."

"You said you'd been here before. Aren't they in there? Eating people? Or whatever they do."

"I did see something once," Freeber said, rubbing his chin. "But I'm still not sure what it was. Could've been anything. Look, laborers have been in those mines for years. There can't be many of those things left, but there's other stuff, synthetic stuff."

"You mean there's a lab out there manufacturing scary things for New Brittia?"

"Probably more than one." Freeber shrugged. "Free testing."

"Bioweapons," I said, scowling. "It's not just Old Earth. I've had enough of xenos lately, too."

"Then maybe you shouldn't go in there," Freeber suggested lightly. He was starting to enjoy this. He still didn't understand.

"I'm a laborer now, remember?" I plucked at my amber suit. "I'm going in no matter what. Do they arm you?"

"You must be joking."

"Do you have a shiv I could borrow?"

Freeber laughed. Loudly. So loudly that it echoed around the grotto.

"That's uncalled for," I said. "So I've got pros in there that want to kill me for a bonus. And *they* have weapons. And bioweapons that are designed to be scary. Sounds painful."

"Don't forget the traps," Freeber said.

"Is it really random?"

"Is anything? Rich people buy in and manipulate it. They're not supposed to be allowed to do that, but everyone knows they do."

That wasn't good. If all it took was money to get access, Evagard had plenty of money. Would that task force out there be at the controls of something in the mines, with a personal hand in taking me out?

Freeber gave me a pitying look, and I glared at him. "Forget the rich people. What do you do when you're in there to stay alive? What's the secret?"

"There's no secret. It's just luck and paying attention. Mostly luck."

I'd been afraid of that. "How long do you think it would take to get to the other side?"

"Dunno," Freeber said. "You seemed like you were in a hurry before. What happened to that?"

"I'm not in a hurry," I lied. "Not in a hurry to go die, anyway. So what's hot right now?" I asked, reaching out to key the broadcast. "I want to stay away from whatever everyone else is going after."

"You can't," Freeber said. "Look. You can see the scavenger items, but you don't know where they are. That's the point."

I found the listing and looked at the top item. "A knife?" More of a dagger, actually. Probably an antique. "What's the point of this?"

"It doesn't matter what they are," Freeber said. "They don't have value. The value is that getting them buys you time."

Macguffins? Who knew the most successful entertainment network ever was so lazy?

"I know, but it seems patronizing," I said. "This one is literally a rubber duck."

"It's an excuse. It gets you in there looking for it. It doesn't matter what it is. If you find it, it buys you twenty-four hours," Freeber explained. It was nice of him to be so patient with me.

"Oh, and there's a cash bonus for the duck. And this—this is just product placement," I said, indignant. It was an old bottle from a limited release of a Trigan whiskey. "Did someone pay to have this here?"

"Probably."

I shook my head. "Idiots."

"Are you sure?" Freeber said, looking up. I followed his gaze. Baykara City glowed against the stars. It wasn't idiotic. It was profitable.

"I know if I saw some prisoner get killed chasing this whiskey on a broadcast, I'd buy some right away," I said.

"I don't drink whiskey."

"I could use some right now," I said, looking back toward the stairs.

"You *are* still in a hurry," Freeber said. "Just move fast as soon as you go through the lock."

"Why?"

"Because those guys you saw down there? They're waiting for you. They'll see you go through, then they'll go through the next door over and try to find you before you get anywhere. It'll be three guys. A kill on another laborer buys twenty-four hours. The other two can get a piece of you to claim an assist and get twelve each. So it's always crews of three. And it's easiest to secure a kill close to the locks. It's more dangerous deeper in. This way is quick and easy. It's how you farm time safely."

"So I have to get some distance before they can jump me," I mused.

"If you're lucky. And don't forget your way back," Freeber said. "None of my closest calls were ever when I was in there knowing what I was doing. Things always get bad when something pushes you off your plan. You die when you're running around blind."

I was a little annoyed to hear him say that, but he wasn't wrong.

"I'm not coming back."

Freeber shrugged. "Good."

"What?"

"Good luck."

"You say that like we're done," he said.

"We are."

"That's the thing." I cleared my throat and looked over my shoulder. "See those guys over there? By the taps? They're the ones staring at us." And they'd certainly taken their time getting here. "I just killed Spirluck a few minutes ago. Maybe I should've led with that. Anyway, from where they're standing, you and I are obviously good friends. So I'm going to go now. You can stay if you like. I don't really know what they have in mind, but it looks like Spirluck had some friends after all. Who knew?"

I'd played it out as long as I dared. I *was* still in a hurry. I'd known I couldn't get Freeber to come along because he'd want to, but now that people thought we were friends, he was a dead man if he stayed on Balkin strut.

I didn't wait to see his reaction; I was already making my way back across the grotto, heading for the stairs. Even before I'd heard what he had to say, I hadn't been looking forward to the mines. I didn't *want* to do this, but even without Spirluck's people to complicate things, Griffith was on Alpine Strut, so that was where I was going, and this was how I had to get there. Sometimes, in certain ways, my life was very simple.

I hurried down, remembering what Freeber had said about vultures pouncing on people just through the gates. It was an obvious tactic now that he'd brought it to my attention. The loiterers looked different to me now, and the peculiar quiet of the gate area had become a bit sinister.

I didn't hesitate. I went to the nearest airlock and started the cycle.

I was leaving Balkin Strut for good. Even if I could escape retribution for Spirluck's death, I was running out of time to reach Griffith. I'd played my hand.

FOURTEEN

EIGHT YEARS AGO

"How does this work?" I asked.

"Is that a trick question?" Griffith didn't even look as he stripped down. We were already late. We'd known the caterers were going to make us wear uniforms for this, but I'd expected something a bit more ordinary. These weren't uniforms, they were costumes.

"I mean this part," I said. "There's no fastener."

"You use this." He pointed at a pair of odd little things in a box.

"But *why?*"

They were such weird black and white clothes. They didn't look weird when I saw them in period dramas, but they definitely looked weird here and now.

The gala outside was surprisingly noisy. It was an awards ceremony for drama actors being held in Cohengard because a particularly coveted award had gone to a fact-based drama based on the revolt.

A lot of people were divided on whether this was in good taste or not.

I didn't care, and Griffith didn't seem to mind either, which was a relief. I was tempted to ask him if he was sure he wanted to do this, but that was just a reflex. What was the point of asking? He was here, wasn't he?

We were there to serve, but it was just a one-time thing. Neither of us had ever seriously considered a career in servitude. It was a prestigious and lucrative field, and an interesting one, at least to me.

In history, working to serve other people in the private sector had been a task for the proletariat. And indeed, Griffith and I *were* the proletariat, but in modern Evagard, skilled human help was greatly sought after and richly rewarded.

Griffith and I weren't pursuing it as a career; tonight was just for fun. And money. I'd been looking forward to it, but I wasn't sure how Griffith would feel about it.

However he felt, he was making much better headway than I was with this ridiculous uniform.

"Help," I said, struggling with my waist fastener. He was already working on his neck scarf. He turned distractedly, saw me, and choked.

"Empress," he said, tossing his scarf aside. "We watch enough dramas, don't we?"

"What?"

"Old-timey dramas. You *see* how people wore these clothes."

"Yeah, but you don't see them putting this thing on," I protested, holding both ends of it and feeling silly. "You just see them take it off for a love scene."

He took the ends from me and fastened it, making sure my shirt was properly tucked. "It's not exactly five space nav."

"Hey, *I'm* the brains of this outfit," I said defensively. "Get it? Outfit? We're getting dressed."

"Empress save me."

"Hey, I'm *funny.*"

"Here." I put out my hands, and he used the little objects to fasten my cuffs, then put the scarf on me and tied it. It reminded me of the ropes that people used to execute each other on Old Earth.

He straightened it and brushed me off, though there was nothing to brush. Griffith tied his own scarf and pulled on his vest, and I did the same. We looked each other over.

"The scarf is cute," I noted. "How come mine's different?"

"It's a tie. It works for you," Griffith said. "I look like I'm trying too hard."

"Only to someone who knows you."

"Touché."

We left the dressing room and emerged behind the drinks counter. I picked up my tray and keyed my holo, circling around as Griffith stepped in with the other servers and got to work composing beverages.

"That looks good," I said, eyeing a particularly elaborate one.

"I'll make you one later. Take these."

I picked up the tray and balanced it, and my holo drew lines in the air that would guide me to each drink's intended recipient. The tray was heavy and the balancing was tricky; I hadn't had long to practice, but it was also fun.

Or it would be until I dropped it. I had to be careful.

Griffith was better for mixing drinks; he knew a little about that. Even with a holo to guide my every move, I knew I'd be awkward with it. But for strolling around and smiling, *I* was the better choice. In the working world, it was definitely better to play to our strengths.

Not that we partook of the working world often.

Griffith and I weren't drama enthusiasts, and Griffith actually preferred older ones, but we were familiar enough with what was popular to recognize plenty of the people present. Some of these famous actors and actresses were Cohengardian, but most of those had grown up and left here before the revolt.

The trick was dodging chairs when they slid back to let someone stand up. The rest was easy.

The circular stage in the center of the venue was raised and lit, and there was an unbroken line of synchronized human dancers up there, at least forty of them. From the corner of my eye they seemed natural, like a part of the gala, but if I looked at them directly, their movements were a little hypnotic. I didn't want to trip.

I made my deliveries and went back for another round. I'd never felt quite this invisible before; no one saw me at all. They smiled and thanked me, but they weren't really noticing me. I didn't mind; I understood my role, and I'd only have been uncomfortable if these people *had* actually paid attention to me.

Although there were Cohengardians among them, these were not Cohengardians. They came from all corners of the Imperium, and they were the elite in their field. People on every Evagardian world would recognize these faces.

They were genuinely important. I'd never been so close to any important people before, much less so many. It didn't bother me, but it was good to see. They were real. They were also ordinary, mostly. It felt good to see them in front of me instead of in a feed. Tangible evidence that success was attainable, even if I didn't want their kind of success.

Obscurity suited me better, though I wouldn't have minded having a little money.

I'd never done any acting, but I was a pretty good server. That was something to think about. These clothes were silly, but it wasn't like all servants dressed this way. In fact, in dramas, the really high-end ones were some of the best-dressed characters. Appearance was a big part of that career.

Lots of money. Good bloodline prospects. Not the fastest way to elevate, but actually quite a reliable way. Servants were artists; it was all about mastery of the craft. Personal refinement. Serenity. Practical skill.

It was a good career and easy to get into because despite the rewards, nobody wanted it. I could find a servitude apprenticeship, even in Cohengard. It might even be a good fit.

Griffith would lose his mind, of course. But he lost his mind on a pretty regular basis anyway.

True, I wasn't much good at this stuff right now, but I wasn't *bad* at it. Even without prodigious natural aptitudes, these skills could be learned.

I could learn to tie funny scarves. I was good with people.

The gala went on around me. Music and laughter. The dancers continued to dazzle, but none of the guests were even bothering to look at them. I'd heard these dancers were homegrown, all Cohengardian youths. I wasn't offended, though. The acting elite would take entertainment like this for granted at their events. They weren't trying to be impolite.

In fact, the simple detail that they were taking our dancers so lightly was an implied compliment. They were up to the standard. They were good enough despite being from Cohengard. That was really nice.

It was a beautiful night.

Something was going on when I got back to the counter. I put down my empty tray and found Griffith.

"What is it?"

"One of the dancers messed up and fell," he said, wiping his hands with a cloth. My heart sank. I didn't have a personal stake in any of this, but I'd have liked for our dancers to give a good showing.

On the bright side, no one was ever *too* surprised when Cohengardian young people screwed up.

Griffith touched his ear, then looked up at me. "Come on," he said, hopping over the counter and stopping me from loading my tray. "We need to take her outside."

"Is it serious?" I asked, leaving my tray behind and hurrying after him.

"She's flagged with a health condition, so she has to actually go to the hospital."

The dance had resumed; presumably the line was slightly more spaced out with one of the dancers out of action.

The dancer in question was being supported by an actor that I recognized instantly and a woman that I didn't.

"We'll take her," Griffith said, moving forward. I was impressed; he wasn't showing any nerves at all. He was talking to these people the same way he'd talk to anyone else.

"You sure?" the actor asked.

"We've got her. Enjoy the party." He jerked his chin at me, and we took the girl, forming a two-handed seat. It looked like her problem was with her foot or ankle. She let us pick her up gamely, putting her arms around our shoulders and wincing in pain. I could almost hear her teeth grinding. That wasn't the pain, though. I couldn't even begin to fathom her shame. Messing up, messing up in front of a lot of celebrities, then being helped by one of the most recognizable actors in the galaxy. It would make a good story for her friends someday, but tonight there wasn't anything amusing about it. For her, at any rate.

"Thank you," I told them. The dancer tried to bow. The actor and the woman just smiled, linked arms, and headed back to their table.

"You all right? Is this carry okay?" Griffith asked the girl. She was thin, almost bony, and she didn't have a very good complexion. Her hair was a shade of red that I'd never seen before. She was no beauty on her best day, but she was in too much pain even to be pretty.

She was very light, and she smelled incredible. I was going to ask about her fragrance, but she spoke.

"It's fine. I'm sorry," she said, making a real effort to keep her expression under control.

"What happened?" Griffith asked.

"I slipped," she said, eyes staring ahead, flat.

"It happens. This way," he told me, steering us away from the action. We'd circle the edge of the gala and go out through a street exit. I got my holo ready for security.

"Why are you going to the hospital instead of getting it set here and going home?" Griffith asked the girl.

"My heart's prosthetic."

Just that much said a lot about her. She was probably the daughter of immigrants.

"I'm a backup," she said.

"What?" I didn't follow.

"A backup dancer. I'm not supposed to be here. I'm not even in the club. I was filling in."

"That's good," Griffith said.

"No, it's bad to make an excuse," she said grimly. "I shouldn't have said anything. I can't do anything right."

"You pick good fragrances," I told her.

"I didn't pick it," she replied, sighing.

"What's it called?"

"Velvet Valmont."

"Oh. That's expensive," I said, quickly revising my assumptions about her.

"It was a graduation present. If I could afford Old Earth perfume, I wouldn't be living in Charlie."

Griffith and I exchanged a look. You couldn't go anywhere in this city without finding sustenance graduates like us.

"What about you guys?" she asked. "Are you apprentices?"

"No, this is just a placement."

"Is that the thing where they get you paid gigs to let you try things?"

"It's pretty fun so far."

"I should've signed up for that," she grumbled, scowling. "I wish I'd been serving tonight."

"It's definitely safer," Griffith said.

"And I need a drink."

I snorted. "How about some painkillers first?"

We left the venue and went out onto the walkway. Night had fallen, and there wasn't much ground traffic. Why would there be? This was Cohengard. It was quiet. I gazed up at the lines of flyers in the sky, and Griffith tilted his head slightly. His holo was telling him something.

"Your pickup's delayed," he told the girl. "Only the best care in Cohengard."

"They'd have gotten here fast if it had been an actual emergency," I said.

"Sorry," the girl said again.

"What's your name?" I asked her.

"Inge."

"Come on," Griffith said. He looked past me. I turned and immediately saw what he meant.

"What?" Inge looked puzzled.

"We can take you there faster than they can come get you," I said, and Griffith and I started to walk.

"Are you sure?"

"If you were heavy it would be different," I said.

She laughed. "Why are you guys doing this? You've got work to do."

"No one will even notice," Griffith said. "We'll still get paid."

"It's for the karma," I added.

"They'll be here in five minutes."

"It's an emergency," Griffith replied, yawning.

"I have a sprained ankle," she said dryly. "I'll live."

"Not that," I said, following Griffith's lead. "Those were really famous people back there. It was a big deal. Messing up there's pretty serious."

She groaned. "Don't remind me."

Griffith nodded. "You know, it's rough when people mess up in a high-pressure situation. Especially Cohengardian people. Especially recent graduates in sustenance."

"Yeah," I agreed, trying not to laugh. "That can be a blow. Better not to leave someone alone after something like that."

"Definitely," Griffith said sagely.

Inge opened her mouth, but then she closed it. She looked at Griffith, then over at me. She swallowed. "Oh," she said weakly. "Well, I am feeling very distressed."

"See?" I sighed. "I knew it."

"Uh, yeah. Maybe you guys are right. Definitely. I shouldn't be alone."

"You think so?" Griffith asked.

"Yeah," she said. "Maybe like until morning. Just to be safe."

FIFTEEN

Now

"Don't bother," I told Freeber as he appeared at my shoulder. He wasn't happy, but of course he wasn't; I'd set him up. I didn't know exactly what would happen in the aftermath of Spirluck's death, but it seemed like a safe bet that being good friends with his killer wasn't such a great idea.

I couldn't *make* Freeber come with me, but I wasn't going to listen to him complain or threaten me. I'd spent enough time on my sales pitch. No more.

The doors opened and I stepped into the airlock, turning to look back at him. I looked past him to see shadows moving on the stairs.

"Make up your mind," I said.

He didn't have a choice, and he knew it. Freeber didn't look back. He just stepped into the airlock and pulled the release. His face was a little scary.

"Lighten up," I told him, facing the other doors. "We're in this together, and you owe me. Look how tall I am."

Freeber raised an eyebrow. "You're not that tall."

"I used to be shorter, though."

I watched the doors while mechanical things happened around us. The airlock was cycling, but it wasn't really an airlock, it was a security lock. It wasn't that they didn't want us getting into the mines; it was more likely that this was a measure against the wrong things from the mines getting into the grotto.

It also guaranteed a certain amount time for the transition, which would make it more difficult for the predatory sorts to pounce on people going through. The timing of the locks was probably randomized. One cycle might take one minute, and another might take two or three, all to give people a fighting chance and keep things from getting too predictable.

Freeber was giving me a funny look. He was still upset, but that wasn't blinding him.

"What?" I asked, folding my arms.

"We all used to be shorter." He looked worried.

"I've been augmented. I used to *actually* be shorter."

"Why'd you do something like that?"

"To become Prince Dalton."

He stared. He knew who Dalton was. And now that I'd brought it up, he had to pay attention to the resemblance. He'd noticed it when he'd been dragging me and Sei around Free Trade space.

"Why'd you want to be him?" he asked carefully.

"You really don't keep up with the news, do you?"

"You don't like to answer questions," Freeber replied, glowering.

"I didn't *want* to be him. But nobody cares what I want." I tapped my foot impatiently. A real airlock wouldn't take this long.

"You're trying to tell me that was you?"

No. No, I wasn't trying to tell him that.

I was telling the whole galaxy.

"You know what they say," I said to Freeber. "You want to make pancakes, you have to break some grapes."

"What's that mean?"

"I don't know. It's an Old Earth idiom."

"What are grapes?" he asked.

"What are pancakes?" I countered.

"Flapjacks," Freeber said.

"Whats?"

"It's a," he began, gesturing with his hands. He indicated a triangle, then shook his head. "Forget it."

I rubbed my chin. "Just something I heard when I was being Dalton."

"You're insane," he said, but his heart wasn't in it. My resemblance to Dalton forced him to consider the possibility that I was telling the truth.

"Are we moving?" I asked, looking around the airlock. I'd only just noticed.

Freeber stopped eyeing me and looked up. "If we just came out on the other side, everyone in the queue would know where we were."

"That's sweet of them."

"Is that the word?"

There was a heavy noise; the doors were about to open. My holo came online, but it didn't do anything. I had no interface and it wasn't displaying any information, but if Management wanted me to know something, they had a way to tell me. Freeber's eyes flicked; his holo had come on as well. I'd have to keep an eye on him in case some Evagardian official managed to bribe the Baykaras to order Freeber to kill me.

That *was* happening at this very moment. Baykara was being bombarded with requests and demands. To kill me, hand me over alive, and other things, I was sure. By now, Abigail Baykara herself might be paying attention to me, and she might be fielding those demands personally.

She probably wouldn't be impressed. She was already the richest person in Free Trade space. How did you go about bribing someone like that? What could you offer her?

And for some reason, there were a lot of galactics who liked seeing normally aloof imperials grovel. I didn't *think* the Baykara family would turn on me, but it wasn't out of the question.

"You said we have to move fast," I said to Freeber. "You lead."

I didn't want him behind me.

Freeber looked bleak. I couldn't expect him to be pleased about what I'd pulled back there, but at least he was still talking to me. What else could he do? He wanted to live. It had been obvious that in his partnership with Willis, he had been the voice of reason. He had gotten out of New Brittia alive once before. That spoke well of him, and he wanted to do it again.

He had the sense to swallow his annoyance with me and focus on the bigger picture.

The doors opened, revealing dimly lit walls that reminded me of the housing blocks of Balkin Square. The tunnels were smooth and vaguely round, or they had been once, hollowed out by mining robots using chemicals to dissolve material that turned up negative for anything valuable.

That was as much as I could judge for myself. There was a lot of damage immediately evident as we stepped out of the lock, and lots of metal structures built into the tunnels that I had no context for. Probably equipment and infrastructure, but asteroid mining wasn't exactly my area of expertise. It looked like a lot of neglected junk.

The light came from tiny emitters placed by small maintenance robots. They were spaced out frugally, and none of them were white; the lights were all colored.

The dominant hue was red in this section. I opened my mouth to remind Freeber about what he'd said, but he was trying to take his bearings.

"We're in the middle," he said.

It was still and quiet. This was a low chamber, but wide, and there were no fewer than eight ways out. I guess only seven ways would've been too easy. I was glad that I wouldn't be coming back; I'd never be able to find my way.

Freeber started forward and I followed, immediately stopping and looking down. I wasn't sure what I was stepping on. It was light and powdery.

There were dark stains on the walls, obviously old, dried blood. The maintenance robots weren't meticulous about keeping the mines clean; that would spoil this lovely ambience. But with the frequency at which people died in here, they couldn't just leave these tunnels choked with bodies, so maybe they disintegrated them. I'd seen something like this on Nidaros. I hoped this powder wasn't the remains of fallen laborers.

Freeber walked briskly, but he was taking some care not to be noisy about it. There was no plan. No strategy. We weren't here to push back our sentences. We weren't trying to find some object arbitrarily assigned value by the people who now legally owned us. We weren't trying to kill anyone. We weren't trying to impress the spectators.

We were just trying to get to the other side.

That was likely a more daunting challenge than any of the normal tasks. The demands of the Baykara Mines might be serious, but at least there was precedent. For all we knew, what we were doing had never been attempted before.

There were running footsteps, and Freeber immediately go out of sight behind a metal support. He was a little big to hide, but the dim light worked to our advantage.

I'd never given the dark the appreciation it deserved before New Brittia. I'd never take it for granted again. I was running out of friends, but at least the dark wouldn't turn on me. That was comforting.

There was an odd detonation, like a shot, but too soft. It was still loud enough to echo through the tunnels, but I'd never heard anything quite like it.

"What was that?" I whispered.

Freeber cautiously emerged, shaking his head. He didn't know. He looked back, then pointed. It looked like his sense of direction was on the same page as mine. Of course, that meant we were moving *toward* the single entry point where most of the nasty people and things populating the mines came in.

Which obviously hadn't occurred to Freeber during the planning stage and had only just now occurred to me. Maybe this wasn't so clever after all.

It seemed like something to mention, but a sudden and growl cut me off.

We froze.

There was no way to know where it was coming from. Worse, we weren't on a single level; there were tunnels above and below us. We could occasionally see light filtering through heavy grates. I didn't know how many levels there were, but considering the number of active laborers that New Brittia boasted and the fact that the spectators still weren't tired of this place after all these years, it was probably quite a few.

A colored light overhead blinked, then went out. A grate squealed as it slowly opened, and a hazy mist emerged. A motor coughed and the recycler came to life. That was all it was. Harmless.

Freeber started to move again, and I went after him.

"That doesn't bother you?" I asked him quietly. I'd never heard anything like that growl.

It wasn't that I'd led such a sheltered life, but I'd never had to go up against bioweapons before. I thought of the Evagardian dramas, the ones about Old Earth, before the Unification.

As a boy, I'd stayed away from those dramas. Too scary.

"It's not close," Freeber said distractedly. "Use your ears."

That stung a little, but he was right. The acoustics were even stranger here than they were in the blocks thanks to the shape of the tunnels and the incredible number of them. It seemed like there was a junction every ten steps. It was overwhelming.

Freeber went to a ladder and knelt at the opening, peering down. He listened, then looked up, touching his ear. He was different now, nothing at all like he'd been out in the grotto.

"What is it?" I whispered, watching the tunnel.

"Something's coming. We have to change direction." He looked up. "Go up."

"I thought we had to go down."

"They heard me say that," he said. "They're setting us up." Freeber mounted the ladder.

If he was being sincere, I was impressed with his instincts. If he was trying to pull something, that was a pity.

I climbed up after him. We emerged in a narrower tunnel, half of which was paneled with stained metal. The red light was starting to hurt my eyes, but they adjusted, and the pain receded. My hands tingled, and I could hear something.

A high-pitched whine filled the tunnel and a shape appeared in the junction ahead. It was obviously a robot, a very old-fashioned one, running on rollers.

There was a loud noise, and Freeber leapt aside as a metal projectile trailing a cord glanced off the side of the tunnel.

The robot had just shot a harpoon at us.

We ran for it, taking the first turn.

Freeber stopped immediately, looking back. "I don't like this."

"It's slow. Don't worry about it, let's just go."

"It's trying to corral us. We have to do something they won't expect or it'll push us into something else. Something worse. That's how this works."

This was why I'd brought him. This kind of insight was on the short list of things I couldn't convincingly fake.

"What won't they expect?" I asked, listening to the whine of the robot's treads growing louder. Freeber didn't have an answer for me. Going back would put us back in the line of fire, and the robot probably had another harpoon. Or worse.

So there was only one thing they wouldn't expect.

"Fine," I said, turning around.

"What are you doing?"

"Three laws safe," I replied, stepping into the open. "Read a book." The robot was right there. It was a mining assistant with two mechanical arms, each holding an old-fashioned spear gun. The robot had no means to reload the one it had fired at Freeber, but it had one more. "You don't mind, do you? Ahab?"

I walked forward, hoping I had my references to Old Earth fiction straight. People were watching, after all. I didn't want to look uncultured.

I hadn't read half this stuff; Griffith was the one who'd spent all his time with ancient literature. But I'd always listened to him talk about it, and I'd picked up some things.

The spear gun was pointed straight at me, and I was in clear view of the robot's camera.

It didn't fire.

I plucked the loaded spear gun off the rig that had been specially built onto the robot to operate it.

Freeber was peering around the corner, eyes wide. I just beckoned; I wasn't taking questions at the moment. This wasn't the best time for it.

The robot accelerated suddenly toward Freeber as he emerged, reaching out with its arms, but he dodged past it, and it struck the side of the tunnel. It would take a moment for it to turn around. So it still had some fight in it, not that it would do any good. Something so clumsy wasn't likely to do anyone any real damage.

"How?" Freeber said, still staring at it as he stumbled after me. "Why didn't it shoot you?"

I ignored the question. "If that's the best they've got, I wonder if you guys aren't doing some exaggerating," I said, hurrying down the tunnel.

I was still carrying the spear gun. I'd never even touched a modern spear gun, much less an old one, but how hard could it be?

"Which way?" I asked.

"We're just guessing."

"So guess," I snapped.

"This way." We clattered over a hatch no longer attached to anything and onto an alarmingly noisy stairwell. At the bottom was water, or more accurately, fluid.

Whatever it was, it was bad news. It wasn't deep, but that was still more than enough to make it impossible to move quietly.

There was also a slight current. Freeber and I splashed into a tunnel with metal on either side. I checked the holo on my ear, wishing I could wear it on my wrist, but it wasn't doing anything.

Chains hung from the ceiling. They served no purpose but to block our line of sight and force us to push them aside so they would rattle loudly. As if it we weren't already making enough noise; they could probably hear us up in Baykara City.

I noticed an opening as high as my waist to our left and backed away, nearly tripping. There was a dead man lying in the water with his throat cut.

A loud banging echoed through the space, metallic noises ringing from the walls. It sounded like someone had a metal rod or something, and they were cruelly taking advantage of the acoustics by hitting things at random. Not a bad idea; it would cover their movements.

I understood what Freeber had been trying to tell me. There was a lot of luck and randomness at work in the mines, but it didn't end there. Management was watching, pulling the strings to keep the proceedings interesting. That meant they were either pushing us toward a threat or pushing threats toward us. They might not sell me out to the Imperium, but I couldn't expect them to clear the way for me.

Passing through the mines without a ripple, unnoticed, as I would have liked—that would never happen.

Freeber believed that the way to counter them was to do what they wouldn't expect, and doing what they wouldn't expect meant taking the least inviting course.

There had to be a system to all of this, and any system could be exploited, but only if I had the time to figure it out.

And I didn't. The key to winning is never to play anyone else's game. Always make sure they're playing yours, and by your rules. The house always wins.

Easy to say, but not always easy to do. Especially in prison.

I ducked and moved into the low opening, hurrying forward and trusting Freeber to follow. He was supposed to be leading, but he was more cautious than I was, and I wasn't satisfied with his deliberate pace. I had places to be.

We splashed into another canal with high metal walls. I didn't think it was water we were standing in now, but water had been used here at one time at high pressure to filter the particles and reduce waste.

It had been a long time since this mine had been used for mining. Used properly, at any rate. We were following the current, but I'd lost my sense of direction.

There was light ahead. Lots of it, at least compared to where we'd just come from. It was more of those portable fixtures, and they were lining the walls just above the surface of the shallow water. It was a pretty sort of bluish green, and though it wasn't anyone's idea of bright, it was still more than we'd had before.

Freeber hadn't liked the enclosed space we'd just traveled through, but he seemed relieved here. It was probably the light. I caught his shoulder as he started forward.

Something wasn't right.

Why would there be light here? Did someone need it to see us by? Unlikely.

Freeber gave me a questioning look, but I was thinking. We could still hear the banging echoing through the crawlspace. Earlier, I'd thought that might be random. Some aggressive laborer laying down some sound cover.

But maybe not. The noise was harsh and intimidating. It made you want to move away from it. It was meant to push us forward. They wanted us thinking about what was behind us, not what was ahead.

We had to think. *I* had to think.

The lights were low on the walls. Were the lights positioned to draw our eyes down? I looked up into the gloom. There was a ceiling up there, and a complex network of beams and supports.

"We have to go," Freeber whispered. I nodded and started forward, watching carefully and getting a better grip on the spear gun. What an odd choice of weapon. Flashy, painful, and not very practical.

Someone's idea of entertainment.

I took aim and fired, clearly feeling the point strike home through the wire connected to the gun.

I swiftly wrapped the wire around my hand and gave it a firm pull, yanking the man from his perch on the support up in the dark.

As he splashed down, the spear buried in his chest, I saw that he wasn't a he at all. Not that it mattered; I dropped to my knees, got my arm around her neck, and snapped it with a single twist. She was masked, and dressed from head to toe in a dark gray.

Apart from a startled curse, all Freeber had done was watch. He stared at me as I patted the woman down. She was obviously some kind of mercenary, here to prey on the laborers. She didn't appear to be a very *good* one. Her weapon was a long knife, and her gimmick was hiding in the dark. I took the knife; she wouldn't be needing it. She'd probably been the one to cut that man's throat back there.

Placing the lights low to draw our attention downward when the threat was above? These weren't groundbreaking tactics, but down here they were probably effective.

Most of the time.

I found a disposable holo on her wrist, probably to let her navigate the mines or receive instructions. Maybe I should've kept her alive and forced her to show us the way.

Too late now.

Sixteen

"Hey," I hissed, and Freeber looked back. I pointed at the tripwire ahead, and he gave me an annoyed look. I hadn't been sure that he'd seen it. What did he want from me? I was just looking out for him.

We stepped over the wire and ducked through a malformed doorway into another steep shaft. The light here was blue, and we'd just managed to avoid another pair of laborers, but they were still close. There were two of them and two of us, but they were following anyway, so they had to be desperate. It was likely that they needed to get a kill to reset their execution timers; they were getting short on time, and I knew the feeling.

Maybe we'd get lucky and *they'd* hit a tripwire.

I drew the knife I'd taken from its sheath and weighed it in my hand. It was metal, not polymer or ceramic.

We'd been lucky so far. The reputation of the Baykara Mines had to be inflated, but not to the point that I didn't have to take it seriously. Most of the men in New Brittia wouldn't have training like mine, but there would be plenty of ex-military types, and some of them would be pretty good. The mine was equipped to handle guys who knew what they were doing as well as clueless idiots.

There was a low mist ahead, probably to hide more traps. At least, that was the impression it was meant to give. More likely, that route didn't lead to any choke points that would force an encounter, so Management preferred to have it less traveled.

I'd figured this place out, but luck wasn't on my side.

Two points of red appeared in the mist. The dark figure that stepped into the open wasn't as huge as Freeber, but he was big.

Freeber saw him and squared himself.

This was obviously one of Management's headhunters. He wore black impact armor and a full helmet with theatrically glowing red circles for eyes. I didn't see a weapon, but he'd have more than just his bare hands. Probably something without much range.

He was alone. At a glance, all that armor was probably a disadvantage. It would inhibit movement, and the helmet would reduce situational awareness unless he had some kind of scanner in there, and that would be *too* unfair.

We outnumbered him, but I didn't like it.

This guy wouldn't have confronted us this way if he didn't think he had the upper hand. No matter how I looked at it, the upper hand was ours, which meant he knew something we didn't. My go-to weapon was bluffing, but I had a feeling that wouldn't do me much good here.

"We can take him," Freeber said. He was giving me a lot of credit.

"But we shouldn't," I replied, staring the armored man down. Maybe we could.

It was still a risk, though. I preferred to strike from the shadows. Tangling with people head-on wouldn't work.

During my short time in New Brittia I'd accumulated a bit of a body count, but not by fighting. My way had worked so far; no reason to change it now.

I took a step back, then another.

"Come on," I said to Freeber. He understood. "Don't mind us," I called out to the headhunter. "We're going to go another way."

We rounded the corner, and the armored man followed.

"You didn't think he'd fall for that," Freeber said as the headhunter stepped over the tripwire. Of course he'd known about it; he'd probably put it there.

But he *had* fallen for it. I stopped retreating and moved in front of Freeber.

I turned the knife in my hand, catching what light I could on the blade to make sure he saw it. Now I moved toward him, and that stopped the headhunter in his tracks.

The tripwire was behind him. He realized that and paused before he could begin to backpedal for a better position.

"I'm sure you've killed a lot of people," I said to him, still advancing. "But not as many as I have." Probably not even as many as I had in the past hour.

I still didn't see a weapon. No blades or anything, but he had something. We'd have to overpower him, but going in close would be playing into his hands.

He still had that tripwire behind him, and he didn't have eyes in the back of his head, although he would have a rear-facing camera in that helmet. It wouldn't help him, though. It would only divide his attention.

I looked down. Stone underfoot, not metal. The headhunter's boots wouldn't have any magnetism.

Freeber was ready to fight. I'd never seen him in action, but it was safe to assume that he could handle himself.

I couldn't risk this. An injury, even a minor one, could inhibit my mobility. That would hurt my chances of reaching Griffith. We had to keep this clean.

No mistakes and no fighting. A fight could be lost.

I haven't always made the best decisions, and there's an argument to be made that I might not be the nicest person.

But I don't *lose*.

I waved Freeber back and he gave me a doubtful look, but I wasn't worried about him as I faced the man in armor.

"We're only trying to get through. We just want to get to Alpine Strut," I told him. "You—" I started to go on, and abruptly threw the knife.

A thrown blade was no threat to a man in full armor, but the action was so sudden and vicious that he flinched regardless. That was all I needed to skip forward and kick him solidly in the chest.

The knife had been our only weapon against him; obviously we could batter that armor for decades without even tickling him, but I wasn't trying to give him a bruise, just a push.

The headhunter staggered back, overbalancing.

No Evagardian ever would have tried to fight with a lethal trap behind them. All the equipment in the world can't make up for bad positioning. He should have retreated when he had the chance, but he'd been greedy.

The armored man fell onto the wire, and the blades came out of the walls so fast that we couldn't even see them in the blue light. The headhunter's body flew into pieces.

I, naturally, was splattered with his blood.

I picked up my knife and wiped the blood out of my eyes.

"That was good," Freeber said, sounding impressed. He was trying to play it cool, but I could see the way he was looking at my new makeup and paintjob.

I had a nice quip ready, but a laborer rounded the corner at a sprint, and it wasn't his lucky day. I made the most of his irresponsible momentum and tripped him. He tumbled to the ground, saw the headhunter's head, and recoiled.

He was down and unarmed. I raised the knife, getting ready to finish him before he could do anything else, but I paused, turning to look back.

Strange, heavy footsteps were approaching along with a wet, guttural panting.

The laborer scrambled up and leapt for the supports above. I read between the lines and followed without hesitation, pulling myself up to balance in a crouch on a metal beam over the corridor.

Freeber was a little behind the curve.

He jumped as the thing came around the corner. I'd never seen anything like it: built low and heavy, with no visible eyes. Its skin was pale, but thick. The mouth was massive and lined with short, stubby teeth. It had to weigh two hundred kilograms.

It chomped down on Freeber's dangling foot without any hesitation at all. The big man cried out and let go of the beam with one hand but held on with the other. I leapt over to his beam and pulled him up as he kicked the creature free.

Grimacing in pain, Freeber got his arm around the beam and looked down at the creature.

Though I still couldn't see eyes, I had the impression it was looking up at us. Its head—it didn't really *have* a head.

Well, it had no neck. But whatever was supposed to be its head was angled upward, mouth open.

The other laborer stared down at it with wide eyes. He'd been running from it, and he didn't look like a loner. He was one of the two who had been following us. Had this thing gotten his friend?

"Thoughts?" I asked Freeber, who clung grimly to the beam. The thing padded around beneath us, filling the tunnel with its breathing.

It was onto us, and it wasn't going anywhere.

"I got nothing," Freeber said, visibly shaken.

"There's an Old Earth idiom for this," I replied, looking down at it. "But there's an Old Earth idiom for everything. Get ready to run."

"Run?"

"Yeah. While it's eating him," I said, jerking my chin at the laborer, whose eyes widened.

"Hey," he started to say, but I'd already hopped over to his beam to push him off.

He crashed to the floor of the tunnel, and the creature was on him instantly. It wasn't nearly as slow as its slightly chubby appearance had led me to expect.

It was fast and vicious, but it wasn't hungry. The creature had no interest in eating anyone; it just clamped those jaws down on the back of the laborer's neck and applied pressure, instantly cracking his spine. I winced.

Then it was looking back up at us. There hadn't even been time to drop down, much less make a run for it.

I swallowed.

"Even if that worked," Freeber gasped. "I can't run."

"What? Oh." Right, his foot. It wasn't even broken; it was crushed. At least he was being stoic about the pain.

The thing growled at us, and the rancid smell of it was starting to get to me. It was marginally less intimidating than the things I'd dealt with on Nidaros, but probably more dangerous. At least those spindly Nidaros natives had mostly been slow and lazy. Mostly.

This thing wasn't lazy. This wasn't the reason the mine had failed, though. This thing was someone's bright idea of a bioweapon, and seeing how efficiently it had dispatched that laborer, we could safely say that it was good at its job. Some laboratory's idea of a success story.

"We can't stay here," Freeber said.

"Tell that to him."

He wasn't leaving; that much was obvious.

"What *is* it?"

"I don't know. People pay to watch this? We have to kill it," I said.

"How?"

I was working on that. We didn't have much to go on; there was a lot of power in the thing's stubby little legs. And it wasn't just the jaws we had to worry about; a blow from that body would pulverize bones.

The hide looked tough. Even if I still had that ridiculous spear gun, it wouldn't help. We had to do this the old-fashioned way.

"You're going to jump him," I told Freeber.

"What?"

"You're heavy. Jump on him, then I'll be there to finish him off," I said, holding up my knife.

Freeber narrowed his eyes. "Why don't we do it the other way around?"

"I'm not big enough to buy you the time." It was true. Even with my added height, I was still half his size.

He searched my face. "I don't trust you," he said finally.

"I don't blame you." I sat back on my beam. "I hope you brought snacks."

"How do I know you won't just stay up here while it kills me? Or try to run?"

I shrugged. "You don't. But there won't be *time* to run, you saw that. There might be time to kill it. And staying up here doesn't help me."

He didn't say anything. He just stared.

"You think they'll just let us sit up here until he gets bored?"

Freeber didn't look convinced, but he repositioned.

The thing panted up at us, its massive gray tongue hanging out.

Freeber gave me a look.

"Hey," I said. "You can do both parts if you want." I took the knife by the blade and held out the handle to him. He eyed it for a moment, then shook his head. "Then go," I said. "I've got you covered."

Freeber dropped down, crashing into the thing's back and crushing it to the ground. There was no doubt that it had the power to throw him off and crush his backbone with ease, but I was already there, touching down and ramming the knife into its back near the head. I angled the thrust upward and twisted sharply.

With the anatomy of bioweapons, you were just guessing, but this thing had a spine, and a spine had vertebrae, and you could usually get a blade in between those. This was supposed to be a military weapon: it was built to stop bullets because its creators expected it to fight armed men. It *had* to be vulnerable to a knife. If it was completely indestructible, that would stretch fairness too much even for this place.

The thing shuddered and dropped. Freeber got to his hands and knees, eyes wide.

"See? You worry too much." I wiped the blade on the thing's skin and picked myself up. Freeber really had expected me to try to pull something. He'd probably intended to defeat this thing himself, then deal with me. Now he didn't know what to think.

"Thank you," he said.

"Don't mention it," I replied, putting out my hand. He took it, and I pulled him to his feet. He winced, but managed, grimacing at the carcass of the creature. It was bleeding something dark that smelled even worse than the rest of it. "Hear that?" I asked.

"What?"

I kicked his knee from the side, breaking it and sending him to the floor of the tunnel. He cried out, but it wasn't enough to drown out what I was hearing: more of the panting and thudding footsteps.

That thing had friends, and they were coming this way.

I saw the way that he was looking up at me.

"Why do you people always seem so surprised?" I shook my head. "You didn't just sell me. I wouldn't take that personally. You sold my date." I shrugged. "And that's just rude."

I didn't wait for him to reply; the things were getting close. I dropped my knife, and it clattered on the stone floor.

"You talk to them."

I kicked it over to Freeber and walked away.

Seventeen

I hadn't intended to cut Freeber loose so quickly, but I hadn't counted on him getting a foot injury. I could drag him along for his expertise, but he'd slow me down, and ultimately, I probably wouldn't profit much from that.

Besides, I'd more or less gotten a feel for the mines. I climbed a ladder and jogged down another tunnel. The temperature was lower here, and there was more blue light.

Freeber was no different from Idris. I wasn't thrilled he'd ruined my plans for Tessa Salmagard, and I didn't appreciate being sold to a sketchy cult to be sacrificed to an imaginary space octopus.

It hurt to give up my knife, but it was for the best. It wasn't charity; the better Freeber could defend himself, the more time he'd buy me to put distance between myself and those things. After seeing that bladed trap with the tripwire, I wasn't keen to move too quickly.

Or too slowly.

It was probably still a long way to Alpine Strut, and now I'd have to make the trip alone. That was familiar, at least.

"Hey," said a voice.

I didn't jump, but I was genuinely startled. I knew at once it was coming through my holo. I took cover and looked back down the tunnel.

"You surprised me," I said, curious.

"Isn't that something?" It was a man, and he didn't sound Evagardian.

"Who are you?" I asked.

"I don't know if my name would mean anything to you," he said.

"Try me."

"Mark Drexler."

Of course I knew his name. He was a Ganraen, a benignly corrupt entrepreneur with close ties to the Royals. The business-minded Royals, anyway. I'd never had anything to do with him as Dalton, but he was a big enough deal in the Commonwealth to be on my radar.

Frequent investor, occasional philanthropist. Well-regarded, if I remembered correctly. Extremely rich.

He sounded younger than I'd have expected.

"How would I not recognize that name?" I asked.

"I don't know. You don't seem to have much regard for Ganraens," he said.

"I love Ganraens," I said.

"So much that you murdered twenty million of us?"

"Love hurts," I conceded. "Have we met?"

"Actually, we have."

"What? At some event when I was being Dalton?"

A pause. I'd taken him by surprise. Freeber had seemed a bit surprised, too. That I would admit to it with the whole galaxy watching. I'd confirmed what so many were speculating about. Yes, the imposter was still alive, if not completely well.

"That's right."

"Don't be offended that I don't remember you." I leaned out to check the tunnel. "It's not personal."

Why was this happening? What was Drexler doing, talking to me?

I hadn't planned for this.

"You know everything we say is being broadcast," he said slowly.

"Naturally." How could I not know? It looked like I wasn't the only one feeling a little off-balance.

"Do you know how hard I had to work to get through to you?" Drexler asked. "What it's costing me?"

A staggering amount of money. I doubted they normally let fans call in like this, but Drexler was rich enough to make an exception for, but there had to be more at work here. Someone must have determined that letting him do this also had entertainment value. All the same, he was probably paying by the second, and he had to be outbidding some very deep pockets.

"Don't look for sympathy from me," I told him. "You can afford it. And if they bill me for Little Norwich, just put it on my tab."

"You seem surprised. Were you expecting to hear from someone else?"

"Is this practice fair? Doesn't it compromise the game?" I asked.

"Depends on what I do with it," Drexler said.

"I guess. So what do you want?"

"I'm not sure," he said. "I can't decide if I want to help you or just get you killed."

"Why would you want to do that?" I asked. "Don't tell me this is about Little Norwich."

There was a pause. "It *is* about that."

"For the love of the Empress," I said in mock exasperation. "How long are people going to hold that over me?"

"Well, here's the thing," he said, doing a good impression of matching my drollness. "My wife was there."

"Way to make it awkward," I said. He was doing a good job trying to keep the emotion out of his voice, but it was still there.

"So was my daughter. And my son. My parents," Drexler added, and I could picture him counting on his fingers. "My wife's parents."

"Bet you could live without them," I said, but he ignored me.

"Nine of my cousins. Assorted nieces and nephews. One uncle. My sister." He paused, and I opened my mouth, but he wasn't finished. "More or less all of the people that I would've called friends. My cat. You even got my mistress."

"Was she cute?"

"What?"

"The mistress. I'm in prison, remember? Tell me about her."

He wouldn't let me get to him this way; each minute he was probably paying the cost of a yacht just to talk to me. He'd come prepared. And he'd come with his mind made up, no matter what he said. He wasn't really on the fence; he had something in mind, and he was going to try to get it.

Drexler was keeping the tone light, but he wasn't doing this to joke around. I didn't have a say in it, though. I was stuck with him.

I had to find out what he wanted.

"That wasn't very nice," he said. "What you did to that big guy."

"He messed up some plans I had with a nice girl."

"Did he really?"

"Yes."

"Huh." I could picture Drexler's shrug. "I felt like I was the only person who saw that coming."

Everyone who'd been watching me saw it coming, but Freeber hadn't been watching me. No one I met in here would know anything about how I'd dealt with my last few acquaintances.

"I'd love to chat, but I should go," I said.

"Who's stopping you?"

Maybe this was his angle: distracting me to get me killed. This wasn't going to make things any easier.

I got moving, pausing by the next ladder to listen, then sliding down and pushing forward.

"I need your help," Drexler was saying.

I didn't reply. His voice in my ear wouldn't give my position away, but mine would. I stayed quiet and kept to the side of the tunnel.

"I need you to clear some things up for me. The capital goes down, Dalton disappears. The imperials say they have nothing to do with it." I inched down the corridor as he spoke; someone was coming. If possible, I wanted to avoid as many encounters as I could, but if Drexler was a part of this, the people was using would know exactly where I was. I changed directions to be safe. Or less unsafe.

Maybe I was overthinking it.

"And suddenly you're in New Brittia for everyone to see, and the imperials are saying you're a terrorist instead of a spy, or at least most of them are."

"Sounds pretty straightforward," I said quietly, looking up a shaft that was missing its ladder. That would be a good way to go to stay out of harm's way, but I also had my destination to think about. I crept onward.

"Are they disavowing you, or are you really what they say you are?"

"What do you think?"

"I think it's the wrong question. How did you get to New Brittia?"

"Funny story," I replied. "That big guy back there? It was his fault."

"There are some idealistic Evagardian journalists sticking their necks out for you," Drexler said. "Saying you're a hero and that the empire's stabbing you in the back. Throwing you under the shuttle."

"Not a very risky thing to say," I told him. "They throw a lot of people under the shuttle. Don't you read?"

More tripwires. I almost felt insulted. The mines would have to do better than this if they wanted to keep me from reaching Griffith.

Which, at this point, they probably didn't. It was like Drexler was reading my thoughts.

"Griffith Karlsson," he said, and that was my fault. I'd said his name earlier, and the whole galaxy had heard it. He was a part of this now. "I can't find anything on you, but there's plenty on him."

"You could've just asked," I said quietly. "He's a New Unity terrorist."

"Like you?"

"Do I *look* like a New Unity terrorist?" I asked, emerging from the shadows to step through a low archway. There was a footstep in the dark, and I moved back into cover, pressing my back to the cold wall. Maybe I shouldn't have given up that knife after all.

Whoever was out there, he'd heard me, and now he was keeping still as well.

Drexler had access to the New Brittia broadcasts—that was how he was watching me. That meant he could also watch Griffith. Griffith's name had been in the news quite a bit.

"I don't understand you," Drexler said. "Are you setting up the Empress? Or did she set you up?"

I snorted.

"Sounds like something she'd do," I said.

"That's not an answer."

"I'm busy."

"He's in the doorway two meters up from you and to your right. He hasn't got a weapon. You've already killed millions of people. What's one more?" Drexler asked.

"I feel like I've heard that before," I said, thinking fast. After a moment, I drew back and retreated into the tunnel. I couldn't take Drexler at his word. I didn't have a feel for him yet, and he was holding all the cards. He could have the brains of a bulkhead and he'd still be able to get me killed in here.

If that was what he wanted—but I wasn't sure it was.

"Those dog things are down there," Drexler warned when I paused by another ladder.

"So now you don't want me dead?"

"Whether you did it under orders or not, you're guilty of war crimes," he said. "Dying in prison would be getting off easy."

"Under whose law?" I asked. "I'm not a soldier."

"You're guilty of crimes," he amended.

"Nobody's going to argue with that." I climbed up instead of down. Someone was following me. It was probably a laborer, and I could shake him off if I moved fast. There was something sticky on the metal rungs. Blood.

I kept climbing.

"How did you really end up here?" Drexler pushed.

"Karma?" Left or right? I went right, stepping over a body. The tunnel sloped downward.

"I did tell you that this was expensive, didn't I?"

"You mentioned it," I said under my breath, crouching beside a maintenance cover. I pulled the release, and there was a quiet hiss. The panel slid up, revealing a dark opening. No lights in there, and barely enough room to crawl.

What were the odds it led anywhere? I decided against it.

"You also mentioned that your wife and mistress are dead," I added. "Think of all the money that's saving you. You can thank me later."

"Don't try to bait me. Because of how much I'm paying, they've given me some tools."

"Tools like what?"

I already knew. And he knew that I knew.

"Answer my questions. Tell the truth to me, to everyone who's watching you right now. And I know exactly how many people that is."

"Why do I care how many people it is? I don't get stage fright. I used to be Prince Dalton. I did four shows a week. I had a dozen number-one singles." I snorted. "Actually, I'm curious. How many?"

Drexler ignored me. "I can guide you. I don't care about Griffith Karlsson. I don't care if you break him out."

"Do I come off as dishonest?"

"I want a confession."

"To what?"

"You're responsible for the single largest mass murder in history. You beat the Trigan Islamic Genocide by ten million. Twenty million people are dead, and it was you. *You.*"

"Nobody's perfect," I muttered, crouching to move beneath a twisted beam that bristled with spikes and razors intended to catch on clothing and flesh.

"You want to die in there that badly?" It sounded like Drexler had actually expected me to cave.

"Oh, this is charming." There were sharp protrusions set in the tunnel ahead, each about ten centimeters high. One wrong step, one scuffle, anything that led to a fall, and I really would be in trouble.

I could turn back and look for another way, but I was making bad enough time as it was. I started to pick my way through, choosing my steps and being careful with my balance.

"This is harder than it looks," I said, glancing up. "For everyone watching at home."

"Don't trip," Drexler said dryly.

"I didn't think you cared."

I reached the other side and paused. This was no different from that tunnel with the lights. Those lights had been low to keep me from looking up. Here, they'd used the blades on the floor to deliberately slow my pace. The expectation was that I would speed up now that I was past that obstacle. There was probably something up there for me to run into.

"It's an android," Drexler said.

"What?"

"An android. If you go past that junction it'll activate. It's a humanoid. It's had all its skin taken off to make it look scary. Looks like the hands have been upgraded. It'll try to choke you."

"Kinky," I said, wondering if I could believe him.

"Go to the right."

"I'll take my chances with the android."

"You can't," Drexler said. "I'm looking at a replay of the last guy it ran into."

"Yeah? What happens?" I was curious.

"It's not pretty."

"I handled your entire star system," I told him. "I can handle one android."

The silence was telling. He'd been holding himself together, but I was wearing him down.

"How," he ground out, "do you plan to do that?"

I advanced slowly.

"My charm," I said.

Eighteen

Drexler was telling the truth.

The android was set in an alcove hidden in shadow. The skin had been peeled away, revealing artificial muscle and a polymer skeleton. It weighed less than I did, but it would be considerably stronger.

That wasn't an issue as long as it had no reason to bother me.

"How?" Drexler demanded as I approached, perfectly safe.

I reached out and rapped on the plastic skull with my knuckles. Nothing happened.

"You're very good with robots," Drexler bit out.

"Machines can be unreliable," I said. "Maybe you should've bought Kakugan."

"Not Evagardian?" he snarled.

"Realistic Evagardian androids are hard to find," I told him. "The Empress doesn't believe in them. But of course, if there *was* an Evagardian android industry, you can assume it would the best. They would be the androids least likely to develop ghost code and turn on you to strangle you in your sleep. Like in that drama." I looked up at where I imagined the feed was. "So everybody out there with comfort androids from second-rate makers—sleep well."

"You did this back there too," he accused. "Someone's helping you."

I snorted. "But that would be *cheating*."

"I had to outbid a lot of other people to get this airtime with you," Drexler said. "Who do you think they were?"

"I used to be Prince Dalton. Maybe I still have some fans." I moved past the android, but the tunnel ahead narrowed, and the walls were rough. I wasn't sure why it looked this way; it didn't seem deliberate.

I didn't see anything threatening. No tripwire, no obvious sensors. And Drexler had actually tried to guide me away from that android back there.

"So that's what you were doing," I said.

"What?"

"That's why you didn't want me to come this way. You knew that android was malfunctioning. You wanted me to go somewhere dangerous instead. Sorry to disappoint. Not that this seems safe," I added, squeezing through the gap.

"What?" he said, taken aback. "It's— *is* it malfunctioning?"

The light ahead was purple. My holo indicated that there was something recoverable nearby, perhaps one of the objects placed for laborers to search for.

I wasn't interested. I passed that turn and took the next available right.

"Nice try," Drexler said, recovering. "Nothing's malfunctioning. Who's helping you? Evagard? Or New Unity?"

"Look at me. *Look.*" I kept walking. "Do I *look* like someone with a lot of friends?"

"If you *do* make it out of there, you've got all of Ganrae wanting you dead."

"Don't forget all the imperials who want me dead."

Drexler wanted me dead. But he wasn't going to be the one to do it. If he'd been going to do anything, he would have already. He wanted answers to his questions, and he knew that if something happened to me in here, he'd never get them.

He really was just one man. One very wealthy man, but still just a private Ganraen citizen.

He was talking to me for his own reasons. He didn't know the stakes.

I didn't want to think about the storm that was brewing outside New Brittia right now. No, it *wasn't* brewing. I remembered that news feed I'd seen in the grotto, the one with the New Unity attack in progress. The storm was already in full swing.

And New Brittia was doing a nice job insulating me from it. Nothing Drexler said surprised me.

This was a good time to be in prison.

"Someone's put a bounty on you," Drexler said.

"What?"

"I said that someone's put a bounty on you."

I stopped, puzzled. "You mean out there? I bet there's a lot of bounties on me."

"No, I mean in there."

"In here?"

"Are you deaf?"

I rubbed my chin. "No, I just didn't know you could do that. Is that another cheating thing for rich guys like you? Take down an inmate they don't like?"

"Does it matter?"

"How do you know there's a bounty?"

"Because I have a map," Drexler snapped. "And there is a team of *bounty hunters* on it."

"Isn't there always? Welcome to my life."

"And they're coming straight for you."

That got my attention. I turned to look back, but I didn't know that they were behind me. They could be anywhere.

A distant scream echoed through the grating underfoot. The lights flickered.

"How?" I asked, keeping still.

"They're tracking your radiological footprint."

"My what?" I was baffled. Was he stalling? He *was*. He wanted me to stand here thinking when I needed to be moving. I broke into a jog.

"Your— your— I can't say it," he said, frustrated.

"What? Why not?"

"Because they're telling me it's a secret."

Cute. New Brittia was supposed to be all about chance. They weren't above letting in a little interference for the right price, but embedding a method to track the inmates independent of the broadcast was fundamental enough that it would defeat the purpose of letting us run around freely.

The broadcast was on a thirty-second delay; the viewers wouldn't hear what Drexler had said. He had access to secret information, so Management would censor anything sensitive. They wouldn't censor me, though.

Radiological footprint? They couldn't inject me with a traceable isotope; that would go against the prison laws that New Brittia so reluctantly adhered to.

But I wasn't a prisoner anymore, I was a laborer. An indentured servant wasn't protected by those laws. But they hadn't injected me with anything when I became a laborer; all they'd done was give me this suit.

I looked down. Radiological footprint? *Literal* footprint?

I was going to regret this.

I kicked off my boots and started to run.

"What am I up against?"

"Well, they look Trigan," Drexler said.

"Why? Why always Trigans? And can you not even do them the decency of profiling them by system?"

"Montoya," Drexler guessed. "I don't know. They do seem to use a lot of Trigans here, now that you mention it."

"Right?"

"It's a business. They're here to make a profit, not to be politically correct."

He had a point. I held up and listened for a moment, eyeing the next passage.

"Look," I said, "you want to see me tortured and talking, right?"

"More than anything."

"Then get me out of here."

"I'm *trying*. They won't let me buy you out."

"I'm worth more here."

"Just keep moving, you're going the right way. And they're hurrying up."

"So someone's doing for them what you're doing for me."

"These aren't robots. They won't ignore you. How *are* you doing that, though? With the robots? Do you have a team of breakers clearing the way for you?"

If I had, we wouldn't be having this conversation. I looked into the dark.

"Go right," he ordered.

I did. There was a loud noise, painful to the ear, and something whipped past me. I threw myself to the side, skidding across the floor and rolling into the next tunnel.

"Oh, *now* you're taking things seriously," Drexler was saying.

A tripwire caught the light, and I just managed to avoid it. At least without my boots, I could run without making enough noise to wake the dead. I probably should've gotten rid of them sooner.

"Watch your step," Drexler said.

More shards underfoot. I skidded to a stop and started to make my way through as quickly as I dared, my arms out for balance. I'd chosen the worst possible route.

"You're just lucky they've never heard of caltrops here. Well, I guess they just did," Drexler added.

"Whats?" I wiped the sweat from my eyes.

"Primitive area denial technology. Get some culture. *Christ.*"

"I know who that is," I said proudly.

"Get down!"

I dropped and caught myself on my hands, but not without picking up a nasty cut to my side. Another shot sailed overhead.

"Have they got *guns?*" I demanded, scrambling up and getting clear.

"Obviously!"

"But they can't," I said, slipping around a corner and pressing my back to the metal bracers holding up the tunnel. "That's *cheating!*"

I leaned out to look, and someone fired again. Their aim wasn't very good, but maybe they couldn't see in the dark.

"It's an antique."

"From when?"

"Twentieth century," Drexler said.

"It's New Sochi all over again," I replied.

"I thought all you Evagardians were supposed to be pretending that never happened."

We were, actually. The mighty Evagardian Service had been humiliated by a pack of galactic insurgents with primitive weapons. Most imperials found that pretty difficult to live with; it was easier to just forget.

The thought of it sobered me. "You're right. Forget I said it."

In a place like this, those antiques were just as dangerous as modern weapons. It was hardly different at all; less refined, but the principles were all the same. The old stuff had been replaced by smart weapons ages ago, and then smart weapons had become too easy to break into remotely, and everyone had gone back to handheld weapons that depended on the skill of the user. It was all about trust. You could never trust a gun that someone else could take control of remotely. Only an idiot would use a smart weapon in combat.

"How is this fair?" I grumbled.

"This from the guy that destroyed a station full of people who didn't have even a chance to say anything, much less defend themselves," Drexler said.

"But we've got a ceasefire now," I pointed out. "So we've got that going for us."

A pause.

Drexler spoke softly. "The war had cost a hundred thousand lives, *maybe*. Most of those were soldiers in uniform. Total. Both sides. Little Norwich was all noncombatants. You murdered twenty million innocent people."

I stood in the dark for a moment, not moving.

"Well, when you put it that way," I said tiredly, "it sounds kind of bad."

The man behind me fired, and I dodged across the tunnel and doubled back through a vent.

"Not to an Evagardian. After all, a single Evagardian life is worth a hundred of ours. Isn't it? Have you done the math?" Drexler demanded.

"Never liked math," I whispered distractedly, peering through a grate that was miraculously intact.

"That's how your Empress thinks, isn't it?"

"Actually, that sounds more like the High Command to me," I murmured, feeling at the vent overhead. There was a vertical shaft. I started to climb up. "Or Public Affairs. But what do I know?" I clambered into the next crossway.

"He sees you."

"How?"

A shot punched through the vent in front of me.

More shots followed, and I tumbled backward, swearing.

"All right," I said, falling into the same cavity I'd just climbed out of. "Bad idea." I kicked out the grate with both feet, straight into the face of the bounty hunter, who recoiled. I leapt out and shoved him hard toward the stretch of tunnel with the sharp things on the floor. I didn't bother to watch the aftermath; I didn't have that kind of time.

"That wasn't nice," Drexler observed. "Oh, sorry, there I go using words you don't understand again."

I just ran. There was nothing to do now but take a few corners and hope for the best. Even Trigan bounty hunters should've known better than to split up.

"Tell them whatever the bounty is on me, I'll double it," I said.

"Think they'll buy it?"

"They're in the Baykara Mines by choice. How bright can they be?"

"The pay's probably good."

"Only if you live to spend it. If you're out there watching and thinking of being one of these people, don't. Best advice you ever got," I said, hurrying deeper into the mines.

"You're all heart," Drexler growled.

NINETEEN

"How am I doing?" I asked, sagging against the tunnel wall.

The light here was bright pink. It might've been nice under different circumstances. I looked at the grates on the floor, the wires strung up overhead, and the patterns carved in the walls. There were no obvious clues about what lay ahead.

"You're asking me?" Drexler sounded taken aback.

"Why not? Are they getting my good side?"

"You look fine for a mass murderer. The fact that I'm not getting you killed is not making *me* very popular," Drexler said. "In fact, I didn't think about this coming in, but my life is probably in danger now."

"People don't respect what you're doing?"

"It's odd to me that *you* seem to get what I'm doing," he said, and I could picture the way he was probably rubbing his face in frustration.

"Anyone would want closure, Drexler." I retreated deeper into the shadows, listening.

"Do you have any idea how many people are trying to get through to me right now? I wouldn't be surprised if one of these transmissions is from your Empress."

"Go ahead and take the calls. I'll wait."

He just sighed. "I wish I could see what's going on in whatever office is in charge of dealing with you right now."

"They've probably been having a rough couple of weeks," I admitted. "I'm sorry, guys."

"Are you really?"

"No, but they stop terrorists all the time," I said. "They'll stop me too."

"You're past the halfway point," Drexler said, sighing.

"Then Freeber was right about how it all fits together."

"It's the only way that makes sense."

"You know an awful lot about this place," I said suspiciously. There was another low mist up ahead, and I didn't like the look of it. The light was changing to green, and it reminded me of Nidaros. That wasn't very inviting, but I had a worse feeling about the alternative. "Don't tell me you're a spectator even when your favorite Dalton impersonator isn't here."

"I wrote a *paper* on New Brittia, you jackass. It was about ethics."

"Really?" I thought back. "You're also a pretty outspoken anti-war guy," I added. "But not anymore, am I right?"

"No," he said tightly. "Not anymore."

"Then it's extra messed up that you can't get behind me ending the war. Isn't that what you wanted?"

There was a long silence. I grinned.

"You don't think there might have been a better way?" he asked at last.

I opened my mouth to reply, then dodged, narrowly evading a lunge from a laborer who had been crouched in the mist. He turned on me, and I knocked away his next thrust. I didn't know what was in his hand, but it looked sharp. I got out of the way again and he crashed into the wall.

"You want to kill me to push back your sentence," I said as he straightened up, shaking his head. "How long have you got?"

He gave me a funny look. He was probably wondering why I hadn't finished him off.

"Two hours," he said, hefting his shiv.

"That's two more than you'll have if you don't walk away now," I told him.

He gazed at me for a moment, but I didn't move.

He turned and jogged off into the gloom.

"Is that your solution to everything?" Drexler asked as I watched him go. "If you can't get them from behind, lie to them? Do you even know what the truth is?"

"You're hurting my feelings. Maybe I'm really good at fighting and I just wanted to cut that guy a break."

He groaned. "Are you?"

I started forward. "Like I was saying," I said, making my way into the green mist. I felt a vague, nostalgic nausea. "I'm glad you understand. Because if we're being totally honest, I've been feeling a bit underappreciated lately."

"Words fail me. Make this next right."

"Sure. What have I got to lose?"

There was light up ahead, glowing on the curvature of the tunnel. I moved to the side, pausing to listen. There was someone up there.

"Is this a trap?" I whispered.

"Depends on your point of view."

What was that supposed to mean? I advanced cautiously, finding an open chamber with light in a very natural blend of white and yellow. It was still dim by the standards of the rest of the galaxy, but for the mines, it was quite bright.

There was a conspicuously feminine man locked down in a crudely constructed device that I knew had its roots in Old Earth history.

"What's that thing called?" I whispered. I was still hidden, and the man appeared to be unconscious.

"Stocks," Drexler replied.

The guy's head and hands were immobilized, keeping him low to the ground. He was nude, and as I got closer, I saw that he had all the physical characteristics of a man and a woman. You almost never someone like this in the Imperium, but they were pretty common everywhere else. The terminology varied by system, but in the Commonwealth, they tended to use female pronouns.

She was in bad shape, with bruises, dried blood, and other bodily fluids visible on her skin.

"What is this?" I asked quietly, staying out of sight. She was definitely unconscious, so if this was a trap, she wasn't the threat.

"A lure. And a way to push back your execution."

"I have plenty of time," I said. "What's it worth to kill someone who's chained up? Where's the entertainment in that?"

"You don't get an extension for killing her," Drexler said.

I squeezed my eyes shut. "Is there not enough of that in here already?"

"Apparently not."

"You people need help," I said to the viewers.

"Oh, *you're* judging people," Drexler said. "You."

I winced. And I understood why she was locked up this way. Obviously there was temptation for the laborers who happened upon her, which might keep them stationary at least for a short time, and that would increase the odds of someone or something else stumbling onto the scene, and then things would get messy and colorful.

"Which way? Get me out of here," I said.

"Kill her," Drexler said.

I blinked. "What?"

"Kill her."

"What's she ever done to me?" I asked.

"What did my people ever do to you?"

"Are you trying to make a point? Because if you are, hurry it up."

Drexler groaned. "She doesn't deserve to be there any more or less than anyone else in New Brittia."

That was probably true insofar that any person could judge. Because this was the mines, one way or another, her actions had brought her here. Even New Brittia couldn't put someone in this situation unlawfully.

"She's already dead," Drexler said.

"What?"

"She might as well be. She'll just be stuck here until someone spiteful kills her to deny the next guy to come along. That's how it always ends. That or they get too rough with her. So kill her now. Spare her that. You can make it quick. I've seen you do it."

"I don't want to."

"Of course you do."

I folded my arms. "Why did you really bring me here?"

"For this."

"Sorry to disappoint."

"You're just going to leave her? Help her."

"That's not how I want to help."

"There's no other way."

I hesitated, but only for a moment. I made up my mind and stepped into the open.

"How do you know?" I asked.

"Because she's locked down."

I made my way over to her. I didn't see anything obviously dangerous.

"I guess I have to get her out of here. Just to spite you," I told him.

"What?"

"Out of the mines, at least. She'll still be in New Brittia, but it can't be worse than what she's got going on here. Don't you think?"

Drexler was speechless. That was fine with me. I checked her pulse. It wasn't great, but it was there. She was badly dehydrated, and that made me wonder how long she'd been here. She'd obviously had quite a few visitors. Maybe that was what attracted spectators to New Brittia.

The glamour.

The stocks were remotely locked, and solid in their simplicity.

I knelt to examine the device and its locks.

"You need to get out of there," Drexler said. So he'd been bluffing. Cute.

"You're the one who brought me here. How much time have you cost me? Could I have been on the other side by now?"

"You need to go. Now." Something in his voice bothered me.

"Why?" I looked up. "What's coming?"

"Headhunters," he said. "They're right on top of you."

Like I didn't already know. He was in the archway, and he was bleeding.

He wasn't a laborer; he was a freelancer. He was clutching a weapon with a long ridged blade.

"Are there any headhunters in here that aren't Trigan?" I wondered aloud.

"They're a flamboyant and passionate people," Drexler said, trying and failing to capture that spark he'd had a minute ago. "Who would *you* pick for your entertainment?" That was what he said, but he was too worried to banter.

He was concerned for me. He'd wanted me to kill this prisoner and get out of here before this other guy showed up. He didn't want me dead; he wasn't finished with me yet.

How sweet.

"Yeah, but they're just feeding the stereotypes," I said.

The Trigan grimaced and sagged against the tunnel wall.

"Hey," I said to him. "Go ahead, get out of here. Just don't bother me. Or her. You're good to go. Go get that looked at." I pointed a finger at each of the exits.

"It's not his blood," Drexler said.

I straightened up.

"Oh. Sneaky," I said; it was a pretty good act.

The Trigan looked surprised.

No one could hear Drexler but me, and maybe the viewers. "Where are you from, man? You're obviously Trigan. Or are you? Did they just give you that armor? Maybe he's actually Evagardian," I said to Drexler. "A master of disguise."

"Quit joking around. He's serious."

"So you do care." I positioned myself between the Trigan and the stocks, not that he had any interest in her. "I'm not into confrontation," I warned.

"You don't mind murder," Drexler noted.

"You don't know me," I replied, and I slipped. It was something I hadn't done in a long time. I said the words, and they came out in my voice. My own voice, not Dalton's.

Drexler shut up.

The Trigan straightened up; his ruse wasn't going to work, and he knew it. He put both hands on his weapon and readied it.

"But don't think that'll stop me from killing you," I told him. "Just because I don't like it doesn't mean I don't know how."

"You can't bluff your way out of this," Drexler groaned. "Just run."

"I think I can handle a Trigan with a knife," I said. "Is it politically correct to say that?"

He charged, and I dodged out of the way. Predictably, he was startled to find his blade hurtling toward the helpless prisoner in the stocks. He probably didn't care if he hurt her, but this was the power of the unexpected. He tried to adjust, but that was what I wanted, that subtle shift in momentum. His technique was compromised. I lunged in past the knife and struck him in the temple with my elbow, all of my weight behind it.

He went down in a heap, his knife clattering across the ground. More of a sword if you were looking at the length. And what were the hooked bits and the ridges for? Looking more frightening?

Not very practical.

I heard Drexler swallow.

"What?" I asked tiredly. The Trigan was out cold.

"I was going to ask you if you'd ever been in a fair fight," he said. "But I thought better of it; you probably wouldn't understand the question."

"Which part?"

"Explaining fairness to someone like you would be like trying to explain passion to an AI."

"I could do that," I said. "Explain the concept, I mean."

"Shut up!"

"Half the androids out there are intended to simulate passion anyway. It would be easy."

"It was a bad example. So shut up," he repeated.

"You shut up," I said. "I didn't ask to hang out with you. Do I even get a share of the money I'm generating for the Baykaras right now?"

Drexler snorted.

"Now talk to me about fairness," I muttered, turning back to the prisoner.

I gazed at her for several moments, drumming my fingers on my thigh.

The lights went out, leaving me in the dark.

And the locks opened.

TWENTY

ELEVEN YEARS AGO

"Everyone else is going to have a parent with them."

"That's why I have to go alone," I said. "It shows autonomy. Agency. It'll help my chances. You don't know how early they start looking."

The overseer put her arms around me, and I wasn't too proud to hug her back gratefully. She straightened and put her hands on my shoulders, looking down at me. The emotion on her face was a little much. Where was this coming from?

"It's an aptitude test. I'm not going away to war," I reminded her.

"Your scores will get you in no matter what."

I was pretty sure of that myself. Did she think I was worried?

"I've got it," I assured her.

She looked me over critically, but finding nothing to correct, she just smiled.

"Is there not a Corinth Academy in every system?" I asked, looking over my shoulder at the school.

"Honey, there's one in most provinces on every planet in the Empire. Doesn't mean it isn't the best."

"Third best," I corrected, looking up at the white walls. "Let me go. I should be fashionably early."

"I'll pick you up after."

I gave her an awkward little wave and trotted off.

The walls were high and there was a lot of traffic. There was no danger from all the passing vehicles, but it was still unnerving. There was all this fuss made about Corinth Academy's beautiful grounds, but how could they maintain that illusion in Cohengard? On the city's single largest boulevard?

I looked back, but the overseer was already gone.

This wasn't anything to be afraid of. *An exercise in nerves* was what my dorm father called it. It had actually been his idea for me to come by myself.

I liked it, though. I'd always been at my best on my own.

There weren't many people filing through the gates; this was only the first day of testing. I was a special applicant, so I didn't have the luxury of dragging my feet. People with money could do what they wanted. People like me had to follow the script.

Again, the dorm father's words. The silver lining was that I wouldn't have to deal with any crowds.

I passed through the gate, bowing to the woman greeting everyone. She had an elaborate Corinth emblem embroidered on the breast of her perfect blazer.

I entered the dampening field that was muting the sounds of the city. There was artificial ambience, the sounds of wind and birds. Even the colors changed, as though the lawns and buildings were being holographically augmented to look pretty. Maybe they were saturating the colors, like they did at the Institute to make it seem cheerier.

The campus was massive, and there was no automated transport. Wherever I went, I'd have to walk.

I consulted the holo on my wrist and made for a building with an elaborate garden. Sweeping staircases led up to a row of doors made of glass that folded away as I approached.

Quiet music played in the lobby. There were too many doors, too many stairs, and not enough people. None, actually. This wasn't the right building, but I'd been hoping to get some directions from a human. So much for that.

I checked my holo again, but all I had was the building number in my invitation. If I'd been an actual student, I'd have access to the school's network, and that would do all my navigating for me. Maybe this was another test.

I'd have to go back through my messages to find the more specific instructions with names and room numbers. It was no surprise that my destination would be tucked away somewhere obscure; there were only a few special applicants each term.

"Hey," said one of the boys on the second floor. They were gathered at the railing up there. I looked up curiously.

There were three of them, a year or two older than me, and very well-dressed.

The one in the middle wasn't the leader. The leader was the one who'd spoken, the one on the right. The one with dark hair and the jacket that cost more than all of my physical belongings combined. They'd been watching me since I walked through the door, but I preferred to ask for directions from an adult.

I smiled. "Yes?"

"Are you lost?"

"A little. I'm looking for the aux admissions office."

A moment passed. I was taken aback by how interested they seemed in me.

"We can take you," the leader said, starting toward the stairs.

I disengaged my holo and straightened up. "That would help me out," I said.

The other two followed the dark-haired one without a word. Bizarre.

"This way," the leader said, and I joined him. He guided me back outside.

"So you're special? A test score kid?"

"I don't know. Maybe. I still have to take the test."

"Us too."

I couldn't stop a snort at that.

They obviously weren't here on test scores; they were real Corinth kids. Unlike me, they actually belonged here. I was willing to bet that none of them had even been born in Cohengard. They were probably from Loston or Casta, relocated here. Maybe their parents were part of the stimulus. Maybe *they* were the stimulus.

I sensed that I'd upset them. Maybe I was supposed to pretend to believe that they were special applicants, but what would be the point? Why would they pretend to be something they weren't? I felt as though I'd missed something.

We went around the side of the building and cut across a lawn, passing a pair of human security guards in very handsome uniforms. There was another big building up ahead, probably the library, which would presumably contain books printed on paper.

I couldn't wait to be a part of a private school. Corinth Academy was going to be amazing. Those would've been positive thoughts, but even in my excitement, I couldn't fail to notice that something was wrong.

We descended an outer staircase to an enclosed walk that led up to a sublevel entrance.

I'd sort of been hoping that this was a shortcut, but it probably wasn't. I should've picked up on the way they were letting me draw ahead a little sooner. This door was probably locked, and now they were between me and the stairs.

I sighed and turned on them. This was just weird.

"Is there a reason for this? I just want to take my test."

Now they weren't hiding their distaste for me, and it was time to read between the lines. Were they insulted by what I'd said? I hadn't been trying to be insulting. In fact, I was supposed to be the one with the low ground. These boys had genes and families, but they thought I was looking down on them because of some test scores? What were test scores next to an actual bloodline? Maybe they didn't understand that.

Or maybe I was reading it all wrong. Maybe this was a shortcut and they just weren't having a good day.

"Tell you what," I said, raising my hands. "I'll get there on my own."

They were speaking quietly.

"Guys, you haven't known me long enough to have a problem with me," I told them frankly. I honestly couldn't guess what they had in mind. There were guards all over the campus. Not so many or so near that calling for help would do me any good, not that I'd call for help anyway.

I was supposed to be here alone for a reason. These three were my genetic superiors but perhaps not my cultural ones. I clearly had a better grasp of propriety than they did, and that made me the voice of justice. That was a core precept of the Grand Duchess' writings: that the voice of justice must never back down, regardless of the odds.

Of course, the writings of the Grand Duchess weren't exactly worshipped in Cohengard.

Whatever these three did, the blowback on them after I'd reported it would be disproportionate to whatever satisfaction they took in causing me trouble. What was the point? Where was the profit for them? Or were these three protected in some way? Immune?

No.

You heard about that sort of thing: privileged kids wreaking havoc with impunity, but that was the melodramatic nonsense you saw in dramas, and I had no time for it.

This was just a bluff; they weren't going to do anything. It wouldn't make any sense.

"It was nice meeting you guys," I said, moving to push past, but the leader gave me a hard shove.

I brushed myself off, a hint of queasiness bubbling up. Okay, maybe not a bluff. I still wasn't completely convinced, though.

"I'd rather not do this. It's not dignified to apply force to a fellow imperial. And I don't believe in fighting," I added hopefully.

"You're not a fellow anything," the leader said.

A minute later I was on the ground, spitting a mouthful of blood. Dizzily, I got to my hands and knees.

"Okay," I gasped. "You win." Like I needed to tell them.

One of them grabbed me by the hair and yanked me to my knees. It wasn't the leader that moved to stand in front of me, it was the other one.

They all looked up at the same time; something had moved above. A figure had appeared at the railing, another boy. I saw curly blond hair.

"Whoa," he said. His eyes were bright, blue, and very wide. "What am I looking at here?" he demanded, leaning over to gaze down at us.

The leader scowled at him and gestured for him to go away.

The blond boy didn't go. "He's bleeding," he pointed out.

I opened my mouth, but the one holding me twisted my hair.

"Yeah. You can go now," the leader said firmly, repeating his gesture.

The blond boy was closer to me in age than to these older boys, and he looked incredulous.

"Is this the hazing I've heard so much about?" he asked, trying to hold in a laugh.

One of the boys started to say something, but the blond boy vaulted suddenly over the railing, forcing the boys to let go of me and get out of the way. He landed between me and them, getting to his feet.

"Are you serious?" the leader asked, scowling.

The blond boy planted his hands on his hips. "I was just looking for aux admissions. I didn't expect to see oppression of the underclass on day one. I knew I'd see it eventually if I got in, but you guys are getting an early start."

"You mean you *weren't* expecting a beating today?"

The blond boy shrugged, grinning. "Beatings and stuff kind of come with the territory when you're a revolutionary. It's like an occupational hazard." He shrugged. "You're lucky I'm a pacifist." I tried to pick myself up, and he looked back. "You're fine there," he told me. "I've got it."

I groaned, still trying. "I'm all right."

The blond boy was bigger than I was. He looked strong and he was clearly bursting with energy, but he was no match for these three. Maybe we could take them together.

"You're kind of slow, aren't you?"

"What?" I looked up at him, puzzled.

"I'm white knighting."

"That's not a verb," I pointed out, straightening up. He rolled his eyes.

"Just go with it." He smiled at me. "But I guess we can do introductions while we still have teeth. I'm Griffith."

TWENTY-ONE

Now

"It still counts as white knighting," I told Drexler stubbornly. I was being extra mindful of my footing. I had the unconscious prisoner in my arms, so she wasn't making my life any easier. I was barefoot, and I still didn't know if discarding my boots had been necessary.

The tunnel ahead was dimly lit, but it looked clear.

"No," said Drexler. "For it to be white knighting it's got to be a girl."

"That's a primitive way to look at it," I argued. "It doesn't matter, but I'm doing the princess carry and everything, and it's not like I can ask her, so I kind of have to guess on pronouns," I added, halting in my tracks.

"What is it?" he asked.

"I thought I heard something."

"Go right."

"I don't see lights that way."

"Go anyway. You're close."

"How close?"

"Maybe forty meters from the next junction. You've got guys coming in on your right, but as long as they don't see you, they'll never know you were there. I think they're going to go down to the next level. You should go out the way they came in."

It had been a long walk from one end of the mines to the other, and without Drexler, it would've been a lot longer.

I couldn't put this off any longer. There was a narrow shaft branching from the tunnel, and I slipped into it.

"Where are you going?"

"I can't take her out there like this." I laid the prisoner down and drew the ridiculous sword I'd taken from the Trigan headhunter. "I hope she doesn't wake up anytime soon, because she's going to be *pissed*." I used the blade to saw off some of her hair, then more. "This might be the worst haircut in all of broadcast history," I said.

"Oh, it is."

"It's because this knife is silly."

"It's called a machete."

"Whatever." I finished. The haircut wasn't exactly masculine; in fact, I wasn't sure what it was. But she no longer had lovely flowing locks, and that was the point.

I put the long knife aside and started to struggle out of my suit.

"What are you doing?"

"Try to keep up," I snapped. "I can't take her out there like this. People need to think she's a guy."

"Fine," Drexler said. "Just hurry."

"I am."

"How does this work?" I asked, peeling the suit off. "Will they just leave her in here? Or pull her out or what?"

"I don't know."

"Just buy her out."

"I'll try." That was decent of him.

"This is awkward," I complained, laying out the suit.

"Which part? That the whole galaxy is seeing you naked, or that you're using a machete to play tailor?"

"I guess both," I said. It was nothing the galaxy hadn't seen before; Prince Dalton hadn't been shy, so I hadn't been either.

"You're going to a lot of trouble for one person."

"What part of white knighting don't you understand?" I asked, annoyed. "And don't let anyone sneak up behind me, this is harder than it looks."

"It would have to be."

"Grow up," I said.

"What? I'm sure she cleans up well."

"Do you have that answer for me?" I asked, finishing my cut to sever the left sleeve from the rest of the laborer suit.

"No. This might be unprecedented. I don't think anyone's ever tried to rescue someone like this before," Drexler said. He was still off-balance, and that was how I needed him to be.

"There's a first time for everything." This would have to do; I'd made some cuts to the sleeve to make it into strips. Her chest was too generous to strap down completely, but my suit would be a bit loose on her, so that might help a little.

"Concentrate," Drexler said. "Or you'll embarrass both of us."

"Relax," I told him. "This place kills the mood. For some reason."

"It wasn't a problem for the guys that found her before you did."

She was tied up as well as I could manage and still breathing, somehow. I started to put the remains of the suit on her.

"That's not a classy thing to bring up. And they were criminals," I said.

"And you're not?"

"I'm a terrorist," I replied. "Which is worse? Doing something terrible, or doing something terrible that you believe in?" I picked up the prisoner and went back out into the tunnel. "Am I good?"

"Compared to what? You're a little pale."

"You're going to feel bad if I get stabbed while you're objectifying me," I said.

"Go."

I got moving, leaving the strange knife behind. I didn't like it much; something about a weapon designed explicitly to inflict pain didn't sit right with me.

It wasn't the cruelty or even the impracticality, because pain was not impractical. It was a powerful weapon, but only in the hands of someone who knew how to use it.

That Trigan back there hadn't understood.

The airlock to Alpine Strut was up ahead. I knew absolutely nothing about it, but I was going to walk in naked and carrying an unconscious prisoner who would double as my expedited death sentence if anyone so much as suspected what she was.

"They're going to cut me off," Drexler said.

"It was nice chatting. Thanks for the help."

"What choice did I have? If you die, we'll never get the truth. You're not going to tell me, are you? Why you did it? Who gave the order? That's what it all comes down to. We all know you're one of them. Maybe there's no proof, but no one out here doubts it. But why?"

"I don't understand the question."

"At least tell me *how* you did it."

"Did what?"

"How you got by that robot, and the android. How you opened those stocks."

"You saw."

"I *didn't*. Someone's helping you," Drexler accused. It wasn't the first time. "Even if I hadn't been here, your friends would have gotten you through."

Something cut the connection.

I was alone again. Drexler was wrong; I had no friends.

Well, maybe I still had one.

Drexler was, or had been, a philanthropist. Whatever his losses had done to him, once a bleeding heart, always a bleeding heart. I'd tipped my hand to free the prisoner, but it had been worth it. When Drexler first contacted me, he hadn't had any intention of letting me leave the mines alive. He'd made a mistake when he led me to this prisoner. His desire to end her suffering by provoking me had handed me a free ticket out of the mines. He'd shown his hand first with his naked compassion.

When I freed her, I became her only chance of survival. Drexler had guided me through the mines for her sake, not mine.

Anyone can be used.

He hadn't *really* known what he'd wanted when he called me. He'd just been compelled to reach out and touch the man who had taken everything from him.

But Drexler wasn't stupid, and I'd given him enough. Barely.

That was all I could do for him. I couldn't bring back the dead. No one could really help him, and he and I were more alike than he realized.

The airlock doors opened as I approached, and I stepped in. Even dressed, I wouldn't have looked like much. The journey was starting to take its toll, and it had taken time I wasn't sure I could afford. But I was still whole, with no broken bones, and nothing bleeding so badly that I couldn't keep going.

I was still in it. For now.

To everyone watching, I had nothing but time. Only I could see things for what they were.

The chamber sealed and cycled. There was a scan, and I worried that the prisoner would pose a problem, but there was no alarm, no indication that anything was wrong.

I should have predicted that. This was a business, and the viewers would be dying to know what happened next. Management wouldn't delay that just because this prisoner probably wasn't supposed to leave the mines.

At the end of the day, New Brittia was just the same cycle of butchery, rape, and cruelty. It was be fundamentally repetitive by nature, and the entertainment value lay in the people. It was all about finding someone you felt strongly about, whether it was love or hate, and then wondering what would happen to them.

This prisoner was an unknown. She wasn't technically an inmate or a laborer; she couldn't be. I didn't know what she was in technical language, only that she must have been sentenced to death in a Free Trade courtroom to end up here.

I knew what was going to happen to her next, but I couldn't see any farther into the future than that. I was hoping that Management would be obligated to extract her from New Brittia, but after that? Who could say? Maybe Drexler could buy her out then.

The doors opened and I stepped through. This place was different, but only a little. It was that same long, spacious chamber as the one on Balkin Strut, but a bit narrower, a bit brighter, and more populated.

It was likely that laborers were used to bedraggled-looking people emerging from the mines, but a nude man carrying a clothed one probably wasn't the norm. And the prisoner's haircut was even worse in good light.

I felt a twinge of guilt, and I hefted her to angle her face into my chest. It was better if these guys didn't look too closely.

Out in the square, I wouldn't last five seconds, but Alpine Strut's labor grotto might prove a bit more civil. I might have a chance of getting through this gracefully.

But only if I could find Griffith quickly. And for that, I would take the direct route.

Not only did I stand out, but I was also a stranger. There were lots of laborers and high turnover, but not so many that they didn't get to know each other. I made for the nearest cluster of men. Were they predators, like Freeber had warned me about, planning to follow the next solo laborer who went into the mines?

I didn't care.

They didn't know what to make of me, and that was fine.

"Griffith Karlsson," I said. "Is he here? Evagardian guy with blond hair. Tall, handsome. At least, he used to be." I looked at them expectantly. No, that wasn't true. The look I was giving them was expectant, but there was more to it. One of them stepped back. "Please," I added politely.

"He's here," one of them said. "Somewhere. I know the guy you're talking about."

"If you see him, tell him the naked guy carrying another guy wants to talk to him."

They stared at me. One of them nodded.

There was nothing for me to do but look for him. Ideally, I'd do that while maintaining a low profile, but at this point I barely remembered what the word ideal meant.

I'd been spending entirely too much time walking around in the nude lately, and I'd have liked to complain, but there was no one to listen.

Apart from the whole galaxy, obviously. *They* were listening. By now I had to be close to the top of the New Brittia standings.

I carried the prisoner past the trio of men and started up the steps. It wasn't much brighter in the Alpine grotto than it was in the antechamber below, and it was similar to the one on Balkin, but with a different shape. It might've been my imagination, but it seemed slightly less shoddy. I wondered if Alpine Square was as spectacularly chaotic as Balkin Square. By the sound of things, it was. I looked at the wall separating the grotto from the blocks, then turned and looked back toward the mines.

The view was the same. The asteroid was vast, and Baykara City was still up there. I could see the glow from big festive holograms lighting up the city.

There were too many eyes on me. Not the viewers, the laborers. I'd have to hope that if the Alpine labor corps was cleaner than the Balkin one, maybe it was also better behaved.

At least I was the one getting all the attention, not the prisoner in my arms.

The Baykara Network had billions of subscribers, and by now there wouldn't much going on that was higher profile than me. Galactic and imperial news would be talking about this as well, providing wonderful free publicity for the Baykara Network. There would an enormous spike in subscribers as more and more people started watching. I wasn't just some guy in prison; my every move carried profound political consequences.

That made me wish I had some trousers, but wishing had never gotten me anything before. I'd tried.

I continued to scan the grotto. A laborer almost as big as Freeber was ogling me, not the prisoner. My white knighting was working. I kept searching, and it didn't matter how many men there were in the courtyard. There could have been millions of laborers; I'd still have been able to pick out Griffith with a single glance.

It had been seven years, and he had changed. Not as much as I had, but that was a given. It wasn't any one thing—hair, posture, gait—it was all of it. I'd have spotted that anywhere. It wasn't a matter of picking him out, though. Not really. There was nothing to pick him out of, because I couldn't see anyone else.

Twenty-Two

His hair had grown out quite a bit, and he had some stubble, but it was all the same shade of gold that it had always been.

We'd been seventeen the last time we'd seen each other. Even with my added height, he was still taller than I was. He'd gotten taller too, and even a little broader.

He hadn't noticed me yet. He'd glanced over at the naked man carrying another man, but then he'd just gone back to talking to the guy leaning on the wall beside the taps.

I walked up and cleared my throat. He turned to look, and this time he didn't dismiss me.

"Give us a minute," I said to the other one. "I have to talk to this guy."

How easy had that been? What if I'd just been processed on the Alpine side to begin with? This was my life.

Griffith stared at me. I didn't look at him. I kept my eyes on the other one, the guy that I needed to leave us alone. Finding Griffith didn't mean the end of my troubles; they were only beginning.

"It's me," I told him. "I know, I'm really tall now. Tell this guy to go away. We don't have a lot of time."

He was speechless, and I couldn't blame him for that, but it wasn't helping. We just didn't have time to do this right.

"Seriously," I said, glaring at the other guy. "*Griffith.* Wake up."

"Okay," Griffith said. He hadn't blinked since laying eyes on me. There was something terribly weak and distant about his voice, which wasn't like him. It wasn't as though I expected him to be the same as I remembered, but patience wasn't really an option at the moment.

I prodded his arm with the prisoner's feet.

"Go," I told the stranger firmly. He gave me a dangerous look, and I sent it right back.

He bristled, but seeing how profoundly thrown Griffith was, he seemed to deflate a little. He tried to catch Griffith's eye, but that wasn't working. He gave up and backed off.

I watched him go, then looked at Griffith.

"Please," I said. "I don't have time for you to do this."

"Is it really you?" He was looking me up and down. "You don't look like you."

"You better hope so." The suspicion was understandable, and my body was different in ways that couldn't be explained by time alone, but he *knew*. He couldn't mistake me any more than I could mistake him.

"How are you here?"

He still thought he was going to wake up from this, but I didn't have any sympathy for him.

"That can wait."

"Who's he?" He stared at the prisoner. I'd never seen him so bewildered. Griffith had never lacked assurance. Under different circumstances, there would have been some humor here.

"Doesn't matter," I told him. I kept my voice brisk. If I wasn't forceful, we wouldn't get anywhere. "Do you know anyone with a conscience?"

"What?"

That was what I expected.

"Griffith, *focus*. We don't have time to be sentimental," I snapped. The irony made it hard to say the words, but it hadn't been an easy day. And if I got any louder, I'd be shouting.

That seemed to wake him up a little. He'd never heard me raise my voice before.

I lowered it.

"This is a prisoner that's not exactly male," I murmured. "I brought her out of the mines, but I can't look after her anymore. We need to hand her off. Who do you know that'll do the right thing? It's got to be quick. It's got to be *right now*. This is time we don't have," I added, giving him a look that he was quite familiar with, even after all these years.

"Do the right thing?" His brows rose. "No one."

No surprise, and we couldn't agonize over this.

I started toward the covered area with the sleeping pods, resisting the urge to swear.

"Where have you been?" Griffith demanded, hurrying after me. "Why aren't you dead?"

He was asking questions that I couldn't take the time to answer, as much as I'd have liked to. I stopped in front of the first empty pod and knelt. "The pocket. Left side, chest." I indicated the prisoner's pocket with my eyes.

Griffith opened the pocket, but froze when he realized that what he felt wasn't a guy's chest. Maybe he hadn't believed me. It wasn't like him to get shy about these things, though. He hadn't been in prison *that* long.

He took out the money card and swiped it. The sleeper opened and I laid out the prisoner inside.

She was going to be confused when she woke up, and if Management or Drexler didn't get her out, she wouldn't have an easy time ahead of her. In fact, this predicament probably wasn't survivable unless she was rescued.

I put the money card beside her and shut her in. She wasn't my problem anymore.

I straightened up and turned on Griffith. I'd made a decision not to do this, but armchair decisions are always easy. I put my arms around him, and he hugged me back fiercely.

There was a horrible familiarity, a sudden and ruthless nostalgia that had the potential to put me off my game. I couldn't let that happen.

No one expected me to be perfect, but no one would begrudge me this, would they?

I would.

I pulled free and gave him my look that told him I was being serious. When we were teenagers, it had meant *No, I'm really not going to wear that.* Or *No, I really am going to class today. No, we aren't spending the last of our money on concert tickets.*

I remembered how to do the look and he remembered what it meant. Now that we were in New Brittia, it meant something a little different: that I was in charge, and I wasn't taking questions.

This would be a new experience for Griffith.

"You can wear this," he said, plucking at his suit. "I'll wear my old one."

"Save time, just give me the old one."

We went to his locker and used his palm to open it.

Griffith's first labor suit was worn, and quite loose on me, but I could actually wear it. That was bizarre; our wardrobes had never been interchangeable before. It was my height that allowed this.

I rolled up the sleeves. I was still barefoot, but I was getting used to it.

"We're leaving," I told him. "Are you ready to go?"

He stared at me with an entirely new sort of confusion, but I wasn't giving him any more time to adjust. He was a grownup. I grabbed a fistful of his collar and pulled him down to eye level.

"Are you *ready?*"

"I don't understand," he said. "I don't understand what you're doing here. Where you've been. Where you got that—*her.*"

"She was in the mines and it's not important." I let him go, and he straightened.

"What are we doing?"

"I told you. Leaving. Were you expecting Larsen?" I remembered the last time I'd seen him. I'd never have believed the brokenhearted boy at that graduation afterparty—my *friend*—would have been the one to go places in New Unity, but Larsen had.

The boy from Cohengard.

And Griffith had followed in his footsteps. I should have seen it coming. There was so much now that when I looked back, it should have been obvious.

I had been so blind.

I cleared my throat. "Who's got things on this strut? We have to go into general. Do you have money?"

"Not much."

"Where do you go to get things?"

"Things like what?"

"Chems. Someone here has to have a chemistry set."

I saw Diana Kladinova's face in my mind: her white skin and red eyes. I was about to make a big play, and I had her to thank for it. Her and Tessa Salmagard. I already owed them my life. Now I owed them Griffith's, too.

"Homebrew?" Griffith looked puzzled.

"Ideally," I said, leaving the shelter and starting off across the grotto. "You got anyone here you need to say goodbye to?"

"Why are you *alive?*" He hurried after me. He had never been big on listening—well, he'd never been big on listening to me. He'd always loved listening to revolutionaries and imperial dissidents. New Unity speakers and critics of the Empress. Larsen. He'd always had time to listen to Larsen. In any case, he wasn't going to stop asking questions just because I told him to.

I sighed. There was no getting around this. I kept walking.

"What did they tell you?"

"That you died. You and some other cadets."

"Training accident?"

"No. That you tried to help some galactics that had gotten into trouble."

"That's heartwarming," I murmured. "I was never a cadet. I never wore a uniform. I don't even know what half the rank insignias are. The Service has too many ranks anyway. I don't know why it has to be so complicated. They didn't recruit me to be an analyst. That's just what I had to tell you."

He started to say something, then caught himself. That was encouraging: his brain was working, and he did *have* a brain. He just liked to act like he didn't.

He remembered, though. He remembered when we'd been recruited, and our recruiter's cloak and dagger act. He'd never taken it seriously. He didn't understand yet; he still hadn't made the connection between me and Dalton; after all, he hadn't been watching the news in prison.

"If you wanted to see me back then, all you had to do was turn on a broadcast. I took Prince Dalton's place before the war started." I glanced upward. "For those of you at home, stay in school. Don't try to have a career like mine. It's not as fun as it sounds."

Griffith had stopped, and I looked back.

"You want me to believe that was you?"

He was trying my patience. "You asked," I said, cutting him off. I beckoned.

He started to follow me again.

"But they say the guy who was faking Dalton was the one who destroyed Little Norwich," he said slowly.

"I don't know why you're acting shocked," I replied, "it's not like you're in here for handing out literature."

He said nothing to that. In a more rational galaxy, this might have been the most difficult and painful conversation of my life. As it was, I wasn't even paying attention to Griffith. Now that I'd found him, I had to stop fooling around.

"That's what they did with you," he said finally.

He could see it. Now that he was looking. Finally.

"What happened?" he asked.

"It didn't end well."

"You killed those people?"

"I hope that's not judgment I hear," I replied coldly. This felt familiar.

He opened his mouth, then closed it. The look on his face was a new one, and it stood to reason. Back in Cohengard, the worst adversity we'd ever run up against was getting beaten up by rich kids. Failing to get into Corinth Academy. Not wanting to get out of bed and go to school. Being poor. Bemoaning our lack of prospects, not because we truly lacked prospects, but because we were both so sure we would fail that it was just easier not to try.

"How?"

We were approaching the labor gates.

"The resemblance was coincidence. They picked me on aptitudes."

"Not that," Griffith said. "How did you *do* it?"

"What? The capital? Don't you watch the news? There's a million recordings of it. Kind of grim, though."

"*Not*— Not that. Why— *Why?*"

I looked over at him.

"People keep asking me that," I said.

We passed through the labor gate into Alpine Square.

General population on Alpine Strut was louder, brighter, and more aromatic than Balkin Square, but otherwise the same. It was packed with crude stalls manned by inmates who didn't want to risk the mines, stocked with wares priced outrageously, smuggled in by Oversight and Management.

Lots of inmates and plenty of laborers. The grotto was cleaner and safer, but the square was where the gambling and the contraband were.

"They did this to you," Griffith said. He was coming around. This was something he would have to make peace with before he'd be able to pull his weight, and I was going to need him pulling his weight if we were getting out of here. This would be harder for him than for me. "You really want to escape."

"How close are you to getting out?" I asked.

The question took him off guard. "I don't know," he said.

"I'll spoil it for you," I told him. "You're not that close. If you were, I wouldn't be here."

"Larsen sent you to get me out?"

"I think he owes you that much."

At last, Griffith stopped gazing at me and looked out at the square. "What do we need to do?"

I listed a few of the chems that would do the job.

"Are you dependent?" His eyes widened. "Dalton was a user."

"I'll let you wonder," I said.

By myself, I was probably the hottest item in New Brittia. Now I was with a convicted New Unity terrorist. That only made things juicier for the viewers, particularly in light of the fact that there wasn't typically much imperial flavor on the Baykara Network. Most Evagardians had enough sense that they didn't even end up in Free Trade space, let alone New Brittia.

My viewership had been growing since I set foot here, and at this point I could safely assume that everyone who was anyone was watching. Even people who normally shunned the prison and just watched the games in Baykara City would have their eyes on me now. This wasn't just a New Brittia event anymore.

All eyes were on me, and all ears. I'd been choosing my words the entire time I'd been here, and I couldn't stop now.

Oversight wasn't listening because they couldn't, but Management was. Drexler was. Evagard was. Along with plenty of other people. It was unlikely that any of them fully appreciated just how tricky all of this was. I was used to that. When it came to credit, no one had ever given me much.

Well, I *was* the recipient of a Rothschild Mark, even if it had just been a trap to get me into the open so Evagardian

Intelligence agents could kill me. It was still the most prestigious award someone could get.

So of course, once they realized I was still alive, they'd stripped it from me. They'd stripped a medal from an alias. I didn't mind that so much. Status was only a word, and at least for me, it wasn't a word with a lot of meaning.

Frankly, the Rothschild Mark was a bit of a slight. If one believed the narrative of the heroic imperial spy daringly destroying the Ganraen capital station to save Evagardian lives that might be lost in a longer war, the Rothschild Mark seemed like a small reward.

Losing it didn't bother me. Killing people wasn't something to be rewarded.

"So?" I pressed Griffith.

"I'm thinking," he said. "I don't use, so I don't know the dealers. We might have to do some asking around."

"How much do you have?"

"Not much."

"Enough for a knife?"

"Part of your plan?"

"You can pretend it is if it helps."

"You're so different."

"That's funny coming from you."

TWENTY-THREE

"We can't," Griffith said quietly. "We have to wait."

He was a vastly better native guide than Idris had been. He'd been in New Brittia for almost three weeks. He had none of Idris' disadvantages; he was big, strong, and driven. By the look of things, he'd been doing reasonably well by stealing into the mines with a pair of like-minded laborers and making his way by treasure hunting.

He hadn't been making enemies. He knew people, and he knew his way around.

I couldn't risk invading another kingpin's block this time, not with Griffith in tow. The close quarters and large number of people inside the blocks was more than I could handle; I couldn't keep him safe in there.

Out here, maybe I could figure something out if we ran into trouble.

We were among the stalls. The sounds of Alpine Square were almost a roar in the narrow pathways, filled with people jostling each other. Frankly, I was surprised there weren't more fights. Maybe New Brittia's culture was evolving despite the turnover.

Griffith and I were under the awning of a vendor who wasn't at his stall. It was just standing empty. Maybe the owner had stopped paying whoever was protecting him and natural selection had taken care of the rest. Maybe he had nothing to sell. Maybe the stall didn't actually belong to anyone; it was built out of defaced components of pressure crates. The awning was made out of a couple of inmate jumpsuits adhered together and colored with some kind of homemade dye.

I could smell ethanol from the next stall over.

"You'll know this guy when you see him," Griffith told me.

"Why?" I asked, watching the flow of people.

"Because no one ever explained to him what a cliché is." He was looking at me again, and I wished he'd stop. I needed him to keep a lookout. "So I guess it didn't work out between you and the Empress."

"You could say that."

"I just don't understand."

"I don't want to hear that from you," I said, glancing at him. He would never know—no one would ever know—how hard I was working to keep my temper under control. It was one thing to hear it from someone else, to merely become aware of what Griffith had become. Now he was right in front of me, and it was different.

"I always knew you had it in you. I just never thought I'd see it happen," I said, and it was the truth.

"Don't try to lecture me. I don't know who you are anymore."

"I didn't come here to catch up."

Griffith went back to watching the men pushing their way through the square.

"Is that him?" I asked.

"Yeah."

We moved forward together. Griffith had been right: I knew the courier at once. There were lots of systems, lots of planets, lots of cultures, but people selling illegal chems all tended to act alike.

This guy probably worked for whoever was the equivalent of Spirluck on this strut, and he was making deliveries to the blocks. We'd staked out his route, and he'd shown within ten minutes.

Not fast enough for my liking, but it could've been worse. Robbing a chem dealer. If I hadn't been a criminal in the classical sense before, I was about to be.

I grabbed him from behind and turned him around. He was surprised, and twitchy. He went for a weapon, and I flicked out the knife that Griffith had bought for me and put it to his throat.

"Got any Bergen?" I asked. "Optics? Anything with a high pH? You can nod."

He was in a lot of pain from my grip and was looking at us as though we were insane. Yes, shaking down someone like him was probably akin to suicide on this strut, but I didn't plan to stick around long enough to suffer the consequences. That was what no one understood.

"Just give me what I need and you can go," I said.

It hurt to say it. I didn't want the chems to use; I needed them to get Griffith out of New Brittia—but even after all this time, my ego chafed at the idea of being reliant on this stuff again. It chafed even more at having to say these words, to embody this cliché. In all the galaxy, all of history, what was less dignified than robbery?

But what was dignity to me at this point? Dignity had never been a concern for Dalton. He'd always struck me as being terribly enlightened in that way.

I looked at the hypo he gave me with his good hand. "What is this?"

"A stim."

I wanted to laugh, but it wasn't funny.

"What *is* it?" I demanded.

"It's homebrew," Griffith cut in. "He doesn't know what's in it. It's probably mostly amphetamine."

I pocketed the hypo. That would do. I let go of the guy and looked over at Griffith. "The White Square Special?"

"How long are you going to keep going back to that?" he asked. "At least when you were dead you couldn't guilt me over stuff."

I still couldn't believe he'd tried those chems that day, years ago. What an idiot. Well, one of us was.

The guy hadn't left. He was still standing there. We'd shaken him down for one hypo; that would be an inconvenience for him, but it wouldn't ruin his day.

"Hey," he said.

"What?" Griffith and I both turned to him.

"You guys are imperials," he said.

"Go away," I told him firmly. "We're not going to hurt you. We've got what we need."

"Wait—can't you help me?"

"No."

He grabbed my sleeve. "Come on, I'm going to die in here. Evagardians have to stick together," he said desperately. I tried to shake him off, but he held on.

"I don't know if you've heard," I said, "but the Empress and I aren't speaking at the moment."

He opened his mouth, and I hit him. The punch threw him back, teeth and blood flying. He crashed into the stall behind him, spilling small packets of protein snacks to the ground and nearly knocking two men out of their seats.

He was unconscious, but the men that I'd just displaced were not. They didn't look happy.

Griffith's shock evaporated, and he steeled himself.

"Brilliant," he said, getting ready to fight.

"Shut up." I stepped in front of him and faced the inmates. I was still holding my knife, but I kept it at my side.

"Let's make this quick," I told the two men, who had gotten to their feet. "I'm in a hurry."

Seconds went by. They weren't going to attack me.

I had found Griffith. I had gotten through the mines. I had done a lot of things that I hadn't particularly enjoyed.

We were close to the finish line, and I was all out of patience.

These people could see that bothering me was not in their best interests. They were inmates, and they didn't want to tangle with two laborers.

I led Griffith between two stalls, into another aisle, then past a crude curtain to a counter similar to the one I'd stopped at back on Balkin Strut to figure out Gingham's little holo—which now belonged to that prisoner because I'd forgotten to take it out of that suit, which she was now wearing. Alas.

I sat down.

"Will you buy me a drink?" I asked Griffith, rubbing my eyes.

He was capable of having a poker face. He'd never had one back in Cohengard, but he had one now. He wasn't the same person.

Griffith was capable of a lot of things; he just wasn't at his best. It wasn't New Brittia that had done this to him—it was me. I didn't blame him for lagging a few steps behind or for being horrified by me.

I didn't blame him for floundering in his shock, and I didn't blame him for the turns he'd taken after I left him and Inge behind. Judging him was the height of hypocrisy, but that wasn't stopping me. Despite everything, I was still disappointed in him.

He probably felt exactly the same way.

"When have I ever not," he said weakly.

There was no time to waste, but I was wasting it, looking at him.

Griffith handed his card to the man behind the counter, who began to mix drinks. Under the counter, I broke open the hypo of homebrew and drizzled the contents on my forearm.

I had Diana Kladinova to thank for this in more ways than one.

I flicked out the knife and opened up a shallow cut. My blood and the stim mixed, immediately bursting into a painful froth.

Chemistry. Two things, harmless when separate, dangerous together. Kind of like me and Griffith in reverse.

I grimaced, but it was better not to show too much distress. I smeared a little of the bubbling mixture on the underside of the counter, then undid my sleeve and covered it, fastening it securely. I dropped the broken hypo and pocketed the knife, then brought my arms up to rest them on the counter.

I'd learned that Diana and Salmagard had gone on quite a journey to reach me and Sei, back when we'd been in the hands of Cyril and his people. They wouldn't have reached us at all if Diana hadn't come up with this maneuver.

Griffith handed me my drink.

"I thought we were in a hurry." He wasn't looking at me; he was looking at a little decal on the wall that showed a stratoplatform and a starry sky, some artist's representation of a rich person's vacation home. Drexler probably had a stratoplatform somewhere.

"Don't worry," I said. "We still are."

"I never thought we'd get to do this again."

For a moment, I didn't know what he meant, and then I realized where we were. It wasn't by accident that I'd gravitated toward these small, enclosed counters. It was my subconscious at work. The same thing had happened from time to time when I'd been Dalton.

These counters were a relic of Far East culture on Old Earth, so if you wanted the authentic experience, you would probably only get it as a tourist to the core imperial worlds or the Kakugo system.

But the authentic experience wasn't what I was used to; I was used to what we'd had in Cohengard. Little stalls like this, built to look authentic but stocked with modern sensibilities. Proper Evagardian drinks mocked up to seem rustic and tiny portions of novel but mediocre food that was priced outrageously.

It wasn't about the food or the drinks, though. It was about the company, and the experience. In Cohengard, these stalls would pop up around festivals or stimulus events. The permanent ones were all near the canals and only open at night, so you'd have a nice view of the dome, and you could hear the water.

Griffith and I had spent plenty of evenings like that.

This stall was made of corroded plastic. There was no dome up there, just the triple shield, and some stars and nebulae, which were nice. And there was no sound of water, just a lot of swearing and music.

It had no charm at all.

Griffith didn't drink, and he didn't say anything. He just sat beside me, both hands on his cup.

He'd always been able to tell what I was thinking, but he couldn't do that anymore. It worried him, but it was for the best.

He wasn't blind, though. Time was no longer a factor, and he could tell. I'd done the best I could, and the top of the hourglass was empty. The final grain of sand was on its way down, and all we could do was wait for it to land.

Griffith had never been one for making sharp turns. He did better in a straight line, and the more momentum, the better. He needed time to come around to the idea that I was still alive, and when he did, things would only get worse.

It was no different for me. I'd known he was alive all along, but after a certain point, I'd also known that I would never see him again. I'd made peace with that a long time ago.

And here we were, but no one was going to be as patient with me as I was with Griffith. I had to stay on course and keep it all locked away.

Right up to the end.

Griffith was looking up through the tear in the canvas overhead, at the little patch of stars that was visible to us.

There were faint flashes of light and color reflected on the curvature of the shields that kept atmosphere in New Brittia. They had to be coming from fireworks going off over Baykara City. The games were on, although I had a feeling viewership was down up there and up down here.

"Pretty," I said, taking a sip.

"Yeah." He was watching me.

I took a deep breath, pushing away my cup and putting my face in my hands. I focused on breathing.

There was a slight heat near my shoulder, just a whisper of it, enough to know that he'd reached for me but stopped himself.

"What's wrong?"

"Just give me a minute," I said. That wasn't too much to ask for, was it?

Of course it was. This was my life, and I'd been living it long enough to know the rules.

The noise level in Alpine Square was rising.

"What's that?" he asked.

I wiped my eyes and looked up through the tear above us. There were stars, and lights, and something else.

Pale streaks trailed lazily through the air, arcing toward us from every direction.

"That's intervention gas," Griffith said, but I grabbed him before he could get up.

Already, the canisters were landing among the stalls, all across the square.

"It's all right," I said as the gas billowed through the curtains. "I've got you."

Twenty-Four

The man behind the counter had the good sense to lie down; he knew that Oversight's intervention gas didn't give you a lot of time to react.

Griffith probably wanted to say or do something, but he didn't get the chance. He slumped over, and I caught him. How many times had he drunk too much and I'd had to drag him home?

Now— *Now* the nostalgia chose to come, and it was here with a vengeance. Not so much knocking on my door as kicking it in.

Fine. That was fair. I had earned this, and I didn't deserve anything less.

I got to my feet, picking up Griffith and putting him over my shoulder.

The haze had become a mist, and now the mist was becoming a fog.

It wasn't the green haze of Nidaros. Sometimes I felt like I really *had* died back on that planet, among those spires. It was easier to think that I was already dead and this was my punishment.

But that would be getting off easy.

It was quiet. The fog was almost opaque; the stalls and rows were just ghostly shadows in the clouds, and there were unconscious men everywhere. The gas had done its work, instantly disabling every man in the square but one.

I started to walk.

People say a lot of things about Evagardians. That we think we're better than everyone else. That our culture looks enlightened but that our caste system and fixation on genes is fundamentally backward. That there is no true freedom under the absolute power of the Empress, that we're good at everything but so blinded by our own society that we can't enjoy any of it.

There's still one thing that everyone agrees on: Evagardian things are expensive. They're right. It's absolutely true.

But you get what you pay for.

Something dark passed overhead, and I followed that movement, stepping over sleeping inmates.

And *this* was an expensive system, but it was also effective, if not exactly elegant. It was one thing for Oversight to send a few armed men into processing. That wasn't terribly dangerous for them, and it wasn't as though they had no surveillance at all. Oversight didn't share in the broadcast; that would be unfair, but they still had some basic technology on their side.

But not enough to make a visit to a fully populated strut even remotely safe. On the rare occasions when there was an emergency serious enough to mobilize for, the danger had to be neutralized. Management loved a riot, but not if it got in the way of the bottom line.

Management couldn't let Oversight hurt the inmates— well, not in these numbers. Shooting one or two here and there was fine, but slaughtering crowds? That would raise some eyebrows. The inmates were the point; they were the beating heart of the business. They were no different than crops or cattle; without them, there was nothing.

But a little beauty sleep wouldn't bring too many casualties, and it was a short sleep. It had to be. A real sedative would work its way through different people at different speeds, leading to imbalance when it came time for people to wake up, which would lead to all manner of unfairness, and not the kind of unfairness that the spectators enjoyed.

So a continuous supply of the intervention gas would be pumped in until Oversight's work was done. The second it cleared, everyone would be up and about.

When that happened, they were going to be two short.

New Brittia.

It was home to Baykara City, the arena, the Baykara Residence, and the games. It was home to what had once been a very large mine. To a mental health ward, and even a maximum-security pod for people incarcerated in Free Trade space who were considered not only too dangerous for New Brittia but too dangerous for any of the official not-for-profit Free Trade detention centers.

It was an asteroid. It was a business. It was an entertainment phenomenon known to more or less everyone in every system.

It was also, for all intents and purposes, a space station.

And nothing on a space station was more terrifying than a biohazard. Nothing would be taken more seriously.

Most contaminants were scrubbed from the air in recyclers, sterilized by maintenance robots, and taken care of by the miracle of technology before they could ever pose a threat to anyone.

But when one got through, one that couldn't be so easily purged, Oversight had no choice but to step in.

Oversight had a strange and dangerous job. No one was on their side. Not their employers and not the prisoners they were charged to control. They had to be firm, but they also had to protect the inmates and laborers from anything that might threaten them wholesale.

In this case, that was my blood, mixed with the homebrew stimulant. Diana had done it at the Bazaar, and nearly caused a major quarantine. My blood wasn't the same as hers, but my imitation didn't have to be perfect, it just had to be close enough to fool the sensors into thinking there was something dangerous down here.

It wasn't easy to smuggle something into New Brittia, but if you were going to do it, it *had* to be inside your body.

Now Oversight had put Alpine Strut to sleep and descended to save the lives of a lot of men who probably wouldn't think twice about murdering them all in their sleep.

New Brittia was a strange place. I was glad to be leaving.

I'd put enough distance between myself and the stall. I set Griffith down and made a point to remember where he was, then moved silently into the mist.

Oversight would be wearing full containment gear; the audio pickups would be good, but the fog would muffle things, and their situational awareness wouldn't be perfect. They didn't have combat scanners, and even if they did, I wouldn't show up on them.

Evagardian suits had better audio; they could filter and adjust sound so that nothing was lost. But this was New Brittia. If the Baykaras equipped Oversight too well, the inmates wouldn't have a fighting chance. Where was the fun in that?

I could still faintly see the colorful fireworks over Baykara City, even through the mist.

Business was good.

There was movement to my right and I followed it, slipping through a narrow gap.

The figure ahead was bulky but too short. I veered off and kept looking as the fog swirled around me.

Griffith and I had once taken Inge to the Giotto Spa, a Cohengardian stimulus resort opened at Da Vinci Lake. It wasn't really a lake; it was the crater from the detonation that truly ended the Cohengardian revolt. It had been converted into a lake. A perfectly circular lake—thus the name.

We didn't care about the lake; all we cared about were the exotic steam baths that were popular at the time. It was the hot place to go and do romantic things and feel adventurous and trendy while doing them.

But the entrances to the baths were segregated by gender, and they were at completely opposite ends of the space, which was massive and filled with attractions. Slides, soaking pools, statues, romantic aids, and a lot of people.

We couldn't find each other in the steam. Griffith and I had searched, and Inge had no doubt been searching for us, and holo use was forbidden in there, of course. We didn't know that it was customary to look at a map first and agree on a landmark; we had gone in completely unprepared.

It was a trip that we hadn't really been able to afford in the first place; we'd only bought a short amount of time in the baths. After a certain point, even as we wandered blindly in the steam, we knew that if we actually found Inge, we weren't likely to have much time together.

We had found her, eventually. With about two minutes left on our ticket. That was a good thing; if we hadn't found her at all, it would've been even more depressing. With the way things turned out, at least we got a laugh out of it.

Now I was making my way through clouds of white with different things in mind.

There was another figure ahead, and this one would do. I stole up behind him and struck him in the kidney hard enough to make him stagger. Then I got an arm around his neck and squeezed. I couldn't break his neck, although that might've been more efficient. It would risk tearing his helmet's seal, and I needed his suit intact.

He struggled, but I didn't let up. There was no reason to kill him, so I only choked him to unconsciousness.

I knelt in the fog, stripping away his isolation suit and pulling it on. These suits weren't top of the line, but they were personalized. Our physiques didn't match up completely, but that was life. I was used to it.

Once dressed, I went to find a second victim. Griffith would need a suit too.

It didn't take me long to get him one.

Oversight was scared; they'd sent down at least a dozen people to scour the strut, scanning for the source of the contamination. It wouldn't take long for them to find my blood, but it might take them a few minutes to realize what was really going on.

The second man I overpowered was carrying a massive sterilizer meant for use in space station maintenance. It was a big industrial laser cleaner but not quite robust enough to be used as a weapon.

I got Griffith dressed and sealed his helmet, connecting our comms and switching our channel away from what the Oversight cleaners were using. They'd already noticed one of their guys had gone quiet and were trying to find him.

It was hard to know how much cover we had left; if Oversight just wanted to eliminate the threat, they could be done with this quickly. Cleaning up the contaminated surface would be a small job. If they wanted to investigate thoroughly, we could have hours, but the viewers wouldn't like that. Perhaps this was why there were two struts: so people could watch Balkin while things were on hold here.

Management would still be watching, and they could see every move I made. This mist was nearly opaque to the naked eye but not to any real optical technology.

Even if Management could figure out what I was up to, they wouldn't stop me. They weren't in the business of helping Oversight. Oversight had to fend for themselves.

And a prisoner running amok? Good for business. Viewers had to be reminded occasionally that the unexpected could happen. They had to believe it could be done, otherwise they wouldn't be able to hope.

All I had to worry about was Oversight, and I could handle them.

Griffith came around in moments. I held him down.

"Griffith," I said. "Stay calm." He wouldn't like waking up in this suit.

He coughed. "Empress."

"She's not here. Can you breathe? Look at your readout," I said, looking around. Some of these Oversight guys would be armed; I couldn't have them stumbling on us now.

"I can't see," Griffith said.

"It'll clear. Look to your right, the right of your faceplate. Do you see green?"

"Yeah, there's green. Sort of. More like blue."

"Good enough." I pulled him to his feet.

"What's happening?"

"We're leaving. You're dizzy. It's fine. Stay with me, don't panic."

"I can't believe it's you."

"Your head's going to clear," I said, taking him by the hand and leading.

"It's really you."

"Just stay cool," I said, clenching my jaw.

"What am I wearing?"

"Just concentrate," I began, but he stumbled. I caught him. In about thirty seconds, he was going to be completely back to normal, but it would be a long thirty seconds.

I plunged onward.

"Am I drunk?" he asked.

"No," I replied. For once.

We emerged from the rows of stalls, and the fog wasn't quite as thick. It was a pity I wasn't familiar with the suit's user interface; that would've made this a lot easier.

Oversight couldn't land their little hover skiffs among the stalls; there wasn't room. They had to be out here, around the edge of the square. We hurried through the fog, Griffith growing more lucid by the second.

"I have a headache," he complained.

"We all got problems."

A shape loomed ahead, and I dragged him toward it. It was exactly what I'd hoped for, and unattended. There was no reason to guard it; everyone was supposed to be asleep, and only someone with an Oversight suit could operate the vehicle. Two layers of security, neither one of which meant anything to me. The skiff was big enough to carry at least six.

We climbed on, and I powered it up.

These people put entirely too much faith in their system. They were woefully unprepared for someone like me.

They wouldn't be next time, though. I'd set the precedent. This would only work once.

We lifted off and I throttled up, taking us straight toward the wall. Down there in the fog, there had been the illusion of hope: I could *hope* that Oversight wouldn't know what I was up to.

And there was still hope, but less of it. The snipers covering the square would see the skiff, and they'd see me and Griffith, but we were in uniform. I simply didn't know how closely they were looking, or what they were expecting to see. Or what the people down in the square were telling them. They might be putting it together, but they wouldn't fire on people that might be their own without being absolutely sure. All we looked like was two of their guys pulling out.

This wasn't a military installation; they probably had smart weapons. If they did decide to fire at the skiff, they wouldn't miss. I didn't give them enough time to make up their minds.

I took us over the wall, out of the line of fire of the snipers, and into open space. I stayed tight to the side of New Brittia, with nothing but stars on my left. I couldn't stray out too far; I didn't know exactly where the shield was, or even where the gravity field ended.

The Oversight facility curled along the side of the asteroid, and I followed the curvature of it, bulkheads and viewports flashing past in a blur. There was the landing platform up ahead. This area was all pressurized, but only because of the shield. We'd have to get through an airlock to get inside. That would be easiest if our cover held.

"Act hurt," I said to Griffith. "I'm going to carry you in."

"What?"

"If they don't know we're fakes, we might be able to sell it."

"You'll carry *me?*"

"Trust me," I said.

"What if it doesn't work?"

"Nobody's shot at us yet." There were defensive turrets along the exterior armor, and I hadn't known about those. If they'd wanted, they could blast us any time they wanted. They couldn't target me, but they could still target the skiff, or Griffith.

Of course, Management might have disabled them to make things more interesting. The bloodsucking entertainment specialists running this freak show were the best friends I could ever wish to have. I'd never had support this good before. That was irony.

They wanted to see me succeed, but Oversight didn't. This wasn't over.

I took the skiff toward a pad that would carry it into the vehicle bay, but we weren't going to the vehicle bay. We wanted the staging airlock.

I was staying off the comms, so I couldn't call to the controller to open the doors. I couldn't risk it; my voice would be unfamiliar, and I didn't know how these people talked to each other. There would be terminology, a customary way to voice the request. I'd give myself away if I tried to fake it.

I landed the skiff and leapt off, going to Griffith. Ignoring his protests, I picked him up. We'd have to do this the old-fashioned way.

Nothing happened as I approached with Griffith in my arms, but someone had to be watching. Right?

Not necessarily. The ease with which I'd been able to use their biohazard containment measures to my advantage proved that there was a delicate balance in New Brittia.

Management couldn't have the place completely fall apart. An escape could be allowed to succeed, but a riot couldn't. Oversight had to be at least tolerably good at their job. They had to get it done, at the end of the day. Just not *too* well.

And if it cost a few Oversight members their lives here and there—well, the show had to go on.

TWENTY-FIVE

I let Griffith down and pulled the manual release. The big doors opened, revealing an incredibly spacious airlock.

I tapped my helmet to indicate to anyone who might be monitoring us that I was having comm issues. Griffith hit the release to start the decontamination cycle.

I positioned myself near the inner doors, wondering if there was anything I could do to look *more* suspicious.

The cycle ended and the doors began to open.

"Just like that?" Griffith sounded disbelieving.

"No faith," I said. "Remember, we've got friends."

Griffith started to say something, but a klaxon started to wail and the doors halted. I'd spoken too soon; they were onto us.

Swearing, I grabbed Griffith and yanked him through. We were lucky to have gotten this far quietly.

I pulled off my helmet and started forward, tossing it aside. Lights flashed in the corridor and a door hissed open. I ran to the nearest ladder and slid down, coming face to face with a shirtless man carrying a pistol. I grabbed his wrist and turned the gun on him, pulling the trigger.

The shot made my ears ring, and he fell back, looking stunned, still clutching the gun.

Another man entered the hallway and I lunged into him, bashing him into the bulkhead. He slid to the deck, senseless, as Griffith caught up with me.

I didn't stop. More lights flashed, and the holographic signs and advertisements were all strobing warnings, but there were still navigation guides.

Personnel quarters were here, and that worked for me. Doors slid apart ahead, and I leapt forward as a woman peered into the corridor.

I caught her by surprise, forcing her back into the room and ramming my fist into her solar plexus. She doubled over, and I struck her down with a blow to the temple before she could recover, but there was also a man in the room who had been getting dressed.

Griffith was there, delivering a pair of punches with a level of competence that took me aback. A lot could happen in seven years.

We couldn't really call ourselves pacifists anymore.

"I get his trousers," Griffith said, beginning to struggle out of his hazard suit. Fine; I'd get something out of the closet.

It wasn't great to take the time to change, but the bulky suits had to go; they weren't a disguise in here, and they would slow us down.

"Do they have surveillance in here?" Griffith asked as we changed.

"Of course." Having the foxes in the henhouse was probably a rare occurrence; Management would want to get their money's worth when it did happen. Everything we did here, we did on the record.

"There's still a lot of them."

I didn't bother with a shirt. Griffith had one, but he hadn't bothered to fasten it.

They wouldn't be looking for us down here, at least not initially. These quarters weren't on the way to any of the places Oversight would be expecting us to go. They were expecting us to try to escape.

In a moment we were back in the corridor, moving at a jog.

"I could use a plan," Griffith said.

"The plan is follow me," I told him, reading the signs on the walls. This was a primitive facility. There were no guide paths, just holographic words and arrows. Lifts wouldn't be efficient; another emergency ladder would be a better bet.

What approach would Oversight take in responding to us? They had to have plans for this; they had to train for it. They were armed, and they outnumbered us. The element of surprise was our only hope, but it had gotten me this far.

There was only one way to keep the initiative. I was telling Griffith the truth: I did have a plan.

There was the ladder, and someone climbing down. I grabbed his ankle and pulled, bringing him crashing down to our level. This guy had a uniform on.

A pistol clattered to the deck. I grabbed it and pressed the muzzle to the man's side.

"Where's the armory?"

He started to say something defiant, so I fired a shot next to his ear. He cried out and flinched, but I kept my grip on him.

"There—in ops," he shouted over the ringing crashing through his brain. I shoved him forward, keeping him under control.

We were moving back in the direction we'd come, and up a ramp. It made sense; the airlocks, bays, and supplies would all be in roughly the same place.

Oversight was clean and bright. The technology wasn't advanced, but it was lavish. Because these people were cut off from everyone outside this facility, they were kept in comfort. There were lots of amenities, like localized VR, but there was a business component as well.

Because there was no one to help them, no one at all, regardless of the caliber of people that they might be, Oversight had to be ready for trouble.

But they were mostly prepared for escapees. There wasn't anything in their playbook for me. I handed the gun to Griffith.

"We're not going for the shuttle bay?" he asked worriedly, turning to fire a shot back at an opening door. A man got out of the way, sealing the door behind him. Griffith wasn't much good with a gun. That was comforting. I knew it was only loaded with stun rounds, but I still didn't like seeing it in his hand.

I focused on keeping our hostage under control.

"We are," I lied for the broadcast. "Just not yet." Griffith wouldn't know I was lying, but he didn't need to understand. He just had to follow. Someone was always listening, and everything I said was for their benefit. My mind was the only safe place.

That was a scary thought.

Stealing a shuttle wouldn't work; that was exactly what Oversight was expecting, and that was the reason we were seeing so little resistance. Their response was logical: guard the ways out and lock everyone else down for safety. It would be a moment before they got organized enough to start sweeping the facility for us.

Even if they weren't all stacked up between us and the shuttles, we couldn't get out that way.

Corruption was simple, but it could still look complicated. Oversight wanted to stop us from escaping; their bonuses depended on it. Management wanted to see us escape; viewership liked that, so Management's overall success depended on it.

Evagard wanted me dead, and Evagard had a lot of money.

There was simply no way for me to know where I stood, but chances were good that the Imperium would pay or pressure Management to actually get serious about stopping me. Or at least they'd try.

Would Abigail Baykara take the deal?

I was still alive, so she hadn't taken it yet.

And even if New Brittia didn't sell me out, it was absolutely certain that there would be ships out there watching this broadcast of me at this moment. They were waiting for me to poke my head out so they could shoot it off.

When I'd been out there on the skiff, I'd been in the sights of half a dozen Evagardian ships. They wouldn't be warships; they'd be the same yachts and sloops that you would normally see around Baykara City, but hiding weapons and soldiers. They hadn't taken me out right there because they hadn't been willing to fire on New Brittia itself. Taking hostile action in Free Trade space, particularly so close to Baykara City, where so many wealthy and influential galactics were—it wasn't something Evagard would do lightly.

On the other hand, they might risk it. Sketchy black ops and illegal shooting in Free Trade space would be a mess to clean up, but not half as bad as the whole galaxy blaming the Empress for the destruction of Little Norwich. *That* would mean another war, and this new war would be a little different.

Right now, people were asking hard questions. There was suspicion on the Imperium, suspicion on the High Command, suspicion on the Empress. Nothing like this had ever happened before, and Evagard was shaken.

I wasn't the only person alive who could confirm or refute those suspicions, but I was the one everyone in the galaxy was watching at the moment.

Prison walls were protecting me in all sorts of ways. There was only one way that Griffith and I were getting out of here.

A guard was heading for the armory from the opposite direction, but Griffith shot him before he could raise his weapon or go for the door. Griffith was no soldier, but he hadn't survived New Brittia for a month through blind luck. His aptitudes had been good enough that he could've tried for the Service after all.

I could remember when we'd gotten beaten up by three bloodliners at Corinth Academy. We hadn't been able to handle ourselves for anything back then. We hadn't *wanted* to.

Physical violence was undignified. Griffith and I were not fighters.

Fighting was beneath us.

"Open it," I said, pushing my hostage toward the hatch. He didn't argue; he palmed it open, and Griffith shot him in the back, stepping over him to shoot the woman behind the desk several times. She jerked and shuddered as the stun rounds struck her, dropping her scattergun.

She'd been ready for us, but not quick enough.

Her scattergun probably wasn't loaded with stun shells. We were lucky she'd choked; if she'd pulled the trigger with both of us in the doorway, that would've been it.

I sealed the door and surveyed the room. The armory had everything we needed. It was close to the airlocks, and also close to the shuttle bay.

I pulled down a protective vest and threw it to Griffith.

"Put that on," I ordered.

"What about you?" he asked, doing up the clasps.

"Not my look," I said distractedly, looking at the shelves of weapons. There was a broadcast on at the desk, and I could barely hear what it was saying, but it sounded like big news. I looked over and saw a white ship. It was something about the *Julian*, Sterling Station, and New Unity. I'd seen something about this earlier, but there wasn't time for the news now. I wished I could stop my brain from reading between the lines.

"Scatterguns?" Griffith asked. "Or shipboards?" He was looking at the racks of firearms.

"Neither," I said, shaking my head. I was getting distracted. "We aren't soldiers. Just get the breaching charges."

"You know I've already got an ear problem," Griffith said.

"Since when?"

"Since I stopped having reliable healthcare."

I opened a case of charges and took some. "We'll keep it simple."

"Simple?"

I went to the door and palmed it open, tossing out a breacher. These charges were used for clearing rooms: they released sound, light, and disorienting radiation. They wouldn't do much lasting damage, but they'd make it all but impossible for people to shoot us.

There was a flash and a roar, and we went out. Sure enough, someone was ducking around the corner, probably hearing a buzz and seeing stars.

I heartlessly tossed another charge after them and led Griffith around the corner.

As far as I was concerned, my breaching charges meant that I outgunned Oversight. They were only using small arms, after all. Still, it was better to keep face time to a minimum. Prison guards were complacent and incompetent across the galaxy—except in the Imperium, of course—but at least a few of these people would know what they were doing.

We passed another news broadcast, this one also showing the *Julian*, and the Empress's flagship was as impressive to look at as ever.

I'd been so *close* to getting there. I wished someone would change to a different feed.

There was a junction ahead. I tossed a charge and pulled Griffith into an alcove.

"I hope the viewers don't get the wrong idea," I said. "Because I'm probably making this look easy."

"All I see is you leading us away from the only way out."

"Yeah, you didn't think I could get us into Club Deception, either."

"You didn't get us in."

"Yeah, but I could have."

"I thought you were testing me. Trying to make me jealous."

"I was."

"At least you're not insecure anymore," Griffith called over the klaxons. "I'll say that much for you."

"Griffith, if there was time for us to have a touching reunion," I said, but paused, throwing another pair of charges and dragging him into a lounge and pulling him behind a sofa. "Then I'd be *all for it*," I hissed.

"Me too," he said.

The charges detonated. There were cries of pain and more running footsteps—that way was no good. We'd go out through the other door. I grabbed Griffith and we were moving.

I wasn't just making it look easy. It *was* easy, because we just kept doing what Oversight didn't expect.

Most prisoners wanted out. We were going deeper in, and we were nearly there.

There was no one between us and my goal. Because what prisoner would want to go into the very heart of the asteroid?

The main entrance for the core was massive; it had to be to make room for utility vehicles bearing equipment and supplies.

I hit the release. There was a seal, but no security. It would be like putting a lock on an escape craft; that would defeat the purpose.

The doors opened and we hurried through, immediately pulling the release on the other side and engaging the emergency seal. *Now* it would be difficult to get in. Oversight could cut through, but it would take time.

I let out my breath. We'd done it.

I turned around to look at where we were. It was cavernous. We were beneath the mines, beneath all of it. This was the refinery, where the ore was processed.

More than that, it was the power source for all of New Brittia. The old mining stuff was long-abandoned, but the place still needed energy. That meant regular maintenance, which meant there had to be a maintenance entrance: the one we'd just used. Techs couldn't come in through the detention facility; their entrance was here with Oversight, where it was safe.

And the refinery wasn't a part of the prison; it wasn't meant to keep people in. There were other exits, like refuse chutes and loading bays.

It wasn't as obvious as the shuttle dock, but it was still a way out. My heart rate was up. This was it. I went to the railing, surveying the massive chamber. It was loud. There was a lot of machinery; the power station was fully operational, and that meant a lot of moving parts.

It was all decades old, and not lovingly maintained. They were just keeping it running. It was very different from the shining polymer that encased the Oversight facility.

In here, there was only the rock of the asteroid and corroded metal.

This was an observation deck. We were about ten meters above the main floor of the chamber, and it was a maze down there, and all over. Raised walkways and catwalks, broken lifts and staircases. It was dizzying, and not very well lit. That wasn't friendly to techs; it was probably mostly kept running by robots.

I turned back to Griffith and he hit me hard, catching me low with his shoulder. It was a familiar feeling as I struck the railing, which promptly gave—it was just like Cyril's house, not so long ago. I'd broken through a railing there, too.

But that time I hadn't been quite so high up.

TWENTY-SIX

TWELVE HOURS AGO

They pulled me out of my sleeper, and I knew I'd been right.

They hadn't even been dressed like real Galactic Rescue, not that most people knew exactly what uniforms the real GRs wore. Frankly, the impersonation had been a bit slapdash.

I was sore all over. I'd had a pretty rough day before going into stasis at Shangri La, and that felt like just a few moments ago. It must've been straight from stasis to the sleeper. I was disoriented, but I wasn't blind or deaf.

And I wasn't complaining about the stasis; I'd expected them to execute me on the spot.

Two men in civilian clothes were dragging me, and I didn't resist.

We were aboard a ship. It wasn't large, and it wasn't military. I didn't recognize it, but I knew what it was. I didn't feel good, and that made me wonder if they hadn't kept me in stasis a little too long before putting me on ice.

That wasn't supposed to be good for you, but I didn't expect to live long enough for it to matter.

Binders clicked onto my wrists, and I was pushed into the spine of the ship. Ahead was the bridge, but there was an abrupt turn, and I stumbled into a cabin.

The guys holding me didn't know how weak I was. Even with my hands free, there wasn't much I could do.

There was no one there. It looked cozy.

The men released me and stepped back into the corridor quickly. Amused, I turned to look at them. They were visibly uncomfortable, and one of them hit the release. The door closed in my face, and I was alone.

I turned back around and went straight to the bunk to lie down and close my eyes.

"I got your message," I said.

"Which one?" the Director asked. She was speaking to me through a holo on the bedside table, but I couldn't be bothered to pick it up.

"The one where I woke up on Nidaros. Why did you send me there? Of all places?"

"I thought that maybe down the line, when it was all said and done, someone might find your body. And figure out the truth."

"We have to age the truth," I said, suppressing a yawn. "Like wine. So it won't be dangerous anymore."

"That's how I was looking at it," she admitted. "I guess I'm getting sentimental."

"A crisis of conscience. It must've been all that conscience that made you want to kill those trainees, and Tremma and his guy too."

"Don't whine," she said. "Tremma was there to kill *you*."

"I'm not whining about that. I'm whining because you ruined my date. Jealous?"

"I don't know why you're surprised. It was a bad plan. She would've seen through you before you got anywhere."

I stopped smiling. Enough joking around. "What do you want me to say? We can't leave this half-finished. And you can't fake it," I told her. "I need you to understand that."

Silence. "It's crossed my mind."

"But the Red Yonder thing. Where *were* you? You had those freelancers grab us, then what?"

"You knew that was me?"

"I'm not *that* unlucky. Weren't you going to kill me?"

"Of course. But something came up."

"What could possibly come up?"

"An internal investigation. For some reason, all three members of the High Command dying at the same time makes people curious. And half the galaxy wondering if an imperial spy is responsible for Little Norwich *also* makes people curious. We have a lot of eyes on us," the Director said. "Makes it hard to move."

"You still got your guys to Shangri La in time. How did you get rid of the real GRs?"

"That's a work in progress."

I winced. She must've killed them. "What did you do with Salmagard?"

"Sent her back to the *Julian*."

"How, though? What happens when they realize it wasn't the real GRs that dropped her off? IS and EI are going to be all over her," I said.

"And that'll be fewer agents for *us* to worry about. She'll be a good diversion. Let them waste their resources worrying about her. You were spotted at the Bazaar," she added.

I recalled Willis and Freeber taking me and Sei into that hotel, offering us to that woman, who had showed us to someone via a reader. I was convinced that I'd been recognized.

"I wouldn't have been at the bazaar if you hadn't gotten cold feet. You could've trusted me. What were our people doing at the Bazaar buying slaves, anyway?" I asked.

"Do you really want to know?"

I didn't reply to that.

"You look terrible," she said.

"I'm dead. If you look at it that way, maybe I'm looking pretty good. What's the date?"

She told me. I hadn't been asleep long. There wasn't much time left until the peace talks.

"You haven't killed me yet. What's changed?" I asked.

"The story won't hold."

"I told you it wouldn't," I said, but my heart wasn't in it. "You'd better let me go. We're running out of time."

"It's not looking good," the Director admitted. "There's blood in the water. The galactics have a pile of bodies. The Imperium has a pile of investigations. Everyone's saying different things. Some people still aren't even convinced you were a double. They think the real Prince Dalton switched sides."

"That won't last. I left evidence. You sabotaged Tremma's ship to stop me. You sabotaged my date at Red Yonder to stop me. Why am I still alive?"

"I thought I didn't need you anymore. I thought I could clean this up myself."

"Now which one of us needs a lecture about ego?" I asked lightly, massaging my jaw, where Cyril had landed a particularly good punch.

"I thought I could trust you," she said finally. Seconds passed. It had been a long time since we'd spoken. I wasn't sure how to feel about that.

"If you know of a way," I said to the Director, "a *better* way. Something I could've done differently. I'll listen."

"I feel like I don't know anything anymore."

That was telling.

"Do you understand why it had to be this way?" I asked finally.

More silence. I wondered where she was. She certainly wasn't on this ship. She'd mentioned internal investigations. The clock was ticking, and I could sense a tightening vice.

"Yes," she said. "But no one else ever can."

"That's the idea."

"I ruined your plan. You can't use Salmagard. She's off the table."

"I don't need her."

"I have nothing to give you. They know. The High Command is gone, but there are still people who know. They're coming for us. It's over. I can't help you."

"Just let me go." I took a deep breath. "I'll do the rest."

"Do you really think you can still make this work?"

"Do you believe in anything? If so, what?" I snorted. "Because I'm dying to know."

"Empress, save us. I can't *trust* you."

"I don't do well with negative feedback. I'm used to being adored. Everyone loved Dalton."

"I could still just kill you. Then all my problems would go away."

I smiled. "For a while. You *do* want to let me go. Don't you?"

Another pause. "I want you to convince me that I should. Convince me this can work. Convince me you don't just want to destroy the Empress."

I raised an eyebrow. "You think she doesn't deserve it?"

She groaned, and though I couldn't see her, I could *see* her.

"Stop worrying about being executed for treason," I snapped, sitting up. "You're already dead. So am I. It's easier if you just deal with that right now."

I could picture her rubbing her face. Nerves from the Director. I never thought I'd see the day, yet there'd been a lot of days like that. A lot of days that were never supposed to come. Expectations. *Evagardian* expectations.

I snorted.

"You're right," the Director said at last.

"Does that bother you?" I asked curiously.

"I just never thought it would end like this."

"If you think that's bad, think about how I feel."

"I'll cover our tracks for as long as I can," she promised. "But that's all I can do. I'm cutting people loose. It'll be everything I can do to stop to EI and IS from getting everything we have."

"You should have been ready."

"I *was*. But how do we get there? The girl's back aboard the *Julian*, and they're watching her."

I rubbed at my eyes. "I told you. I don't need her."

"You had *another* plan?"

I sighed, then snorted. "It's my last one."

"Let's hear it."

"I know about Griffith getting picked up."

She blew out her breath. "I was hoping you didn't."

Free Trade law enforcement had caught him and a few other New Unity operators buying Mactex in Free Trade space. Mactex was one of those things that was illegal wherever you went. There was no acceptable use for it, and the only people buying it were terrorists. There wasn't really anything *worse* that you could be caught buying.

So of course, that was how Griffith had gotten busted.

"I know IS's on edge," I said, closing my eyes. "I take that to mean they don't know where the Mactex is."

"They don't."

Griffith had been caught, but he was hardly the *only* New Unity terrorist. New Unity had Mactex, and Evagardian authorities didn't know where it was, or where they planned to use it. There was only one way to read it: an attack was coming.

"You think they're targeting the peace talks?" the Director asked. "A lot of people think they are."

I rubbed my hands together and shook my head. "I'm not sure yet."

"I'm surprised too. Hell," the Director said. "Mactex is what pushed Griffith into New Unity's arms in the first place."

I swallowed. "I know."

"Sorry."

"They sent him to New Brittia," I said. The Director didn't reply to that. "Is he still alive?"

"As far as I know. IS probably considers him taken care of, though. They'll pick him up if he ever gets out," she said.

"Think about it. Griffith Karlsson. Mactex." I turned and looked at the holo. "I don't need Tessa Salmagard."

"What? You want me to put you in there? You want me to send a dangerous New Unity terrorist to break another dangerous New Unity terrorist out of prison?" She sounded close to laughing.

I smiled. "Whoever heard of a *safe* terrorist?"

"Even if I thought for one second that you had a real plan," the Director said, "you said it yourself. You *are* already dead. You have nothing to lose. How do I know you aren't just being sentimental? How do I know you won't just use me to get him out and disappear?"

"I have everything to lose," I told her. "And you know I'm not sentimental."

"Well, you're half right." She groaned in frustration. "I *can't*."

"Then why save me from Shangri La?" I demanded.

"You don't understand. I *can't* get you out of there. It helps that Larsen's out there with this Mactex that Griffith bought, but EI and IS aren't totally distracted by that. My fake GRs—I miscalculated. I can't *do* anything else. I might be able to get you in there, but there's no way I can get you out. And for the love of the Empress, why would I want to? How can you expect me to just serve you up to all those eyes and ears?"

"Don't worry about the narrative," I said, my eyes fixed on the viewport and the stars beyond. "I'll handle it."

"Like you handled the High Command?"

"You're the one who killed them," I pointed out. "Is there anything you can give me?"

"Nanomachines, I guess." She groaned. "But even those won't buy you a jailbreak. It won't be enough to get you out of there."

TWENTY-SEVEN

Everything blurred. It all went in and out of focus.

Griffith appeared at the edge of the platform, high above.

There was pain. I could feel the way my body was splayed out on the cold metal. Every detail.

"You thought I wouldn't know?" he called down to me. "Your plan? Your help? Suddenly you can pick me up like I'm nothing? You just walk through the sedative? You're full of imperial nanomachines. You're *one of them.*"

I gasped for breath, tasting blood. "I never said I wasn't."

"And you want to talk to me about Larsen?" Griffith demanded.

Then that had been what tipped him off. It had been a gamble, but I hadn't considered it a very risky one. I'd insinuated that we were expecting support from Larsen.

Griffith wasn't supposed to know any better; it had seemed plausible.

But he did know better. How could Larsen come to rescue him when Larsen was busy launching his attack elsewhere? How could I have known Larsen's attack would go live while I was here? Griffith had known. I hadn't.

I should've known better. I'd seen those feeds about the *Julian*, and I should have put it together.

This was what happened when you tried to do these things without enough preparation, but there was no sense worrying about that now.

There was no such thing as a perfect plan. That was why it was always important to have a fallback. Griffith was my fallback, and he always would have been. He never would have left me.

I'd been the one to go.

I looked over at my bloody hand. I could move my fingers.

Griffith was too far away for me to really see his face, but he was still gazing down at me.

I coughed. "Griffith."

The pain wasn't getting any better. I was having trouble breathing, and my voice came out weak. I was supposed to be a performer. What good was a singer who couldn't project?

But I didn't need to sing or dance. I just wanted to get through to him.

"You *left* us," he shouted down. "This is what *you* wanted."

I closed my eyes. "Griffith," I said. "I came here for you."

"Who's really coming get us? Them? You wanted to rescue me so I could die in an imperial prison?"

He wasn't listening. He had his memories of our time together, and it had to count for something. But his beliefs counted for something too, and I knew exactly how he felt. I was no different.

He couldn't see me as anything but his enemy now, and I didn't want to lie to him.

My right eye started to sting, and I had to squeeze it shut. There was a lot of blood.

"I could never reason with you," I groaned. It was true. Griffith had never been one for deep thinking. Intelligence off the charts, of course, but he'd never wanted to use it. Why think when you can act? And once he was acting, it wasn't easy to talk him out of it.

Impossible, really.

I hadn't realistically expected him to grow out of it. Some things about him had changed, but not the important ones. I was glad; it wouldn't have seemed right if we'd been total strangers after only this long. Even this much familiarity was a comfort.

"I always liked that," I said. "In case you didn't know."

He gazed down at me, the anger on his face slipping away, replaced by uncertainty. I'd just taken a ten-meter fall, and I hadn't landed gracefully. He could see the state I was in.

It wasn't my first fall, but even if it was my last, it was far from over. There was still a long way down.

"But it's not like that anymore," I said. "You have to follow my lead now. I wish you didn't, but you do. I didn't want this, but no one cares what I want."

I sat up.

Griffith's face went white. He could see how I looked, but now he could also see that I didn't look nearly bad enough.

He'd been the one to say it, not me. I *was* full of imperial nanomachines. That was the one thing the Director had been able to do for me. The one thing I could bring with me into this place: my blood, even if I was leaving plenty of it behind.

Nanomachines in the human body was about as un-Evagardian as it could get. Impurity. Playing God, disregarding nature. But if I'd ever had any properly human blood, I'd bled all that away a long time ago. I was an orphan from Cohengard. My blood had never been worth anything to begin with.

"We *are* leaving," I called up to him, rising to my feet and brushing myself off.

He vanished from the edge. I couldn't hear his footsteps over roar of the power station and all the machinery.

"Together," I added, but he probably didn't hear me.

I couldn't manage more than an awkward limp. That had been a bad fall, but the nanomachines wouldn't let anyone take me out so easily. They would mend my body nearly as fast as a physician could, within reason. A bullet in the head, a knife in my spine—I wasn't invincible. But nothing less than that would stop me.

This was the same technology that was given to Acolytes and Vanguards. Most people outside the Imperium didn't even believe it existed.

Griffith had hoped to kill or disable me, but he was underestimating Evagard's commitment to absolute technological dominance.

Superiority at any cost.

I'd fallen onto a walkway. The machinery was generating a lot of searing heat, and it washed over me as I made my way down a set of stairs that groaned alarmingly. Vents opened, bathing the power station in bright orange light.

"I find it hard to believe that you don't already know this," I called out, "but when they want to find you, it's just a matter of time. You've been spending too much time with Larsen. I think you traded down."

A row of pistons ten meters thick chugged ruthlessly, every cycle sending showers of sparks across my path.

"It's cute that you think you can hide," I went on. "I was there, remember? When we watched those Old Earth dramas? The ones with the men with knives and the pre-Unification women? The gene pool's better off without them. You don't have to be an imperial to know that. I know what you're thinking."

There was a flash of movement, and Griffith disappeared behind cover on a walkway overhead. I limped onward, taking the turn and entering a narrow space that wasn't meant for walking.

"Where are you going?" I asked. "It's not rhetorical. This is a prison. Where are you going to go?"

The Director's nanomachines could make me invisible to sensors, like those in robots and androids. They could make me immune to sedatives like the knockout gas used by Oversight. They could save me from being crippled by a bad fall. They could let me open locks, like those that had secured the hermaphrodite. They could even help dull the pain of my physical injuries. A little.

But there were limits.

Griffith was looking for another way out, but he wasn't going to find one.

"Isn't this strange? It used to be the other way around," I called after him. "Back then, I was the one who couldn't get away from you."

Massive coolant tanks were venting into my path. It was too dangerous; Griffith wouldn't go in there. I climbed out of the trench.

"Did you want to?" Griffith wanted to mimic my tactics, to use sound against me. It wouldn't work. I couldn't be beaten this way.

"Of course not," I replied.

He knew the truth, but he didn't believe in it. He thought he had changed, but he was blind to his own reflection. All he had left was bleeding wounds and blind spots. What kind of terrorist had he expected to be? How had he expected to get anything *done* with his head in this state?

It didn't bother me that he had taken this path. It only bothered me that he wasn't any good at it.

He was in the dark, and he thought that was enough to make up the difference. Pain could be a powerful thing. For some it could prove galvanizing, but it weakened others.

Griffith was making his way upward. I knew what he had in mind, and I wasn't going to allow it.

"This is why it could never work," I said, mounting a staircase that rattled violently. "I managed for a long time, but I never could have done it forever."

"You never understood."

"I understood well enough to know it couldn't be as simple as you wanted it to be," I said, and my voice came out very tired.

The entire structure groaned. Sooner or later the Baykaras were going to need new systems. That would be expensive.

They could afford it, especially with the boost I'd given them these past few hours.

No one was watching this, though. There was no coverage down here. The last they had seen was the two of us breaking into maintenance, which was definitely a new precedent.

A lot of people out there who'd been betting for or against us would be very displeased right now.

An alert began to sound. The alarm itself was weak and distorted, like it had been going off down here for a long time. All of this functioned, but the state of it bordered on outright neglect. I'd only seen a handful of maintenance robots. Maybe the Baykaras' profit margins were narrower than I imagined. Or maybe their practical considerations were just as out of alignment as their moral compass.

Not that was I was one to talk to anyone about morals.

Or maybe people who accumulated vast wealth on the backs of suffering people just weren't the brightest. Historically, that had never been a terribly practical strategy—except, perhaps, for Evagard.

These things were best appraised through the lens of history, but Evagard's story wasn't over.

Not yet.

Whether the Baykaras believed in Karma or not, surely they believed in the realities of space. I'd have expected them to have more respect for their facilities.

"Martyrdom's played out," I shouted toward the upper levels. "It's not what it used to be. Trust me."

A martyr was supposed to be killed for his beliefs, but that wasn't how it worked, not anymore.

They were all in such a hurry to be persecuted that they made it their job to create enemies for themselves.

"Revolution is supposed to be about change." I dragged myself to the next landing, looking up. "It's hard to get results when you're dead. At least that's what I hear," I added, stopping to rest. I leaned on the railing, hoping it would hold. It was hard to breathe, and there was a lot of blood in my mouth.

I spat it out.

"I'm serious," I called up to him. "I'm not supposed to be the one doing the chasing. You remember when you tried to sneak into my dormitory? When the Overseer was in my room? And you set off the peacekeeping alarm for the whole floor?"

"Yeah," he shouted back.

"Well, where's that enthusiasm now?"

He didn't reply. One set of conduits running from the reactor to the jagged ceiling went dark, and the others lit up.

"I'm—" I stopped. I had been about to say that I wasn't one of those men with knives from the dramas. That he didn't need to run.

But I was. I reached into my pocket for the folded knife that he had bought me out in Alpine Square, the one I'd used to cut myself and trigger the biohazard alert.

I did have a knife. I *was* the scary man from the dramas. The flashing red lights caught on the blade, and my fingers shook. The knife trembled. I let go of it and listened to it clattering down the steps.

I cleared my throat and looked up.

"I lie for a living!" I shouted. "Why are you taking this so *personally?*"

I began to drag myself up.

"I won't tell them anything," he called down.

"I *know*," I snarled. The railing was slippery. Blood was running down my arm, but I was close to the top. I kept going. Something was going to give, but not in time to stop me.

Griffith thought he could take me by surprise by stopping short of the highest deck. I caught the piece of metal that he swung at me, stopping it as though he'd swung a soft towel. I jerked it out of his hands and threw it aside. He staggered back in surprise, then lunged for the railing, but he didn't have a chance.

Who did he think he was dealing with? Forget the fact that I was an imperial spy. That didn't matter.

What mattered was that I was the one who knew him better than anyone. I knew what he was going to do before he did. I'd even expected him to do something like what he had back there, knocking me from the platform. I'd just expected it a little later on, like *after* we'd gotten out of here. What was the point of turning on me *now?*

But he didn't know what I knew.

I caught him before he could jump and pulled him back, throwing him to the floor. I planted my foot on his chest and held him down. Even if I hadn't gone through so much to reach him, I still wouldn't have let him kill himself. Without him, I had nothing.

"The Empress frowns on suicide," I told him. "Not that we can have anyone thinking that we care what she thinks. Your words. Right?"

A massive detonation shook the chamber, but I didn't even look. The big doors would be opening, and armed men and women would be streaming through.

"Your friends," Griffith gasped.

"It's Oversight, you idiot. I have no friends. Obviously."

His eyes widened. "What?"

"Evagard has its hands full with Larsen," I said, removing my foot from his chest. "No one's coming." I sat down beside him. "Congratulations. You and Larsen pulled it off." I sighed. Griffith just put his face in his hands. "You're not falling into Evagardian hands, Griffith. It's just you and me."

He stared at me.

"What kind of escape *is* this?"

I glanced over at him, then looked out over the machinery. My every word had been recorded in New Brittia. I rubbed at my eyes and leaned against him.

"I said we were leaving. I never said we were escaping."

Escape had never been an option.

The whole galaxy was waiting outside, aiming straight at us. We wouldn't last five seconds out there; prison was the safest place for us, but that wasn't saying much, and we couldn't stay.

There was only one place to go: upstairs. To secure an invitation for two to Baykara City, we had to be special. It was all about getting noticed, and I'd made sure of that.

Abigail Baykara had probably been itching to get her hands on us for a while, but she couldn't just pull us out because she suddenly realized I was more than just an ordinary prisoner. She had to at least pretend to be fair.

I'd made things easy for her by getting us this far from the cameras. No one would know what happened in here, so the narrative was now Abigail's to shape.

She was about to have two new toys to show off, toys that the entire galaxy was dying to see.

I hadn't been lying when I told the Director that this wasn't my best plan.

But it was the only one I had left.

TWENTY-EIGHT

SEVEN YEARS AGO

It was a beautiful Evagardian evening.

I squirmed around to face the tent's opening and reached and swiped to disable the filter, letting some cool air inside.

It was almost fully dark, but the bay was lit up by the gaming island's entertainment district. Even the bridge connecting it to the mainland was shining bright with every color.

Every structure, every dome, every tower, every shape—all of it was perfectly reflected in the bay. Combined, it was enough to light up the coast for kilometers. The tiny specks of light winking in the black were flyers, mostly luxury models ferrying people from attraction to attraction.

Full of fashionable people with genes that mattered.

I wondered what it would be like to be seen as one of those people.

"Are we too close to the water?" Griffith asked, covering me with the blanket. He pulled over his pillow and rested his chin on it, gazing out at the surf.

"There aren't real tides," I said. "We'd all drown."

"Oh."

"If we aren't this close, we can't hear the water. You're supposed to be able to hear it. What part of a spiritual journey don't you understand?"

Griffith snorted. "Right."

"Why this beach, though? Why put your long, natural trail full of—full of spiritual stuff, where it ends with you looking at this," I said, pointing at the lights of the casinos. "Isn't that kind of backward?"

"It's pretty," Griffith said.

"Yeah, but... never mind." The trail had not been nearly as difficult or as spiritual as we had been led to believe. We were also two days ahead of the projected time it was supposed to take. Still, it had been a taxing physical exercise, and I was always pleasantly sore at the end.

Inge would be glad to have us back two days early, but what effect would that have on her studies? I sighed.

"We can stay out here longer," Griffith said, reading my mind. "I don't think we're going to make it over *there*, though."

I gazed at the island, and I thought I could faintly hear music floating across the bay.

"Maybe someday."

"Stop looking at it," Griffith said. "It's not helping."

He reached out and swiped. The front of the tent became opaque. I groaned and turned onto my back, reaching up to swipe the ceiling. It opened up, and we could see the stars. Not the real stars, of course, but the dome's representation of tonight's sky was perfect. We might as well have been on a world without a shield, and it was all much clearer than it would've been with an atmosphere.

Griffith propped himself up on his elbow and joined me in looking up.

"You're the one who pays attention in class," he said.

I pointed. "That should be Burton Station."

"How can you tell?"

"Because that's the Aegis behind it. And you can see the whole Commonwealth tonight."

"Really?"

"Yeah. That's the Frontier system. And then there's Ganrae. And there's Kakugo."

"We'll be at war with them soon enough. I blame Free Trade."

"The Commonwealth is the bad guy. They're the ones who aren't playing by the rules."

"If the Free Traders were more serious about enforcing those rules, it wouldn't be an issue," Griffith argued. "They're just taking the bribes and not giving a thought to the consequences. Their officials will do anything to get elected, they don't care what it means for anyone else. Nobody's thinking long-term. They can't see beyond the election cycle."

"They'd need strength to back it up if they resisted, and where's it going to come from? It would defeat the whole purpose of their culture if their central government actually had any power. What would a Free Trade military look like?" I asked.

"Probably pretty funny," Griffith said.

"Yeah, maybe."

"So out that way, that's Demenis, right?"

"I guess. And I guess we can pretty much shelve any hopes or dreams we had about going off-world," I said. "If it's not in our future now, it's not going to be in our future when there's a war on."

"Trigan systems will still be open. And it's not like the Imperium is *so small,*" Griffith said, smiling.

"I guess. But our systems are expensive."

He couldn't argue with that.

"I've never seen a, well, like, a big war before," I said.

"The last big one was thirty years before we were born," Griffith said, folding his hands behind his head. "This won't affect us. The action will all be on the Free Trade curvature, in that neutral space."

"We are, you know, sort of on the edge."

"But we're not a colony or an outer station. There won't be anything in Evagardian space. The Empress always says something. And she's always right," he added dryly.

"She is," I told him. "Historically, anyway."

"She writes the history books, so of course she is. There's been action in Evagardian space if you count Cohengard."

"I don't," I said.

"Of course."

"Do you think Inge's actually studying right now?"

"Probably," Griffith said.

"What do you think her chances are?"

"I'm not sure it's courteous for us to speculate about that," Griffith said.

"Like we've ever been courteous before. Speculate anyway."

He grimaced. "I can't imagine that her chances are much better than that recruiter lady said they were. I wonder who she really was. I keep thinking about it, and I think she might've actually been someone really important. That was a weird ID she had."

"Focus on Inge. What do you think?"

"I think she's overreaching."

"The blonde called it. Well, it went great the last time we tried to talk Inge out of something," I told him.

Griffith laughed bitterly.

"We have to do something," I said. "She wasn't wrong about that."

"Classic sales technique," Griffith told me. "Sense of urgency. Don't fall for it. Don't let her get to you."

We lay in silence for a few moments. It was too late. She'd already gotten to me, though. No, that wasn't true. I'd gotten to myself. The lights of the gaming island had gotten to me. Tim Woodhouse and his commission had gotten to me. I didn't know.

"I've made up my mind," I said.

Griffith just covered his face and groaned. "*Please*," he said.

"This can work. You stay here and write your political stuff. Keep Inge out of trouble."

"You can *get* your apprenticeship."

"But this is a guarantee," I said. "It's better. I'll be able to take care of both of you no matter what happens."

"It's insane."

"Aptitudes are aptitudes," I said. "Apparently I have some. Who knew? The Empress is never wrong."

Griffith made a strangled noise. "*Isn't* she?"

"I'll fight in the war. And if Inge falls short, we'll still have everything we need. And everything we want."

"Have you forgotten that wars are—you know— *dangerous?*"

"Just wait," I said, lying back and grinning up at the stars. "You'll see. I'll come back a hero."

The Author

Sean Danker conscientiously objects to author bios. Can you believe he used to be in the military? He doesn't seem like the type.

@silverbaytimes
www.seandanker.com